BLACK MONASTERY

WILLIAM STACEY

Beware the foe behind the strange threshold.

BLACK MONASTERY

WILLIAM STACEY

Cover designed by Scarlett Rugers Design
http://www.scarlettrugers.com/
Cover illustration by Jez Art
Image photograph by Studio Berube

DEDICATION

To Marie and Nicole, without your love, I would be lost.

PROLOGUE

Hedeby, Denmark,
October 15, 783.

Asgrim had expected to be left to die where he had fallen. Instead, the others had carried the young warrior aboard the longship and somehow kept him alive during the sail home. And the two-day voyage had been agony beyond description. He had repeatedly soiled himself, begging them to let him die. They didn't, and he didn't. And he'd been returned to his home, where he lay in bed, tended by his mother and their servants. His face burned as though someone held a flaming torch to it, and every breath brought scalding pain. Yet through the haze of his suffering, he overheard someone, a skald most likely, promise his parents he would live.

He wasn't sure he wanted to.

At that moment, another white-hot bolt of fire shot between his eyes, deep into his skull, and he cried out, bolting upright. Then someone pushed down on his shoulders, forcing him back and muttering assurances.

The pain was too much pain, far too much. Surely the skald had lied and this was death—or at least the path to death. But if so, if he were dying, why hadn't they put a weapon in his hand to make sure he was accepted into the afterlife? He may have lost his battle, but he *had* fought it. That should count for something.

Shouldn't it?

Sleep, when it came, was a blessed relief—at least at first. Asgrim dreamed of a longship riding high on foamy waves as men pulled at oars in unison. He smiled, feeling overwhelming camaraderie for these men and a vast sense of anticipation that sent shivers down his spine. Ahead, a green, hilly shore pulled closer, and arrows whistled over their heads: a battle, his first. The dream changed, sped up. Fire, choking smoke, the screams of women and children, the savage clash of arms, and the moans of the dying overtook his senses. Battle lust gripped him. This was living. This was what he had been born for. And then he saw the church in flames again, saw the woman and children burning, and heard their screams once more. Horror replaced his excitement.

He awoke to agony, and his misery endured. But one day became two, and he didn't die. A week of near-constant pain passed, and somehow, he lived. The skald hadn't lied, after all. He would survive his wounds. As one week became two, the pain became less… obscene.

He should have died in Wessex. He knew that. Everyone would have been better off if his corpse, defeated and shamed, had rotted on that beach. Death would have been preferable to disgrace. But obviously, the Nornar, the three withered crones who spun the thread of men's lives, had other designs for him. Death in a foreign land had not been his fate, at least not yet, and a man could never change his fate.

Gloom and despair settled over Asgrim as he lay in bed, visited only by his younger brother Bjorn, his mother, and an endless stream of servants. What would he do now? What would become of a man who, on his first sea raid, had challenged his captain to a duel and lost? What captain would ever sail with such a man?

One day, he heard voices outside his room. One in particular cut through his sleep, and he bolted upright, awake instantly. His father was talking with Hrolf, right outside this room.

In almost complete darkness, he listened intently, staring at the wooden door, but it was no use. He couldn't make out what they were saying.

Would there be blood?

And then, incredibly, his father laughed, and Asgrim's face burned. He looked away, tenderly touching the bandages swathing his face, wincing as he did. There would be no blood and no revenge. His father had nothing to avenge. Asgrim had challenged Hrolf and lost. The duel had been fair.

He sat and waited, knowing his father would come when Hrolf left. His eyes watered, and he angrily wiped them dry, lest someone see and think him a woman. How had he fallen so low, so completely? Once, his life had been filled with promise of a glorious future. What now?

All too soon, his door opened, and his father's large form filled the doorway. Just behind his father, looking over his shoulder, was his mother. Her blond hair glistened in the candlelight. She was still a beautiful woman.

Father and son stared at one another. Was that contempt in his father's eyes? After a long, painful silence, his father spoke first.

"I won't kill Hrolf."

Be strong, he told himself. Be a man.

"I… I know," he muttered, his voice muffled by the bandages.

"He's my friend."

The young man nodded.

"He could have killed you, you damned fool. He *should* have killed you."

Fire built in his father's voice. Despite his attempt to master his emotions and appear strong, a shiver ran through him, and he trembled like a leaf.

His father paused, then shook his head. "*I'd* have killed you."

The pain in his heart burned far hotter than that in his face.

His mother pushed past his father, sat on the edge of the bed next to him, and ran her hand over his forehead, brushing back his hair.

"Leave him be, woman," said his father. "He needs to toughen up, and he's been lying about in bed too long. Sluggard would stay here all winter if I let him. It's done between you and Hrolf, boy. It's over. Now we move on."

"Yes, father," he mumbled.

His father's features softened, if such a thing was possible, and he actually smiled. "Get yourself ready, boy. I've sent for Guthorm. He'll be here in a week with his men, all the best plank-cutters and stem-smiths in Denmark. You and your brother will help. You both need to learn how to do this."

Asgrim sat up on his elbows. "You're going to build her now? I thought you were going to wait another winter?"

His father shook his head. "No. We do it this winter. The best gods-blessed ship any man's ever seen. Even the earl will be jealous. And when she's ready, we'll raid with her, you and *I* this time, maybe your brother, as well. And when we come back, no one will remember what happened. We'll make a proper sword-Dane out of you yet."

His father turned to leave, but then paused and looked back over his shoulder. "I still don't understand why you did it, but Hrolf tells me you faced him like a man. Says you even cut him, and he's limping." His father smiled. "Says you were fast, real fast. *Disloyal and stupid*, but so fast he almost had to kill you anyway."

His father sighed and walked away, leaving him alone with his mother, who sat on the bed stroking his hair. They stayed like that in the candlelight for some time, neither saying anything. Finally, he spoke.

"I was fine with the fighting. The fighting was… exciting. It was *after*, the things we did after we killed all their men. I… I couldn't…"

His mother's gaze was sad, perhaps even understanding, and he felt like a little boy again. "The world can be harsh and cruel. But death is part of it. No man, no woman, no child can escape their destiny. You must accept this."

He shook his head. "You don't understand. They ran into their church to hide, the women and children. Someone set it on fire. Some didn't… didn't come out. They chose to burn instead of… instead of *us*. They were screaming… screaming. There was no honor. No… nothing. And those women that did come out, the men… *took* them, right there in front of their children. I couldn't stand it, not the screaming, not the horror in the children's faces. So… I tried to stop it. I *challenged* Hrolf." This time, his voice did crack, and he turned his face away.

His mother shushed him and carefully held the uninjured side of his head against her bosom. "I don't think Hrolf is an evil man. He's just a man, with the same love for violence and plunder as all Danes. Your father is the same, but he's also a good man, treats the slaves and servants well, does no dishonor to our family."

"I'm sorry, mother. I've shamed us all."

"No, of course you didn't. It took courage to step onto the dueling blanket with a killer like Hrolf the Elder. You tried to defend those women and children, even though they were foreigners. There is so much good in you. You have always had a kind heart. Perhaps too kind. But you are also your father's son." She sighed and hugged him just a bit harder.

"Sleep now." She stood and walked to the doorway. "There will be much blood in your life, I fear, my beautiful boy. And your father is right. You need to harden your heart—else this world will kill you. But... you must always be prepared to be a good man, to do the right thing, and make me proud."

He couldn't speak; instead, he simply nodded. He lay awake a long time, thinking over his mother's words. Eventually, he drifted off into sleep. For the first time since his injury, he didn't dream of the raid and dying children.

When Guthorm and his laborers arrived a week later, Asgrim was strong enough to move about and help with the small tasks. Thousands of little details needed to be looked after. His younger brother Bjorn, not yet twelve but already a foot taller than he was, became his shadow, never leaving his side. The famous Guthorm was a stoop-shouldered grandfather with skin like dry bark and a long, untidy grey beard that looked to still hold most of his breakfast. Asgrim's father greeted Guthorm with much honor, embracing him like a long-lost brother and promising him whatever he required. And Guthorm quickly took over life at the manor, leveling the most profanity-laden curses the young man had ever heard at those whom he considered slackers. The old master craftsman had a better repertoire of curses than the best skald did.

Soon, their home and farmlands became so occupied with laborers that it reminded him of a termite's mound. At first, his wounds pained him, and he found himself often having to sit and rest, but over the weeks that followed, his endurance grew. Breathing was still hard, though, and still painful.

The smell of fresh-cut wood and the pounding of axes permeated the cold winter air. Sawdust and wood chips covered the snow. The workers laid the keel two hundred paces from the inlet of the *Schlei,* which led to the sea. The keel, a single plank riven from a particularly tall oak tree, had been chosen for its slight natural bend. The plank had been soaked for two months in seawater so that the salt had thoroughly penetrated the wood, and as the wood dried, the salt became a natural proofing against rot. Whispering in wonder, men stood about the keel; it was almost fifteen paces long—far longer than any man had ever seen on a ship. To its front, they attached a false keel, a shorter plank that protected the real keel when the longship was beached. That night, when no one was around, Asgrim and Bjorn snuck out to carve their initials into the false keel.

As the days turned to weeks, the day to remove Asgrim's bandages arrived. The skald who had originally tended his wounds returned. Asgrim's parents, his brother, and the skald, his bony arms trembling, sat with Asgrim beside the hearth in the hall. His mother had sent away the servants and slaves. No one but family was present. As the skald carefully unwrapped the linen from Asgrim's face, the man whispered incessantly to the land spirits, beseeching their blessings. As the last bandage slipped from his face, his mother's eyes widened and her face whitened. Bjorn's face twisted in disgust, and he swore.

His father scowled at Bjorn and cuffed him in the back of the head. As Bjorn mumbled an apology, his father shook his head and came closer. "How does it feel? Can you breathe through it?"

He closed his eyes, then inhaled carefully. There was pain, but he could still draw air through the ruined tissue, although it was harder than it should have been, as if the air had to fight to make it through his airway.

"I can breathe, but it feels… blocked."

"The tissue is pushing in against the airway. It'll improve as he grows older," said the skald. "The nose was shattered, as were the bones around the cheek and eye socket. They'll heal, grow harder, even tougher than before. Breathing will remain challenging perhaps, but he'll become accustomed to it. As the years pass, he may not even remember how it was before."

"I'll remember," he said.

"Will it… will it look better?" his mother asked. "In time?"

The skald exhaled, looked down at his hands. "My lady, the wounds… I don't… I don't think—"

"It doesn't matter," snapped his father. "If he can breathe through it, he can fight with a helmet over his face. *That's* what matters. Looks are for women, not men."

"But—"

"Leave it, wife! He'll still be able to do everything a man needs to do. He'll fight and raid and have strong sons." His father draped an arm around his mother's shoulders, pulling her against him. "It's better than dead."

She nodded and placed her hand on her son's knee. "It'll get better."

"I want to see," Asgrim said.

The skald raised his head slightly, and his eyes darted nervously toward Asgrim's parents. "My boy, perhaps we should wait until—"

He reached out and gripped the man's wrist, causing him to wince in pain. "Skald, I danced the cloak with Hrolf the Elder and lived. I am no boy, and I want to see my face. Now!"

"I'd do as he says," said his father.

The skald nodded quickly and turned away to rummage through a small sack he had brought. A moment later, he turned back, holding a polished square of brass the size of a man's palm. The young man hesitated for a moment, then took the metal. When he saw his reflection, a sudden coldness struck at the core of his being, and he gasped. A tingling sensation ran through his muscles as he gingerly touched his face. He thought he was going to throw up. The skin around his nose was waxy, smooth, and discolored brown and black. It felt like melted candle wax.

But when he pushed against it, pain stabbed deep behind his eyes. He turned away, handing the mirror back to the skald.

The silence was as heavy as a chain mail coat.

"It will get better," his mother whispered.

"Yes," he said.

He was proud that his voice didn't break.

As the weeks turned to months, the pain began to lessen, and his strength and endurance grew. At first, the laborers stared at his face in horror. As they grew accustomed to him, they paid him no mind, treating him the same as every other young man. He was grateful for the shipbuilding; it took his mind off his face. Occasionally, on those days when his nose didn't pain him too badly, he even rode out with the laborers to an old-growth forest to cut timbers. Normally, logging was forbidden in the ancient and dwindling forest, but his father and the earl had sailed together when they were young men, and the earl had given his father permission to take as much wood as he needed. They split the tree trunks on the edge of the forest using wedges and hammers, then trimmed the planks with short-hafted broad axes. The much smaller planks were then sent back to the manor by wagon.

They attached the stem and stern planks to the keel with wooden plugs and expensive iron nails. The planks, once attached, were slathered with a pine tar mixture that stained the workers' hands dark brown. Along the length of the keel, they attached the first two strakes, the individual hull planks. With the first two strakes in position, they began to lay the others. Each one was clinkered so that the edge of the one above sat atop the one below. They caulked the spaces between the strakes with a mixture of sheep hairs and the pine tar. The men complained that the mixture stank, but he had become accustomed to breathing through his mouth, and the smell didn't bother him as much as it did the others. When he mentioned this, one of the laborers joked that a man needed a nose, not a lump of wood, to smell it. As the laborers laughed, his skin burned, but he said nothing.

Within weeks, the bones of the longship emerged, like some mythical beast washed up by the waves, and men from all the outlying farms began to arrive, either seeking work or simply coming to watch. Some men helped for free, just to brag they had been involved in the making of a masterpiece of work: the best ship the famous Guthorm had ever built.

When the time came to mount the keelson—a single piece of oak fifteen ells long in the center of the hull to hold the mast steady—they could move it only with a series of pulleys and nets. It needed to be so large, especially for a longship this size because, resting directly on the keel, the keelson transferred the forces of propulsion from the mast to the hull. When the ship's decking was in place, the only part of the keelson that would be visible on the deck was the mast fish, which was named for its distinctive fish-like shape. Getting the keelson into its proper position took the entire day. At one point, a walrus-hide rope attached to a pulley snapped and whipped about like a sword blade. Had it hit anyone, it would have cut him in half. But the gods must have been watching, because no one was hurt. After that, the men agreed that luck was with Asgrim's father.

Once the keelson was firmly in place, the time had come to mount the mast. At twenty-five ells in length and carved from the trunk of a single massive oak tree, the mast was the longest piece of wood any man had ever moved. As the trunk was finessed into position by Guthorm and his laborers, Asgrim's father stood with his two sons, each straining against one of the ropes. As the workers pulled in unison under Guthorm's command, the mast slowly rose. Then, with a single mighty thud that shook the entire ship, the mast slid into position, standing tall and proud. The men cheered, as did Asgrim and his brother. Even Asgrim's father, a normally stoic man, smiled.

His father met Asgrim's eye, and then he squeezed his shoulder. "Someday, she'll be yours, my son, and no man will remember your first raid. She'll carry more warriors than any other ship in Denmark, travel faster and farther with more oars. When men see her sail coming over the horizon, they'll shit themselves in terror and run for their miserable, gods-forsaken lives." His father barked out a single harsh laugh. "And they'll be right to do so, by Odin's fiery asshole."

"What will you name her, father?" Bjorn asked.

"*Sea Eel*," whispered the older man. "And she'll earn her name. Deadly and fast, a predator."

Once the mast was in place, artisans arrived to carve decorative patterns on the planks. Every exposed surface was worked and trimmed with intricate marks to please the gods. A particularly gifted young man was hired to carve the dragonhead prow. It was fierce and howling, its jaws wide, its teeth long. He built it to be removable, so it could be stored below deck when the longship was at home so that it would not frighten the land spirits and foul their luck.

Asgrim and his brother stood back and watched the young artisan finish the dragonhead and present it to Guthorm and their father. The elderly shipwright, with just a trace of approval on his weathered face, turned to his father, who nodded solemnly.

Once all the carvings were finished, the workers painted the hull with a mixture of pine resin and seal blubber that stunk almost as badly as the waterproofing had, but left the wood stained a deep, dark green when it dried. At the same time, other workers built the oar ports and rigging. She was long enough to accommodate thirty rowers on each side. Fully loaded, she could carry more than a hundred warriors, which was an unprecedented number.

She could only be finished in the water, and it was time to launch her. To accomplish this, the men laid a trail of parallel logs, over which they could slowly roll her down to the shoreline. Her sail, homespun wool in a green-and-yellow striped pattern, was already soaking in animal fats and oil. The cost of the wool had been enormous, even for his father, and it had taken their servant women more than a year under his mother's direction to weave it together into a single piece. The tiller and side rudder would be attached last, once she was afloat.

The worst of the winter cold had passed, and within another month, spring would be upon the land. Once the spring planting was completed, the time would come for raiding. Excitement grew among the men. Soon, the right day to launch the ship came. On a day with favorable weather and few crosswinds, they attached long lines of walrus-hide ropes to her, and *Sea Eel*'s wooden planks squeaked as the men hauled her down to the shoreline. Women and children from town left their tasks undone to come watch. Even the earl came. Removing his coat, he stood next to Asgrim's father to help haul on the ropes. Every man knew the honor the earl was paying to his father by his presence, especially since he had left his newborn son, Frodi, to come and help. Under Guthorm's steady command, they rolled her to the water. Her dark-green hull scraped along the wet sand as she hit the shoreline and stuck fast. Men pushed and pulled, but the massive longship stubbornly held her place. Asgrim and Bjorn stood beside one another, up to their thighs in the frigid water, pushing and straining against the hull.

"Get in there! Get in there!" Asgrim screamed as he shoved.

Then, with a rush of foam and splash so fast it took most of them by surprise, the mighty longship slid into the waters of the *Schlei*. Bjorn pitched forward headfirst into the water. Asgrim reached into the waters, caught his brother by the shoulders, and yanked him free. Bjorn was wild-eyed and spitting water, but grinning like a berserker. And *Sea Eel*, perfectly ballasted in advance by Guthorm, rocked gently in the calm waters of the inlet. As one, they all cheered—men in the water, the women and children along the shoreline, his father, and the earl. And this time, finally forgetting his wounds, Asgrim cheered as well, hugging his younger brother.

That night, along the shoreline, Asgrim accompanied his father and the other men to a ritual. There, by the light of a massive bonfire, his father sacrificed a bull to Odin, killing the beast with one blow of an ax. He helped his father and his father's warriors anoint the hull of *Sea Eel* with the ox's blood. The earl was there, as well, having remained for this most sacred of tasks. All the men agreed the gods were pleased. Luck would be with his father and this magnificent longship.

With the ritual completed, the earl approached his father. In his hands, he held a long fur-wrapped bundle, which he handed to the other man. His father took the bundle reverently, inclining his head in thanks. Then the earl bade farewell, and he and his bodyguards mounted their horses and rode off for his own estates. Asgrim's father's bondsmen also bade farewell then, wishing to return to the warmth of their own farms, promising to return early in the morning to help prepare *Sea Eel* for raiding.

Asgrim stood in front of the bonfire with his father. Both men were soaked to their waists, but bundled in thick fur cloaks. His father wrapped an arm around his shoulder, pulling him against him.

"The rigging will be done in days," his father said. "In another week, she'll be ready to sail. Then, I'll teach you all you need to know about being a man."

"I am a man."

His father snorted and hugged him just a bit tighter. "Aye, maybe you are at that."

They stood in silence for a time, staring at the flames as the wood crackled and spit. The frigid wind howled, fanning the flames higher.

His father released him and stepped back. "I'm getting old, son, too old for raiding. This will be my last voyage across the sea. We will sail for Wessex, raid along the coast. And when we return home, I will go forth no more. I will sit in my lodge, drink ale, get fat, and be a farmer."

"Why are you saying this?"

"I didn't build *Sea Eel* for me… well, not *only* for me. I built her for you, for you and your brother."

His father became silent, staring at the fire. He felt his father's discomfort.

"I won't pretend I understand why you did it," his father started again. "But it's done. You fought with honor and courage, and you've borne your loss like a man should. I'll have no bad blood between you and Hrolf. You'll promise me this."

Just for a moment, he saw again the sight of Hrolf's shield rushing toward his face, the iron boss growing in size. He shuddered once and inclined his head in agreement. "Aye."

"Good," said his father. "You and his youngest boy, Gorm, were friends before this happened. I want you to be friends again."

He nodded again. He and Gorm had not spoken since that day, although he had been certain Gorm had tended his wounds during the voyage home on the longship.

"We're Danes, boy. We take what we need. There's not enough good land left in Denmark for all of us, but this is not a mistake. It's part of our destiny. The gods made us strong so we could take what we need from lesser men, and then they put us here, in this harsh, cold land where there was no choice but raiding. If Denmark were a land of plenty, where each man owned his own farm, how many men do you think would choose to leave their hearths, travel across the sea, and face the horror of a shield wall? Damned few, I can tell you. No. This is how it's supposed to be. Why else do you think the gods taught us how to build longships, how to travel for days at a time beyond sight of land? The gods made us what we are, and they're always watching us. They are pleased with battle, even slaughter. Always remember this. Those who are not Danes are not your people. They are not worthy of your pity, your sacrifice. Their lives are miserable and shitty because they have abandoned the old ways. Now they are nothing but prey, barely human. But you, you are a sword Dane, a pillager, a man who honors the gods. You have a warrior's destiny. I know it. Those cattle in other lands who think themselves men will shiver in terror at the very mention of your name. And the gods will watch you and smile."

"I'll make you proud, father. I won't fail… not again."

"I know you won't, boy. But…" His father paused, staring at his face. "If you're going to make a habit of fighting duels with killers like Hrolf, you'll need a better weapon." His father turned away and retrieved the fur-wrapped bundle from where he had placed it on the ground. He began unwrapping it as he approached, and the young man saw a sword hilt extend from the end.

His father pulled the weapon free of the fur covering and held it in front of the fire for him to see. His breath caught in his throat. Never had he seen such a masterpiece. The metal was polished so brightly that the metal gleamed red in the firelight. And it was longer by at least a hand's length than any other sword he had ever seen. The hilt and pommel glistened with intricate silver etchings; it was a treasure.

"It's beautiful," he whispered.

"It's a gift from the earl," his father answered. "Payment for a debt the old rascal owed me. He carried such a blade himself into battle when he wasn't too fat to fit into his armor. It never failed him. Now, my own son will carry one just as fine. It's yours."

He handed the weapon to his son, hilt first. The young man hesitated, his hand inches from it.

"Go on, boy. Take it."

The young man wrapped his fingers around the detailed leather handle and raised the weapon in front of his eyes. The blade was unlike anything he had ever seen before, with a bizarre frost-like pattern smelted into the steel. He made a cut with it, and the blade whistled through the air. Its balance was perfect, like an extension of his arm. He stared in wonder at his father, who beamed back at him.

"It's perfect. Lighter than I would have thought, wider than most swords." He gripped the pointed tip with his fingers and slightly bent the blade. "But lighter somehow, and more flexible—so flexible." He stared in wonder at the blade. A single groove, called a fuller, ran most of the length of the weapon. The indentation carved in the sword made it lighter and more flexible, allowing it to retain its strength the entire length of the blade. Staring intently at it, he saw writing in the hollow of the fuller. Starting near the hilt, a single word read: +ULFBERH+T. "It can't be Damascus steel, not with those crosses. Is it… Frankish?"

His father snorted. "Franks make good swords, boy, but those aren't crosses. They're hammers. Thor hammers. You're holding *crucible* steel, lad, crucible steel, made in the secret ways brought back from the *Volga*. That is an *Ulfberht* blade. One of only a damned few ever made. The metal is special. I won't pretend to understand how, but because it's lighter, it can be made longer, more flexible and thus won't get caught in an opponent's shield as easily as others might. You see the point? It's tapered so it can stab through chain mail."

"Chain mail? Really?"

"Really. Once, I saw the earl skewer a Frankish prince with his *Ulfberht*. A single thrust, right through the metal links, like they were nothing more than wool. Ripped the man's heart in two."

"*Heart-Ripper*," he said in wonder.

"As good a name as any." His father smiled, his eyes gleaming. "I wish I had such a weapon when I was your age."

He stared at his father. "I can't take this. I don't deserve it. You'll need it this spring."

His father seemed to rise in height, and when he spoke, his voice boomed with his authority. "It is a gift, boy. A gift."

The young man lowered his eyes. "Yes, father. I'm sorry. Thank you. I… don't know what to say."

His father snorted. "Then say nothing. But take it, and get yourself home. Your mother will worry that I keep you out too late when you're still injured."

"I'm better now."

His father grinned and shoved him. "I know it, boy, but your mother doesn't."

"What are you going to do?"

His father tilted his large head toward *Sea-Eel*, which bobbed softly in the waters of the inlet. "I'm going to go sit on my ship for a time. It'll probably be the only chance I'll get for a spell of solitude until after this spring's raiding." With a slightly pained expression on his face, he rubbed his bicep, swinging his arm in a circle. "Too damned old for this shit. Go on, then, Asgrim. Off with you."

Asgrim turned and loped away, his new sword beneath his arm. Bjorn would be green with envy. As he approached the lights of their manor and farmlands, his feet seemed to float over the ground. Somehow, life had become good again. That hadn't seemed possible. Soon, very, very soon, they would finish *Sea Eel's* rigging. In another week, she would be provisioned and ready for sailing. This time, under his father's command, he would wash away the memory of his first raid. His scars would remain forever, but his future was bright again.

The next morning, Guthorm, always first to work, found Asgrim's father's corpse, still sitting at the prow of his longship, an arm around the tiller, a surprised look on his dead face, which stared up at the early morning sky.

"Destiny," whispered the workers.

Fate.

ONE

The coast of the Kingdom of Frankia,
August 2, 799,
Dawn

Sea Eel's dragonhead prow rose high above the waves and then smashed down again, throwing cold spray into the air. Asgrim Wood-Nose locked his gaze on the dark tree-lined shore of the approaching island. *Sea Eel's* sail was furled, so each of the eighty-six Danish warriors pulled at a dripping oar, their excited eyes shining in the moonlight. The night was silent, expectant; the only sound came from the waves crashing against the pebbled beach ahead of them.

It was already hot; a promise of the scorcher to come, and Asgrim wedged a finger beneath the eye guard of his helm to wipe stinging sweat away from his eyes. Peering past the wooden prow of his ship, he watched the dark forest beyond the beach, but saw no sign of life. He glanced up, his eyes drawn once more to the flaming tail of the red dragon burning in the night sky.

The dragon had first appeared two days ago, when they were still following the coastline south. Bjorn had told the men it was an omen, a sign that Odin was pleased with their raid and that he would watch over them. Asgrim sighed, and that moment, Hopp, his vallhund, rose from where he had been resting between the seated rows of men and came to him, rubbing his thick body against his legs. He reached down and scratched behind the dog's ears.

Bjorn was wrong. Odin didn't favor cowards and murderers. The flaming dragon *was* an omen, but not a favorable one. It was a promise of doom, of red death; his fate. And what could a man do to change his fate?

Nothing.

Fate was inexorable, like the tides.

The longship's deck creaked as Bjorn moved to stand beside him. Asgrim was a tall man, a large man, but Bjorn towered over him. In his bearlike hands, his little brother held a great two-handed Dane ax, its edge sharpened keenly, its wooden length studded with iron rivets. Both men wore their finely crafted chain mail coats and full iron helms, with the fur-lined cheek flaps tied in place beneath their beards. Only the two brothers, however, possessed chain mail armor. Most of the men wore only padded leather or reindeer-hide coats, even though each Dane carried a serviceable wooden round shield with a sturdy iron boss.

Sea Eel's prow scraped against the sandy shoreline, coming to a jarring stop, and Asgrim roused himself, forcing his attention back to where it needed to be. He didn't know what destiny his crimes had bought him, but whatever it was, he would face it like a man. If murder and misery were all the Nornar would give him, he would play out his part and drown the world in blood.

Hopp pushed against his leg, anxious to go, and Asgrim slapped the coarse flank of the hunting dog. In a moment, Hopp leapt over the prow of the longship and was loping across the sandy shoreline before disappearing into the trees. Had anyone been waiting in ambush, Hopp would have barked.

But the vallhund made no sound.

"Go!" snarled Asgrim.

Without a word, eighty-six Danish raiders launched themselves over the side of the longship, splashing through the water to the shore. Asgrim felt the excitement of coming battle surge within him. He gripped the handle of the iron boss on his shield and drew *Heart-Ripper* from its sheath before dropping over the side of his ship and landing in the wet sand. His men had already fanned out, forming a half ring to defend the ship, but there was no need, they were alone on this beach.

The Franks called this island *Noirmoutier*, the Black Monastery. It sat just off the coast of the Kingdom of Frankia, at the mouth of a great river. The island and its monastery were named for the Christian holy men who dressed all in black and resided here in their great stone home, worshipping their ridiculous One God. Asgrim and his men had sailed for weeks to get here, past the Kingdom of Wessex to the north before turning south to follow the coast. And it had been an unpleasant voyage, plagued by violent summer storms, blistering hot sun, and short tempers—especially Asgrim's. But there had been no choice: the earl had leveled a monstrous wergild on Asgrim. In order to pay it, Asgrim needed profit—else his war band would fall apart as each man felt the pull of home, a home now denied Asgrim. And here on *Noirmoutier* there was silver, a hoard of silver, enough to pay his wergild.

Days ago, at a trading camp along the coast, they had met a group of dark-skinned Saracens, black-eyed easterners. Their leader had whispered of the vast secret hoard of silver the holy men had hidden away on this island. No fool, Asgrim hadn't trusted the Saracen, but he also felt certain the heavy hand of fate was at play. He needed treasure; the holy men possessed treasure.

"Scouts," he hissed, jabbing his sword point inland.

Five of his stealthiest men, led by Steiner Ghost-Foot, the best hunter Asgrim had ever known, darted into the trees, leading the way. Five other men remained behind to guard the longship, and Asgrim led the remainder of his war band into the forest.

Thankfully, the foliage was open, easy to traverse, and they moved quickly. The Saracen trader, generous to a fault, had also provided Asgrim with the details of the island, including the monastery's location, about two miles inland. By the time they came out of the woods and hit the monastery, the sun would be rising. *If* everything went according to plan, which almost never happened, most of the monks would still be asleep.

He needed surprise, particularly since the Saracen had also warned of a small fort built beside the monastery, manned by soldiers sent by the Frankish king, Charlemagne. If the soldiers and priests were waiting for them, the raid could become too costly. Despite the boasts of drunken warriors, most men secretly wanted easy fights with little risk. Clever captains sought one-sided fights and kept their losses down.

As they stalked through the darkened forest, the black night lightened, turned grey. They exited the woods, coming out onto salt fields where the ground crunched beneath their boots. Just ahead of them, framed by the red glow of the emerging sun, they saw the monastery for the first time.

They dropped to their bellies, watching the monastery from behind a ditch in the salt fields. The monastery had been aptly named. In the pre-dawn light, shadows settled over the buildings, blanketing everything in darkness. The structure was surrounded by rows of salt fields and copses of trees. The main buildings, which rose two stories high, were joined together at a right angle, forming a half square. A tall crenellated stone wall met each end of each building, extending out to complete the square. The open space in between would be the monastery's inner courtyard. Sloping tiled roofs reached up to meet a stone bell tower where the two buildings met. The windows in the stone walls were all thin, dark slits, devoid of signs of life. Asgrim peered intently at the tower, looking for a sentry, but saw no one. He didn't see anyone moving about the many sheds and small huts of the monastery grounds. He smiled. They must all still be sleeping. Good.

Just west of the monastery, no more than two or three thousand ells away, sat the garrison's fort—a log palisade surrounding a single wooden longhouse. There was a village to the southeast, Asgrim knew, if the Saracen's description was correct—and everything else the man had said so far had turned out to be right—but it was at least a half hour's walk away, which was too far to influence the coming battle.

"Twenty, thirty soldiers?" offered Bjorn, peering at the dark bulk of the fort.

Asgrim nodded. "Enough to cause us trouble. More than enough to hold the fort."

Bjorn snorted. "I can take that fort from them. Shove those wooden logs right up their Frankish asses."

Asgrim frowned at his younger brother. "They can sit all day in their wooden fort, just as long as they don't try to stop us. We're here for silver, not blood."

"Well… *some* blood," Bjorn muttered in a hurt voice.

"Take twenty killers—none of the un-blooded boys. Stay hidden. If the soldiers try to come out and help, *then* you smash them. Send them running."

"Aye," said Bjorn.

Asgrim stared at the monastery again, seeking signs that the inhabitants were waking. In the east, the sky was beginning to turn red, and far off, a rooster crowed. It was time.

Bjorn reached over and squeezed Asgrim's forearm. His brother watched him closely with an uncomfortable look on his face.

"Brother," Bjorn said. "I… know how you must feel, but the gods will forgive you. Men make mistakes. We do things we never meant to do. *All of us*. A madness took you that night, that's all. You're not a monster. The gods watch over you now: Odin and Thor. They approve of your courage. *That* matters, what we do now. All else will pass in time. You will pay the earl's wergild, and if Freya's brothers—"

"Freya had no brothers, and her father is old," said Asgrim. "But old man or not, if he comes to me with sword in hand, I will not… not…"

"It won't be like that, brother. I will talk to her father for you, explain things."

A rush of shame threatened to crush Asgrim, and he closed his eyes. Bjorn was wrong about the red dragon, and he was wrong about him. Asgrim *was* doomed. The crones spun their damned bloody thread from which dangled the lives of men, and some acts could never be smoothed out or explained away.

Asgrim exhaled and nodded once, quickly, as he pulled free of his brother's grip. "I know." But he didn't know at all, and a thickness clogged his throat. "Fight well. You have my back, as always."

Asgrim was surprised and pleased that his voice did not crack.

Bjorn's face betrayed his doubt, but he nodded and rose to pull together his men. In minutes, they were gone, moving off toward the fort. The soldiers there would not interfere this night, Asgrim knew. He trusted his brother completely. Bjorn was as clever as an otter. Many a fool had made the mistake of thinking him stupid because of his size. More than a few had died for that mistake.

When he was certain he'd given his brother enough time to get in place, Asgrim stood and turned to his men, who also rose. The faces of the younger ones betrayed some trepidation, but he saw the mounting excitement in the eyes of others.

He spoke loudly enough for all to hear him, putting steel into his voice. "Anyone who stands against us dies, but if they run, let them go, let them live to spread tales of us. It's time for these Frankish holy men to know the wolves of the northern seas have descended upon them!"

Harsh laughter and murmurs of agreement drifted from the men. Their heads bobbed, and their teeth flashed in unpleasant grins.

He thrust his sword toward them. "But listen carefully! I'll have no fires until I have their treasure. After, *then* we burn everything."

Asgrim's gaze swept their faces, making sure they understood. When their blood was up, men acted like idiots. Such things were to be expected, but the last thing Asgrim wanted was his silver melted.

Once satisfied they understood, Asgrim slapped his sword blade against his wooden round shield. The sharp crack rang out in the early morning air and the blade of *Heart-Ripper* vibrated. The time for silence was over.

"Let's go get our treasure." Asgrim stood at the center of his men, who formed a long line facing the monastery. The red glow of the rising sun began to burn away the darkness in the east, creating just enough light to see. Again, Asgrim smashed the flat of his sword against the metal boss of his shield and stepped off. Hopp ran beside him, his tongue dangling, and the men followed. After several paces, they broke into a trot. Their hobnailed ankle boots crunched the salt beneath them as they quickly closed the distance to the monastery.

Asgrim knew the men would be building up a murderous rage and getting ready to slaughter anyone they came across. He felt no pity for the Frankish holy men. All men died at their preordained time, but dying in battle, *that* was how real men died, not in some bed, fouling themselves while women cried. The priests should thank him.

As the first of his men reached the wooden gate in the stone wall, he began to sense something was wrong. At first, he thought the wooden gate had been left open by mistake. But then, as he drew closer, he saw the door was smashed and shoved inward.

What?

His men screamed in fury as they funneled through the open gateway, hungry for blood. Asgrim pushed through the throng of men and came out in the monastery's inner courtyard. One of his men tripped over something and fell flat, dropping his spear. The others fanned out, but then faltered. Silence dropped over the raiders as they ground to a halt, their mouths hanging open, their eyes betraying their confusion.

Asgrim lowered his shield and sword and gaped at the inner courtyard. Bodies of armed warriors and unarmed priests lay scattered everywhere. Clearly, the soldiers and priests had killed each other. Many of the corpses were ripped apart, their limbs lying nearby. Entrails lay scattered everywhere, and the soil was soaked in congealing blood. The stench of feces and rotting flesh washed over Asgrim, and clouds of flies buzzed angrily. Although he was no stranger to death and battlefields, the stench still almost gagged him. Beside him, Hopp whined once before turning and disappearing back out the opened gate.

By Odin's ass, what had happened here? What kind of battle had these men fought? The bodies of the priests had been cut down with sword, spear, and ax. The soldiers, though, had been pulled apart, shredded, their guts ripped out and discarded.

All of the bodies of priests had blood-stained hands.

These were the strangest holy men he had ever heard of, more berserker than man.

He pointed toward the stone buildings with his sword. "Move, damn you! Search inside."

Some of the men stood in place, looking about themselves stupidly, but others began to pile through the monastery doorways.

"Get moving!" screamed Asgrim as he shoved a young raider forward.

What had happened here?

He stalked toward the main buildings and pushed his way inside. He was met by complete darkness, the stench of more dead, and a feeling of dread. He stood in place, trying to make sense of this. Inside, the air was moist and thick with the smell of the sea. How was that possible? The floor was sticky with something that sucked at the soles of his boots. Thousands of angry flies poured out the doorway, so many that men covered their mouths and eyes with their hands.

"Torches. Light torches," he ordered.

When the first torch blazed to life, chasing away the darkness, Asgrim found himself facing a foyer with a large curved stone entranceway that led inside the monastery. Over this entranceway, the monks had painted a scene of piety and welcome: a faded and chipped painting of a woman sitting on a throne and holding a baby. On either side of her, men with wings knelt in supplication. The woman wore a smile of serenity as she gazed down at Asgrim and the scene of carnage around him. At least six bodies, monks and soldiers, lay piled in the small foyer. In one corner, the corpse of a priest still sat astride the chest of a soldier. The dead priest's teeth were locked on the savaged throat of the other man, and the soldier's dagger was rammed into the priest's heart. Asgrim stared at the corpses. He had seen men bite each other in combat. Once, he had even seen a warrior, caught up in his battle rage, bite his own arm and tear away a chunk of flesh, but he had never seen a man sink his teeth through another's throat like a wild animal.

His first mate, Gorm Louse-Beard, moved past him and examined a bloody pile of… *something* in a corner. As Gorm bent to examine the mess, his expression betrayed his confusion. Using the point of his sword, he lifted the flayed skin of a man. Impossibly, it was still mostly intact, as if someone had just popped out the bones and wet tissue.

The two men's eyes locked over the bloody skin on the end of the sword. "What orders, Captain?"

Asgrim's skin tingled as if ants crawled over him, and in a voice that was little more than a whisper, he said, "We find the silver. Then leave."

The Danish warriors spread out, moving from chamber to chamber, building to building. Everywhere, they found more corpses. The monastery was a slaughterhouse. The lower levels of the monastery housed storerooms, sleeping chambers, and a large dining room. The dining room, with its long wooden tables, was filthy. Dirty dishes and plates were piled everywhere. Animal bones and other garbage covered the floor. A severed goat's head in a congealed pool of blood sat on one of the tables. Its dead eyes seemed to follow Asgrim as he walked past, mocking him, as if the dead goat knew all the secrets of what had happened here and was amused by Asgrim's confusion. The men muttered oaths beneath their breath, calling on the gods for protection.

Upstairs, they found the monastery infirmary. One of the beds contained the corpse of a priest who had been tied spread-eagle to the posts. Beside the bed was a bloody collection of medical instruments that had been used to torture the man. The skin covering the corpse's face had been cut loose, strip-by-strip, exposing the glistening muscle and sinew beneath. The corpse's lidless eyes stared at Asgrim and his men. His mouth open, one of the younger men gaped at the savaged corpse. Asgrim turned toward the young man to say something comforting, but at that moment, the young man suddenly bent over and vomited.

In another chamber, they found the monastery's library. Each desk held a book; each book was chained to the desk. Asgrim casually flipped through one of the meticulously detailed tomes before letting it drop. Real men had no need for such nonsense, and although the books may have been priceless to the priests, they were useless to him. He could sell them, he supposed, but he had come for silver, not paper. At the back of the library, one of the priests had written something in dripping blood on a wall, but neither Asgrim nor his men could read the runes.

He turned and looked about himself. "Where's Knut? He speaks Frankish."

A young, thin man with pockmarked skin appeared as if by magic and stood next to Asgrim, staring at the writing on the wall.

"Well, man. What does it say?" Asgrim demanded.

"I don't know," Knut answered. "It isn't Frankish. I don't know what it is."

Asgrim frowned and walked away, muttering beneath his breath. Something very wrong had happened here. This place was cursed. He thought it best to find the silver quickly and get away.

The upstairs church was the largest and most grandiose room in the monastery. Tiles covered its ceilings, and the walls were adorned with elaborate tapestries showing scenes of piety and religion, images that were obviously of importance to the priests but seemed pointless to Asgrim. Not a single battle scene was among them. Did these men have no heroes? Long wooden pews took up most of the chamber, and early morning sunlight poured through the narrow windows. But even there, in their most holy chamber, the stench of death was present. More angry flies droned near the wooden platform at the front of the church.

What now?

Behind the platform, they found the naked corpses of six young women, and this time, Asgrim himself almost vomited. He had seen his share of death. In truth, he had killed enough men to fill a mead hall, but this was too much.

Before turning away from this carnage, Asgrim's fingers brushed the Thor's hammer he wore on a thong around his neck. The women must have come from the village. But why were they there? And who had done this, the priests or the soldiers?

The priests, Asgrim was certain.

But why would the priests do such a thing to their own kind? It was unmanly, cowardly even, worse than beasts. Perhaps that was why the soldiers had turned on them? If Asgrim had been the local garrison leader, he would have done the same. By Odin's beard, he would like to kill these priests all over again.

Beside him, Gorm swore beneath his breath as he glared at the corpses. "Who would do such a thing?"

"Doesn't matter," said Asgrim. "Let's find the silver, burn this place to the ground, and go home."

"Aye," said the other man, shaking his head as he followed Asgrim out of the church.

In the rear, they found the abbot's quarters. Much larger than the cells the other monks lived in, the abbot's chambers were spacious and well lit. The abbot himself sat at a desk facing the doorway, his dead face smirking at them. There was not a mark on the corpse, but his skin looked ancient, withered, and rotted, as if he had been dead for years.

They searched the chamber quickly and thoroughly, seeking the monastery's treasure. What they found was a paltry sum: a small purse of silver coins, some brass candlesticks, a small tin cross, and another bag filled with pennies. They found no treasure, no hoard of silver.

Asgrim's anger rose. He turned to Gorm. "Have the men search every room. Tear this place apart. Search all the buildings, everything. The priests have hidden their treasure somewhere. I know it. Search the haylofts, the piggery, the stables, and workshops. Tear up the floorboards, but find that gods-damned treasure!"

Gorm's eyes went wide, and his face blanched. "Captain. We can't… can't stay here. This place is cursed. There's no doubt of that. Their god had forsaken them. If we stay—"

His hands clenching into fists, Asgrim rounded on the other man. "We stay until we find the silver. I'm not leaving without plunder. It's their god, not ours, nothing that can harm us."

"I'm not so—"

"Just do it, man!"

Gorm nodded somberly before turning away to issue the orders. The others left Asgrim alone in the abbot's chambers. He plopped down on one of the wooden chairs and undid the leather ties holding his helm in place before removing it and placing it on his knee. His dark hair was drenched in sweat and plastered to the side of his head. He rubbed his beard where the cheek flaps had pressed against it.

Asgrim's hair was short, well groomed, and shaved at the back of his neck to ease the fit of his helmet. His moustache, though, was long, running past his mouth and into his short beard. He would have been a handsome man, if not for the misshapen lump of scar and tissue that was his nose.

Balancing his helmet on his knee, he glared at the dead abbot. "Don't you laugh at me, priest! I'll find your treasure. You'll see. And after I do, I'll burn your damned home to the ground."

The smile remained on the dead priest's face as a wasp crawled out of his open mouth and flew away.

* * *

Three times, Alda had silently circled the monastery, trying to find the courage to enter it, to find Celsa. But she couldn't do it. She just couldn't bring herself to come any closer. Instead, she spied on its darkened walls from the cover of the night, and her dread grew. Something had happened there. The monastery was no longer a holy place—if it ever had been.

Alda had rushed there as soon as she received word—belatedly—that the monks had taken the women from their homes. A former neighbor, one whom Alda had helped when her little boy had suffered from the pox, had arrived at Alda's hut in the forest, wild-eyed and frantic. The monks had taken her daughter, as well. They burst in on her farm, assaulting her husband and dragging away her daughter. They had not even spoken. That had been the previous night.

Later that same night, while Alda hid in the woods and watched the monastery, the soldiers had come from the fort, demanding the women be released. Instead, the monks had fought them. Peaceful monks fought soldiers. It was impossible. All of this was impossible, but Alda had heard the sounds of battle and the screams of the dying. Since then, she had neither seen nor heard anything moving within the monastery or the nearby fort.

She had been within the monastery's walls as a young girl. Her father had taken her to trade for salt with the monks after they had moved from the mainland seeking solitude and an escape from the plague. The priests had been kind to her, offering her water and an apple, but she had never felt safe within its walls. Something had always felt *wrong* there, as if something dark, something secret was hiding within its walls. She had spoken of her fear once to her father, who had laughed at her and told her she was being foolish. The monastery of Saint Philibert, the home of the famous Black Monks, was a holy place, loved by God, and the island of Noirmoutier, with its happy little fishing village, was as safe a place as any in Frankia. This was why when her mother had died of the wasting sickness that had killed so many others within the city's walls, when Alda and her sister Celsa had been little, her father had moved the three of them here, to become a village healer and to live a simple life among rural godly people, safe from the horrors of living in a town the size of Nantes.

But then, her father had been wrong about so many things. Most of all, he had been wrong about the village and its residents. They had never truly accepted her family. She hadn't realized this when she was little, but she understood it as an adult. Her fellow villagers, Christians all, had made sure she learned this particular lesson well—especially her former in-laws.

She crouched beside a tree near the edge of the woods facing the monastery and its salt fields and shivered, despite the summer heat. Something evil had always been hidden away within the monastery. She had felt it when she was a child, regardless of her father's admonitions, and she felt it now. She had always been very sensitive to omens and the secret world around them. Some hidden thing, some dark force that had been slumbering within the monastery had awakened. She felt this in her soul. And whatever it was, it had passed its evil on to the monks. They were no longer men of God. What were they doing in there to the women, to Celsa? And why couldn't she find the courage to go help her?

Alda tugged at her hair, rocking back and forth on her heels. Her muscles were sore and beginning to cramp from exertion and lack of sleep. She should go inside, she knew, to search for Celsa. She should confront the monks and demand that they let Celsa go, but she just couldn't find the courage to move. She was so pathetic and weak, so cowardly. She would never save Celsa from outside. She ground her teeth together, shaking her head. What were those damned monks doing to her? Why had they taken her and the other women? Celsa was innocent, as good and pure a soul as any that lived, better than those damned villagers they lived among, who professed to be Christians yet abused those weaker than themselves.

Knowing she should go inside, go find Celsa, she stared at the monastery's dark walls, but something stopped her from entering—some sense that there was still something hidden away within the monastery. If she went in there, she would die.

So she did nothing, and hated herself for her cowardice.

And then she saw the warriors arrive, slipping from the woods not a hundred paces from where she hid. When she heard their leader speak, she realized they were foreigners, raiders, Vikings. They had to be Vikings, bloodthirsty murderers all.

Death from the sea.

TWO

The Black Monastery,
August 2, 799,
Early afternoon

Asgrim was pacing in the courtyard when his brother and his men returned from the fort leading a prisoner, a Frankish soldier. Asgrim met Bjorn at the entrance to the monastery. His brother's eyes widened when he saw the corpses lying about the courtyard, and his face wrinkled in distaste.

"What in the name of the gods happened here?" Bjorn asked, indicating the corpses with a jut of his chin.

Asgrim shook his head. "Don't know, but they killed each other. There's none left living here. The fort?"

"Just this one." Bjorn indicated the Frankish soldier with his thumb. "We saw nothing moving within, so we searched it. Empty. Like they all just piled out and didn't come back. Left everything in place, though. Food, belongings, some small coin. We found this one hiding in the woods nearby." Bjorn smirked. "Shit his hose when we grabbed him."

Asgrim considered the Frank. The man trembled like a sheep being led to slaughter. He was short but well fed, with a soldier's solid build. He wore a boiled-leather tunic studded with metal rivets. Dried blood matted his long dirty hair and had crusted down the side of his face. His hands were bound behind his back, and one of Asgrim's men held him in place with a hand on his shoulder.

"Didn't want to come with us at all," Bjorn said. "When he saw we were coming here, he kept trying to run away." Bjorn snorted. "Tried *real* hard to run away."

Asgrim stepped closer to his brother and whispered near his ear. "You'll soon see why. The monks and soldiers fought one another. I don't know what's happened here, but it looks like the monks were crazed, attacking each other and murdering girls from the village. The men are already muttering of spirits, of *draugr*."

Bjorn stepped back, shock on his face. "*Draugr*?"

"This place is cursed, brother."

"Odin's balls," Bjorn muttered, his hand going to the wooden hammer hanging about his neck. "We can't stay. The silver?"

Asgrim shook his head.

"Damn," Bjorn said. He held the great ax between his knees as he removed his battle helm.

Asgrim had inherited their father's stern, dark looks, but Bjorn had taken after their mother. He even had her blue eyes and long straw-blond hair. Like Asgrim, Bjorn sported a short-trimmed beard, but unlike his brother, he shaved his upper lip. He was a good-looking man, who was blessed by the gods and popular. In battle, he may have been fierce, but back home, he would dangle a baby off his knee and bellow with laughter. Long married, he already had three daughters and two sons, all tall and good looking like their father. His younger brother had everything Asgrim could never have.

The gods probably thought that a great joke.

Sighing, Bjorn stared at the carnage covering the courtyard. "How long do you plan to stay?"

Asgrim rubbed the back of his neck. "As long as it takes."

A heavy silence fell between them. The frown on Bjorn's face grew. "Brother… the Franks will come. The best we can hope for is a day or two… maybe not even that."

"I know."

Bjorn leaned in closer and lowered his voice. "The men won't like it, and assholes like Harald will cause trouble, undermine you."

"Harald doesn't have the balls," said Asgrim.

Bjorn snorted. "Don't be so sure about what he'd try."

As if on cue, Harald Skull-Splitter—a nickname Asgrim was fairly certain the man had given himself—stormed out of a monastery doorway, his face white. Just behind him, trailing him like puppies were two of his closest friends, Koll and Mar. Harald was a large man, not as big as Bjorn, but a strong, capable fighter just the same. Unfortunately, he was also a hotheaded loudmouth and saw himself as an up-and-coming war band leader. Bjorn was right to worry, Asgrim admitted. Harald had his own little circle of admirers, and someday, he might become a real threat. But he was not now, not on this voyage.

Asgrim drummed his fingers over his sword hilt as he watched Harald. "All right. Keep an eye on him. If he starts causing problems, then do something. Make an example. But *don't* kill him."

"Someday you're gonna have to," said Bjorn.

"Not today," said Asgrim. Wanting to change the subject, he turned to stare at the Frankish prisoner. "I need to know what happened here. Knut and his father used to trade with these people. Have him question this one."

Bjorn nodded, then walked over and gripped the prisoner's shoulder. As Bjorn led him away, the man went docilely enough, but Asgrim suspected he would bolt if given the chance.

"And find out about the monks' silver!" Asgrim yelled at his brother's back.

Asgrim shook his head and swore beneath his breath. He needed information. The villagers might know what had happened here. They almost certainly knew the Danes had arrived. No doubt they had already run from their homes to hide within the forest. Even now, they were probably spying on them.

The Saracen merchant had said there was a long bar of land to the south of the island that reached most of the way to the mainland. At low tide, men would be able to ride across it. Eventually, the Franks would defend their kingdom; they had to. If Asgrim and his men were caught by horsemen while away from their longship, it could be a disaster—especially if the Franks brought bows. They could stay at a distance and pick them off. Asgrim and his men couldn't stay here, but he was not willing to let go of his chance at plunder.

But the Franks weren't the real problem. As great a worry as they were, at least he knew how to fight men. But there was a supernatural menace here—one that he could do nothing about. *Something* had driven these men to kill one another, something nebulous and invisible, yet deadly just the same. The longer he and his men stayed near this accursed place…

He bent down, picked up a round stone, and hurled it at the stone wall of the monastery. "Gods damn this shithole!"

He wasn't going anywhere without the silver. Fate had driven him here, where he could find the means to atone for the blood on his hands. He refused to believe the Nornar would lead him to the island just to deny him a chance at redeeming himself.

Freya.

"Gods damn their one god!"

He'd lost so much already because of his rage. Without plunder to pay his wergild, he could never go home again. And without home, the men would begin to turn against him. Soon, he would face a mutiny as his warriors demanded to return to their families, to the fall harvest. What then? What destiny waited for a man like him?

"Gods damn the crones," he muttered, closing his eyes and seeing Freya's face again.

* * *

The monastery sprawled over numerous buildings. Some, such as the kitchens and latrines, were kept separate from the rest of the monastery. Other buildings had been added on over the years. The bakehouse, brewery, piggery, stables, smithy, and other workshops looked to be newer buildings than the others. Searching all these buildings took time. Unfortunately, even after hours of searching, they found nothing, and Asgrim's desperation grew. He even ordered his men to dig up the newest graves in the monastery's small cemetery. When the men hesitated, he cursed them, grabbed a shovel himself, and began to dig, shaming them. After that, the men rushed to help. So far, though, they had found nothing but rotting bones. Asgrim was standing in a grave, dirt to his knees and leaning on a shovel, when Bjorn approached.

"Anything?" Asgrim asked.

Bjorn shook his head and glanced about warily at the disturbed graves. "They killed their own horses, still in their stalls. Stabbed them with sharpened staves." His brother paused and spit on the ground.

"Why?" asked Asgrim.

Bjorn sighed and shook his head. "Brother, these men were crazy. For all I know, they killed the animals for sport."

Chills ran down Asgrim's back.

His brother glanced about, making sure none of the others were within earshot. "Brother, these holy men were crazed. We should leave before—"

"We leave when we have their silver," Asgrim said.

"There may be no silver," Bjorn said forcefully. "Not here, but there's still time to raid somewhere else. We can still raise the wergild."

"There's silver here," said Asgrim. "I know it."

Bjorn wiped his palms on his leggings and looked away, his face clearly showing his unease.

"What?"

Bjorn stared at the ground. "There's something down below, beneath the monastery."

"A cellar? Storeroom?"

"Not a storeroom," mumbled his brother. "Something… else."

Asgrim's skin flushed with anger. He climbed out of the hole and grasped his brother's upper arm. "What?"

"A crypt, I think."

Asgrim smiled. "Crypts are important. What's down there?"

His brother looked away, then lowered his voice. "I… don't know. We didn't enter. I was… afraid."

Asgrim let go of his brother's arm and stepped back, staring at his brother's face. In battle, Bjorn was always where the fighting was fiercest. And once, Asgrim had watched with pride and fear as Bjorn, still wearing his chain mail, had danced on the oars, jumping from one to another, risking certain death if he fell in the water.

"Brother," Asgrim said. "What are you doing? You can't act like a woman in front of the men."

Bjorn's head jerked up. His eyes were filled with offence. Any other man, Asgrim knew, would be dead in moments. To call a man womanish was to give him the right to kill you. It was the worst insult Asgrim knew, one his brother could never ignore.

"You say this to me? Your own brother?" Spit flew from Bjorn's mouth, and he seemed to grow in size. Just for a moment, Asgrim feared he had gone too far, but then his brother's gaze lowered, and he stared at the ground.

"You don't understand," Bjorn said. "We found the entrance past one of the storerooms. Stairs cut into the earth. The walls are stone. Not earth, but stone, and covered in their damned Frankish runes. I think it's supposed to be a holy place, but it feels… *dirty*. I almost shit myself, and so did the others. I've never, not *ever*, been frightened like that." He looked up, locked eyes with Asgrim and gripped his brother's shoulders with both hands, squeezing tightly. "There's something down there, something evil."

"Brother," said Asgrim, choosing his words carefully. "I don't know what's happened here, but our choices are few. If there's treasure here, we need to find it. The crypt may be cursed—if a crypt it is—but we need to search it. It's the best place to hide something. This place scares me as well, but we need plunder." Asgrim paused, gripped the back of his brother's neck, and pulled his head down so that Asgrim's forehead touched his brother's. "You and I, we can't let the men see we're frightened. You know this."

A silence stretched between them, and Asgrim knew the other men had stopped digging and were watching them. Bjorn nodded, then tried to smile.

"Okay, then," said Asgrim. "So let's go do this."

* * *

Harald Skull-Splitter stared at the writing on the wall of the monks' library. The blood forming the runes had dripped and run down the side of the wall. Flies buzzed about his ears, making a never-ending droning that disturbed him more than the obscenity on the wall. He was glad no one could understand the runes. He didn't want to know what they said. This was just wrong. What kind of a mad fool wrote messages in human blood? This place was cursed by the gods, and they shouldn't be here. It was all wrong.

Asgrim should have stayed in Hedeby and taken his justice like a man. Instead, he had run away. What was worse, he had forced Harald and the others to run with him. And while it was true that Harald and every other man had just sworn an oath to sail with Asgrim Wood-Nose, they were supposed to have been part of an invading army in Ireland, not a single longship farther south than any man had a right to go. Despite what the others like that toad Gorm said, the trip didn't feel like a raid. If this was to be a true raid, they should have sailed away from Hedeby with their shields hung on the side of *Sea Eel* for all to see. Their families should have been there, cheering them off. Instead, they had skulked away in the dark of the night like thieves. Harald had barely had time to say goodbye to his father before that giant idiot Bjorn had dragged him from his home. The others didn't want to say it, but Harald knew they had run away in the night like cowards, barely escaping the earl's rightful vengeance. Asgrim had been a decent enough captain in his time, leading a number of profitable raids in the Kingdom of Wessex, Frisia, and once even in Breton. But that was in the past. Now, he had nothing but bad luck. Harald saw it; the others must see it, as well. And once a captain's luck went foul, a man could do nothing but find someone else to serve.

They had heard of the earl's wergild soon enough at a trading camp along the Frisian coast; word had spread that quickly. Then all the men realized what Asgrim had done that night, although they had already whispered of it among themselves. No one had ever heard of such a wergild before: one hundred pieces of silver. No man could pay such a price, not even Asgrim Wood-Nose. No. He would never find so much plunder, not if he raided every single village, port, and Christian monastery in the world. Asgrim Wood-Nose would never go home again, and he would always have a price on his head. Eventually, it would catch up to him.

Koll and Mar stood nearby, arguing about a book they held between them. They could sell the books, Harald knew, Franks paid good silver for useless junk like this, but even if they sold all of the books they'd still only make a handful of silver. Not enough, never enough. Harald shook his head and walked out of the library, letting the two men argue over scraps of paper that neither could read.

Sunlight poured through the slit windows of the monastery, casting pools of light across the darkened hallway. As Harald walked and pondered, he considered his options. He was the son of a minor landowner, a poor farmer with progressively weaker fields. He would never, not ever be able to afford his own ship. And in all the time he had sailed with Asgrim, not once had the ugly bastard ever even given him a silver armband to reward his impressive loyalty or his considerable prowess in battle.

Asgrim was jealous of him, Harald knew. He was a better man than that ugly freak. The others must see it, as well. This is why he always gave Harald the shit jobs and let that bastard Gorm give the orders. Asgrim hated Harald because he knew Harald would be a better captain than he would ever be. If only Harald had the chance to prove this. Harald snorted and kicked the severed head of a monk down the hallway, watching it bounce and thud off the walls before rolling to a stop.

They were only there, so far south, because of the stupid whore. Not that Harald blamed Asgrim for what he had done. Any other man would have done the same. But then, he also didn't really blame her for spreading her legs for another man. What woman would choose to lie with that ugly rot-nosed freak? She probably would have fucked Harald, too. He snorted at the thought of having Wood-Nose's wife. Shame *that* hadn't happened; she had been a rare beauty.

Still, it wasn't fair that they all had to suffer because one man couldn't satisfy his woman. Worse, they shouldn't be here in this gods-cursed shithole. They needed to get out before it was too late. Any sane man could see that. But that stupid bastard wouldn't give up his useless search for treasure that didn't exist. He would drag them all down with him.

Unless someone else took charge.

But they had sworn oaths. Men didn't break oaths. No man was more dishonorable than an oath-breaker. Any man who broke an oath would go to Niflheim when he died, not Valhalla.

But hadn't Asgrim also sworn an oath to the earl? Didn't killing the man's son also make him an oath-breaker? It did. That's why the gods had turned away from him. That's why his luck had turned so bad. Asgrim Wood-Nose? No. Asgrim Oath-breaker. Asgrim Ill-luck. Realization dawned on Harald that his future was changing. They couldn't be oath-breakers if Asgrim was already an oath-breaker. It was so simple once he realized it. The gods were giving him an opportunity. All he had to do was take it.

He walked out of the main complex and stepped out into the sunlight, feeling better for being away from inside that damned unholy stone building. He was onto something, he was certain of that. The men were frightened. And well they should be; spirits haunted this place. They didn't want to stay here, but that ugly bastard forced them to. The others must also be feeling the same way Harald was. There was no plunder, nothing worth coming all this way. *But*—they could raid the village on the other side of the island. At least then, they would have women. Butthole that he was, the captain never let them raid villages or take slaves. He was soft. Despite his ugly looks, he was soft and weak.

That's why his own wife had betrayed him. He probably couldn't get it up anyway.

His thoughts tumbled about inside his head as he wandered without purpose. He was vaguely aware that he had walked in the direction of the piggery. The animals had all been slaughtered by the monks, their carcasses left to rot where they had been killed. He shook his head in disgust. Who killed pigs just to kill pigs? Some of the men were searching the piggery. Others rooted about the hay. Harald leaned against a rickety wooden fence and absentmindedly watched them.

Who would still be loyal to Asgrim? Who had yet to come to the same realization he had? He listed the most obvious in his head: Gorm, Steiner, Gils, Snorri, and at least ten more. The most obvious of all though was Asgrim's freak brother. That giant idiot would be the greatest danger. He may have been stupid, but Bjorn was also huge, strong, and a better fighter than any other man present. Harald snorted. Well, maybe not a *better* fighter, but he was bigger and stronger.

A plan began to form in his mind. They were far from home, they couldn't go back, and the captain's luck had turned bad. There was no way he would ever raise the earl's wergild. Even worse, the place was haunted, and if they stayed, they might all die there. On the other hand, the longer they stayed and found nothing, the more likely it would become that the others would begin to see this, as well. In time, they would all come to the same conclusion Harald had; they would have to, also. And Harald could ease them along that path, subtly, safely, until enough of them recognized the truth.

Without Asgrim, they could sail home again. But first, they could make a series of small raids along the coast, make some profit, earn some fame, and get the lads some women. That'll make 'em happy.

Harald smirked, congratulating himself on starting to think like the leader he knew he was. Like a captain.

* * *

Bjorn was right. An evil presence *did* lurk at the bottom of the stairs. Asgrim could feel it from where he stood at the top, holding a lit torch. Behind him, Bjorn and four others waited: Gorm Louse-Beard and three of the steadier men. They carried picks, hammers, and shovels they had found in one of the workshops.

Never in his life had Asgrim felt anything like this. The air was cold and wet, almost misty. Even the stairs were wet. Asgrim bent down and ran his finger in the water on the stone stairs, then tasted it. Salt. Salt water slicked the stairs.

How was that possible?

And then he saw something else on the stairs, vegetation of some type. He stared at it in confusion for several moments, then bent down and picked it up, holding it close to his eye.

Seaweed?

He let it fall from his fingers and hesitated, glaring at the darkness below. He knew he couldn't keep standing there, too terrified to move. It wasn't manly. Tremors ran down his body, and he actually shivered. He wanted to run away, to bolt in fear. Instead, he took a tentative step forward, then another. Slowly, he descended the stone stairs, his pulse racing like the wind in a storm. The others followed.

A large chamber, perhaps twenty ells long by ten wide, met them at the bottom of the stairs. Numerous carved stone arches, each thicker than a man and linked by countless spiderwebs, held up the chamber's high curved ceiling. All along the arches, the monks had carved scores of their crosses and more of their mysterious runes. Recesses, each holding a desiccated skeleton, had been set into the brick walls all along the length of the tomb. Why have a cemetery *and* a tomb, Asgrim wondered. Was this place only for their dead leaders?

The otherworldly presence they had felt from above was unmistakably stronger down there. Its cloying presence threatened to suffocate Asgrim and to crush his faltering courage, yet somehow, he forced himself to move forward. The flames from his torch dampened, as if the fire had to struggle to survive. The smell of the ocean was overwhelming now, and just for a moment, Asgrim thought he heard the crashing of waves. The air he breathed was thick with moisture; the stones of the chamber were soaked, and puddles splashed beneath their boots. Behind him, Gorm cursed, and then whispered a prayer to Odin.

Swinging the faltering torch from side to side, Asgrim stepped farther into the crypt, and a crypt it was. This was, without a doubt, the monastery's inner sanctum, its most sacred place. At least it should have been, but there was nothing holy there.

Asgrim's vision focused until it was tunnel-like. At the far end of the crypt, a figure stood watching them. Asgrim's heart throbbed in warning, and he almost dropped his torch before he realized it was only a statue carved in the likeness of a monk. Just beside the statue was an open stone coffin. The stone lid had been carefully placed on the floor. As Asgrim drew closer, he expected to see a corpse within it, but it was empty.

The statue's face had been carved with a beatific smile, as if he saw secrets others could not. This man must have been important to the monks to have earned a place of honor beneath their monastery. But if so, where was the corpse now? Had it awoken somehow? Had it climbed from its stone coffin and walked away as an undead spirit, a Christian *draugr*? Only scraps of rotted cloth and dust remained.

"Gods help us," muttered Gorm. "What's wrong with this place? I feel… I—"

"We all feel it," said Bjorn as he stepped closer to Asgrim and peered into the empty coffin.

Asgrim walked past the coffin and examined the stone wall behind it, looking for signs of loose stones or perhaps a hiding place, but he found nothing.

"There's something here," said Bjorn from behind him.

Turning, Asgrim saw that his brother had drawn his knife and was using it to poke at the rags within the coffin. Asgrim's fear spiked abruptly, and he was about to lash out at his brother when Bjorn suddenly thrust his hand into the coffin and picked up something. He held a small fragment of bone in front of his eyes.

"Brother…" said Asgrim.

"It's nothing," answered Bjorn, staring intently at the fragment. "Just a piece of bone. Old, very old."

Asgrim stared, mesmerized at the bone in his brother's hand. It was yellow with age and was perhaps just a piece of finger, maybe a knucklebone. Asgrim's skin felt clammy, and he found himself gasping for air. He lurched forward, gripped his brother's large forearm, and felt a shock pass through him. Just for a moment, in place of his brother, Asgrim saw a monster, a green-skinned aquatic thing with an impossibly elongated and hairless skull. Its flesh pebbled, and its giant eyes were all black, like a shark's. Then the vision was gone. Bjorn stared at him in confusion.

"Put… put it back," Asgrim croaked.

Bjorn paused, staring at the fragment in his fingers. His hand shook.

"Now!" ordered Asgrim.

Bjorn, startled at his brother's voice, seemed to see him for the first time and nodded. He tossed the bone fragment back into the coffin, where it struck with a thud that resonated throughout the chamber, as if the bone weighed far more than it should have.

Panting heavily, Asgrim wiped his palms across his sweaty face. He shook his head. "There's nothing here. Let's go."

He turned and walked toward the stairs, resisting the urge to run. At the bottom of the stairs, he waited for the others, trying to act like a leader. The other men must have shared his terror, though, because they practically ran over themselves going up the stairs. Only Bjorn hesitated, still at the rear of the crypt, still staring into the coffin.

"Bjorn!" Asgrim raised his voice.

His brother turned away from the coffin and stormed past Asgrim, heading up the stairs. Asgrim took the stairs three at a time and would have run had it not been unmanly.

* * *

It stood in the darkened woods, staring at its grey hands in contempt and wonder. Scornful of the weakness within these beings, it still marveled at the potential for destruction and carnage. Already, the rot was starting as the body it wore began to die. It had to be careful this time, or else it might become trapped again, existing as nothing more than a shade within the bones, powerless without physical contact. And even this body, a warrior's body—stronger than the others had been—was still not going to last very long, not as long as the monk had. But until then, at least it wore flesh again, flesh that allowed it to move and act, to rend and tear. And act it would. These lesser beings would suffer greatly for its forced inaction.

It sensed life—and wished to crush the offensive foulness of it. An entire village of souls to devour stood before it. A rictus of pleasure, more snarl than smile, spread across its grey face.

So long, it had been locked away for too long. Strong though he had been, Philibert had died too soon, without enough warning. And it had happened while it had been unaware, while its consciousness had been elsewhere, sleeping. Existing in this realm required constant effort and was a never-ending struggle to remain. It didn't belong here, so this reality fought it and tried to push it away. Had it been aware Philibert was that close to death, it would have taken another body—*before* they locked away the rotting corpse within that damned crypt. Even then, when it had awakened and found its servant dead, it still should have been able to escape the tomb, to find another human shell to possess. But the other monks had loved Philibert and had, of all things, believed him to be holy. So they had engraved his coffin with silver etchings—not much silver because they were poor, but just enough to bar its passage in its weakened state. So it had been trapped, just as surely as if it had been locked away within a silver jar. It had been all the monk's fault. The mortal should have been stronger, strong enough to last years. Instead, he had died in less than a single year.

Trapped within the crypt, its awareness drifted in and out, like the waves. Then, while it slept, through some happy chance, those fools had finally released it. They opened the coffin and touched the bones, awakening a portion of it and absorbing some of its influence—not much, just the most infinitesimal portion of it, but far more than enough to poison their souls, to turn them away from their god. Without even being fully awake and aware, it had taken them all, driving them to acts of depravity and joy. And as the priests died, it started to wake, convalescing into the body of their leader, the head abbot. And when a stronger body of the warrior appeared, it abandoned the abbot.

And now it was finally awake. After years of drifting in the void, it was awake and hungry for carnage, so very ravenous for destruction.

It had been so long, too long. Philibert had made promises, yet he had died. All men were liars. It should have expected as much. It too was a liar, a lord of lies, and prince of pain.

And now it was free. What to do first? It should start with the village and skin them all, every man, woman, child, and animal. These thoughts gave it a rush of joy, but then it halted in place as a worry intruded into its consciousness. What of the Eastern men? Where were those fools? They would never give up. It wouldn't, so why would they? If it destroyed the village, would that send a message and lead them there before it was ready for them? No. It wasn't strong enough yet to resist them. They were out there somewhere, it was certain of that. It understood the need for power all too well. They would never stop searching for it. The fate of their Caliphate depended on it.

It wandered aimlessly through the woods, weighing its options. It was on an island, which was good and bad. It couldn't go far inland anyway because it needed to stay near the ocean. But if it stayed there, still wearing the rotting shell, it would be vulnerable to the Eastern men when they came for it—and they would come for it.

And then it felt something new. A small part of its existence still remained within the crypt of Philibert. The piece was so small that it had forgotten it was there. Then someone touched it, releasing its malignance. It felt a connection with the living.

Someone new had arrived on the island, someone interesting.

It turned back toward the black monastery.

THREE

The Black Monastery,
August 2, 799,
Early evening

Koll's and Mar's faces reflected their fear as Harald explained how Asgrim had betrayed them all, leading them here to their doom.

"But we've swuh—swuh—sworn oaths," Mar stuttered, as he always did whenever he was nervous. He ran his hands over his bald head. An ugly little man with pig's eyes, he always looked like he had just been punched in the face.

"He's already betrayed us," said Harald. "Don't you see it? He promised us plunder, land in Ireland." Harald motioned around himself expansively at the walls of the stable where they had been digging near the support beams. "Is this Ireland?"

"You're splitting hairs," said Koll, leaning on his shovel and watching Harald carefully. Koll was a tall, thin man with blond hair that he wore in long braids. "The oath we swore was to serve him for the voyage. None of us actually said *Ireland*."

Harald snorted. "Didn't need to say it. All of us meant it. It was understood, an unspoken promise. One he broke."

Mar's face still showed his uncertainty and his worry, but Koll looked as though he were beginning to get it. "Perhaps," he muttered.

"He'll ku—ku—kill us if he hears what we say." Mar looked about himself.

But no one else was within earshot. Harald wasn't stupid. First, he needed to get his friends onboard and convince them. It wouldn't be too hard, he knew. Neither Mar nor Koll particularly enjoyed doing their own thinking.

"He's done," said Harald. "He just won't admit it. The idiot killed the earl's son. He'll never go home again, but he can bring us all down with him."

"He's a dangerous man," said Koll. "Kill any one of us in a duel."

Harald hawked and spat on the oat-covered earth surface of the stable. "He's not *that* good. Everyone's just afraid to challenge him. If it weren't for that freak brother of his and the ship his father built, he wouldn't even be a captain, just another man, just like us, just like me."

"Yu—yu—you should challenge him," said Mar. "You're b—b—better than any man with an ax."

Harald's mouth opened, but Koll spoke before he could. "Not better than Bjorn. No man can fight him."

"A duel won't work," said Harald. "He'd probably cheat anyway. Or ask his brother to fight it for him." Harald looked away. Even he heard how ridiculous his words sounded. Asgrim Wood-Nose was many things, but he had always been an honorable man.

Could Harald beat him?

"It's this place." Koll pointed his shovel toward the monastery. "He's brought us to ruin, to a cursed land. There's nothing here for any of us but an ignoble death. I bet the gods aren't even watching us this far south." Koll paused and stared at Harald, a smile spreading across his thin face. "Any man that led us away from this place, why, he'd be a hero, a true leader."

"It would take a real leader to save the men, wouldn't it," Harald said.

Mar's face reflected his confusion, and his little pig eyes squinted, but Harald smirked. Perhaps Koll was smarter than he had thought. He would make a good first mate. The three men sat down and began to whisper among themselves, trying to determine whom to approach next.

* * *

When he walked into the stables and saw the three men whispering with their heads together, Gorm Louse-Beard didn't know what they had been saying, but he saw he had spooked them, and he was certain he saw fear in the eyes of that stuttering moron Mar. The back of his head itched, as it always did when he was afraid, but he glared at them and pointed away. "Get your lazy asses up to the main building. We're tearing up the floorboards in their church and need more help."

The three men climbed to their feet and shuffled past Gorm without meeting his eyes. His palm resting on the hilt of his long-knife and his pulse racing, he watched their backs as they walked past. He knew trouble when he saw it. He had to tell the captain.

* * *

Asgrim lurked just inside an open doorway of the monastery, watching the men work in the courtyard. He had ordered them to drag the corpses out of the monastery and pile them outside the walls. They couldn't do anything about the entrails, blood, and feces, but by removing the corpses, they would get rid of the worst of the stench and make searching the monastery slightly more bearable. The men's mood was getting worse. Bjorn had been right about Harald Skull-Splitter. Gorm was certain he had been plotting trouble earlier. Even when Harald should have been helping move the corpses, he and his two buddies, Koll and Mar, were huddled together near a stone wall, whispering.

They needed to be taught a lesson—*before* he had to kill someone. Mutiny was a rot that would only grow if left unchecked. Asgrim stepped back into the interior of the doorway as his brother came up behind the malingering trio. Letting Bjorn administer this particular lesson would be best. If Asgrim had to become involved, somebody might have to die. Oaths were a serious matter.

Without warning, Bjorn stormed forward, grabbed the back of Harald's shoulders, and threw him to the ground, knocking Mar down, as well. His eyes widening, Koll turned to stare at Bjorn, and Bjorn punched him in the face, sending him flying back against the wall before he fell onto his knees with blood streaming down his face. Harald scrambled to get up again, but Bjorn grabbed him by the collar of his leather armor and the seat of his trousers, then rammed him headfirst into the stone wall. The sound of Harald's skull striking the stone made a sickening thud.

No! Bjorn was going to kill him.

Asgrim darted out of the doorway and ran to stop his brother. "Bjorn, enough!" he yelled as he grabbed his brother's shoulders from behind. But Bjorn just shrugged Asgrim off, sending him stumbling back. Trying to overpower the big man was like wrestling a horse.

Ignoring Asgrim, Bjorn lashed out at one of the men on the ground, savagely kicking Mar in the gut. The man whimpered and curled into a ball, all resistance gone. Bjorn lifted his leg, obviously preparing to stomp on Mar's unprotected face. If he connected, he would probably break his neck. Asgrim tackled his brother at the back of his knees, and both men fell forward.

They wrestled together on the ground. His brother screamed in rage and lashed out. His punch only scraped Asgrim's chin, but it still nearly knocked his head off. His brother's eyes were wild, crazed, as if he didn't even recognize him. Grabbing Bjorn's face with both hands, Asgrim smashed his forehead against Bjorn's nose, knocking the larger man onto his back. Moments later, other men rushed forward and piled on top of Bjorn, holding him down with the weight of their numbers.

Asgrim dragged himself to his feet and grabbed at the men holding down his brother, yanking them off him. "Brother, what are you doing?"

From where he squatted on the ground, Bjorn stared at Asgrim as if he didn't recognize him. "I… what?"

Gorm was bent over the unconscious Harald. "He's alive," he called out. "Gods! His head should be cracked in two, but he's alive."

Asgrim got down on his knees and gripped his brother's face. He leaned in and touched his forehead against his brother's. "Are you all right?"

Blood streamed from his nose and dripped into his blond beard, but recognition slowly returned to Bjorn's blue eyes, and he nodded. "I… I what happened?"

Asgrim sat back, staring at his brother's face. "You almost killed these three men."

"What?" The confusion on Bjorn's face made it look like he had just woken up.

Asgrim reached out and squeezed his brother's shoulder. "Go clean your face. Walk it off. We'll talk later."

Looking uncertain, Bjorn got up and stormed away. Asgrim looked to the three men Bjorn had attacked, the ones he was only supposed to teach a lesson.

Well, he'd taught them a lesson, all right.

Harald would live, but he would have a bad headache. The other two men were fine. Koll had a broken nose, but was otherwise okay.

"Get back to work," ordered Asgrim.

The men took to their task with a vengeance, leaving Asgrim to sit and wonder over his brother's rage. He watched Harald's back as he left. The other man's face had held hatred, pure and white hot.

Gods damn this place.

* * *

As the sun went down, the monastery became even more sinister, if such a thing were possible. The western sky was a sea of red flames, and shadows grew across the island. The men, constantly on edge, snapped at one another. Their hands hovered near their weapons, and their eyes darted toward any sudden movement. Even Asgrim found himself on edge, as if spiders crawled across his skin. He stood in the garden, pissing into the monks' stone fountain and watching the darkness grow.

They had been there all day. How much longer could they stay? And where was that gods-damned silver that the Saracen had promised was there? The men he had left with *Sea Eel* would be worried, but they were good steady men and would wait. Besides, they had no choice but to wait. More than five men were necessary to sail a longship that large.

Then he felt the unmistakable presence of eyes upon his skin. Turning his head just slightly, he saw one of the shadows move behind him. Someone was sneaking up on him. Exhaling slowly, he forced himself to finish urinating and move as if he still believed he was alone in the courtyard. He felt a slight dizziness and a churning in his stomach. Forcing himself to keep his back toward his unseen opponent was torture, but he did so anyway. His fingers rose to scratch the left side on his jaw, near the shoulder where the hilt of *Heart-Ripper* was slung. He paused for several heartbeats.

Had they missed someone within the monastery, or was it one of his own men? Had Harald Skull-Splitter found the courage to attack his captain? Or was it a spirit? *Draugr* came out at night; everyone knew this.

A pebble shifted just behind him, making a scratching noise, and Asgrim spun, his sword in hand, his teeth bared.

No one was there.

He panted in place, his eyes darting about. He was certain he had heard someone and seen the shadows move.

Draugr.

Ham and Glum, a pair of young men on their first raid, little more than boys, really, came out the doors of the monastery and saw Asgrim standing with his sword drawn. Both men spun about in place, drawing their own long knives and looking about in all directions for attackers.

"Captain, what?" Glum asked, his eyes betraying his fear.

"Do we… do we call the others?" Ham asked.

Asgrim exhaled, then shook his head. He was jumping at shadows, at nothing. No, not at nothing. This place was haunted.

"No." He re-sheathed his sword. "But go find Gorm and my brother. Tell them to round everyone up. We're not staying here this night."

The faces of both of the young men lit up with smiles.

Only a fool stays overnight where spirits dwell, and the dead did haunt this place. Asgrim was certain of it.

"Back to the ship?" Ham's face reflected his desire to quit this island.

"To the Franks' fort," Asgrim replied. "We'll start the search over again in the morning. When there's no *dra*—when there's more light."

* * *

Alda sat back against a tree trunk hundreds of paces from the walls of the monastery, watching. The northmen had been in there all day, and all day, she had remained hiding and watching. She bit into an apple as she watched. Periodically, she had seen the men on the walls of the monastery. They had gone into all of the outbuildings, and once, she had even seen them up on the monastery's roof. They were searching for something. Plunder, she guessed, but she doubted they would find much. The monks had always been poor. Everyone knew that.

There had been no fighting, no sounds of battle or screams of the wounded. Had the monks surrendered? Would they have given up her sister to the raiders?

She closed her eyes and put her head back against the rough tree bark. Tears flowed down her cheeks. She was lying to herself, and she knew it. There were no prisoners and no fighting because no one still lived within that monastery when the foreigners had arrived. She was certain of it now. Her sister was already dead. She was wasting her time, and she should go hide in the forest until the raiders left. Being this close to them was dangerous, too dangerous.

But Celsa. Was Alda to blame for Celsa?

No. God wouldn't be so cruel. Hadn't Alda suffered enough already? Her stillborn child, her husband, her father. Must the Lord also take her sister?

Wiping her tears with the back of her hand, she glared at the dark monastery. She wasn't going anywhere, not until she was certain about Celsa. She owed her little sister that much.

Then she saw movement near the gate of the monastery. She climbed to her feet, excitement coursing through her. The raiders were leaving. And they had a prisoner.

* * *

As they left the monastery, a vast feeling of relief came over Asgrim. He could tell by the faces of his men that they felt it, as well.

A beaten path through the tall grass led to the fort, and the men followed along it in single file, barely talking. After about a minute, Asgrim saw a familiar brown head poke up from behind some bushes, and a moment later, Hopp ran over to join him. Asgrim dropped to one knee and pulled the hound's head in close. Hopp, normally lively and excited, merely rested his head against Asgrim's armored chest and panted heavily.

"It's all right, boy," whispered Asgrim into the vallhund's ear. "I wanted to run away, as well."

Hopp kept beside him the rest of the way, unwilling to separate himself again from his master.

As they reached the wooden fort, some of the men began to talk and joke, obviously feeling better. The Frankish soldiers had been there for some time, long enough to build an earthen mound and log wall all around their fort. Though small, the fort consisted of a sturdy wooden longhouse, a couple of guard towers, and some huts that no doubt served as storehouses. Asgrim set a watch and had the men raid the fort's pantry. The soldiers had left several weeks' of food, including some live chickens and goats in a pen. The wooden barrels were filled with beer, and even though Asgrim wanted to avoid letting the men get drunk, he allowed them to break open one of the barrels. Sometimes, a man needed a drink. The other barrels, though, Asgrim ordered Gorm to secure. Some of the men grumbled, but Asgrim didn't care. The last thing he wanted was for danger to arrive when his men were too drunk to fight.

Besides, the darkened walls of the monastery were close, too close.

As Gorm turned to follow his orders, Asgrim reached out and gripped the other man's arm. "A minute," he said.

Gorm turned and raised an eyebrow.

Asgrim hesitated while he searched for the right words. The vision of the monstrous face in the crypt flashed before his eyes. “Gorm, down below, in the crypt, did you notice anything unusual, see anything weird?”

Gorm’s eyes narrowed, and he shook his head. “No, but something down there scared the piss out of me. What did you see?”

Asgrim released his arm. “Nothing. I saw nothing but shadows.”

Gorm nodded, then turned and walked away.

“Just shadows,” Asgrim whispered to himself.

* * *

In the fort’s small stable, they found four riding horses. The animals had been abandoned and were weak with hunger, but several of the men set to tending, feeding, and brushing them, then walked them as much as the half-starved animals could take. In the morning, Asgrim would use them to send word to the men guarding *Sea Eel* to let them know everything was okay.

With the sun down and night fully descended, they sat in the fort’s longhouse, eating roasted goat. Asgrim sat apart from the men. Gorm joined him, but his brother sat back in the shadows by himself.

Bjorn had been melancholy since the incident with Harald, who, on the other hand, was suddenly very cooperative and well behaved. He had kept his mouth shut since the beating from Bjorn. But Asgrim still remembered the hatred on the other man’s face. This wasn’t over, and he needed to keep a close eye on him. He shook his head. As if he didn’t already have enough to worry about.

With food in his belly, Asgrim began to feel less irritable, and he ordered the prisoner brought out. Two of his men dragged over the Frank and pushed him down on his knees in front of Asgrim.

"He's eaten?" Asgrim asked his handlers, one of whom was the tall, thin Knut who spoke the Frankish tongue.

"We gave him food," answered Knut, "but he didn't touch it."

Asgrim considered the man kneeling before him. He had been clean-shaven, as was the Frankish custom, but he wore at least two to three days of stubble on his dirty face. He wouldn't meet Asgrim's gaze, choosing instead to stare at the ground. He trembled, and spit ran down his grizzled chin.

He'd seen this before, in men who had seen too much battle. The man probably thought they were going to torture and kill him. It was a valid fear. Asgrim knew some captains tortured their prisoners for sport, but this was not his way. He had killed more men than he could count, but usually in battle.

Usually, but not always.

Damned.

Cursed.

He sighed and concentrated on Knut standing beside the prisoner. "So, what happened here?"

Knut bit his lower lip and ran a hand through his long red hair. "I'm sorry, Captain, but nothing he says makes sense."

"What do you mean?"

"He keeps repeating 'They're taken, they're taken,'" said Knut.

"Who's taken?" Asgrim considered the prisoner. Was he referring to the six young women? He turned to Gorm. "Bring him some beer."

Gorm nodded and stepped away, then returned with a large wooden cup filled with dripping beer. The prisoner looked at it stupidly for a moment before taking it with trembling hands. Then the man upended it into his mouth, guzzling it, letting a large portion pour down his cheeks and onto his chest.

"Get him another," ordered Asgrim.

The prisoner drank the second beer only slightly less quickly.

Asgrim glanced at Knut. "Tell him we won't kill him, that when we leave, we'll release him."

"I'm not sure he'll believe you," said Gorm.

"Maybe not," said Asgrim, "but I don't slaughter helpless men."

The words were out of his mouth before he realized what a hypocrite he was. The others must have realized it, as well, because an uncomfortable silence settled over them, and they looked away.

"Just tell him," snapped Asgrim.

Knut, speaking slowly in the Frankish tongue, repeated Asgrim's words.

The prisoner met Asgrim's eye, seeking assurance. Asgrim nodded and motioned for the man to drink his beer. He sipped and then began to talk, slowly at first, but then faster, rushing to tell his tale.

Knut stopped him with a raised hand and turned to Asgrim. "He says his name is Amalric. He's in the service of a Frankish knight named Cuthbert, from Nantes, along the banks of the Loire River."

Asgrim nodded. Although he had never been there, he knew where Nantes was. It was a large Frankish settlement, less than a day's sailing inland. It would have made a nice prize, but raiding it would have taken ten times the men he possessed, if not more.

"Why are they here?" Asgrim asked.

Knut repeated the question; again, Amalric the Frank provided a long answer before Knut cut him off.

"He says his master Cuthbert was sent here by the Frankish King Charlemagne to safeguard the monks. Says the king was afraid the Saracens would attack them again, and he ordered the monks to move their monastery to the mainland, where they'd be safer. This Cuthbert was sent to see they made it."

Saracens? Asgrim's face felt hot. A Saracen had sent him here with a promise of silver. Why were the Saracens so concerned with this place? He felt the play of destiny, so strong it almost made his head spin.

The man began talking again, and they all watched him. He became even more agitated.

Knut stopped him. "They got here six months ago, built the fort and the longhouse, and waited on the monks to prepare to move."

"How many men did this Cuthbert bring with him?" Asgrim asked.

Knut repeated the question. "Two score. All fighters."

Asgrim frowned. "What took so long? It doesn't take six months to move."

When the question was put to him, Amalric became even more agitated as he provided the answer.

"Says the monks dithered, wasted time. Says they didn't want to leave. Finally, this Cuthbert made them start moving, threatened the abbot. So the monks opened their sealed crypt to remove the sacred bones of—"

"Philibert," interrupted Bjorn, his deep voice booming.

Asgrim turned and stared at where his brother sat, paces away, in a corner, wreathed in shadows. The prisoner's eyes grew large, and he nodded, repeating the name.

"*Saint* Philibert," said Knut, his glance flicking to Bjorn.

"How did you know that?" asked Asgrim.

His brother glared at him before abruptly standing. "I don't know. Who cares?"

Without another word, Bjorn stomped out of the longhouse.

Asgrim knew a bit about Christian monasteries. They each had their own patron Christian ghost. Had the Saracen they met mentioned the name of the Frank for whom the monastery had been built? Maybe. Asgrim didn't remember. He returned his gaze to the Frank. "Why did the soldiers attack the monks?"

Knut repeated the question. This time, Amalric's face went white. When he spoke again, the words poured quickly from his mouth. Knut stopped him again.

"He says the monks became crazed, almost overnight. Fine one day, violent the next. Taken by… *Lucifer*, one of their gods."

"I thought they only had one god," said Gorm.

Asgrim raised a hand, cutting him off. "Go on."

The prisoner looked scared enough to soil himself. Knut asked the man a question. He considered the answer before replying. "The monks barred themselves within the monastery, wouldn't let the soldiers in. They fought among themselves like animals. Every time the soldiers came to stand out front and demand to be let in, there were more wounded monks. None of them would say what happened. They just glared at the soldiers, as if they wanted to kill them. This Cuthbert became angry, yelled at them, but they wouldn't let him in. So the soldiers went back to their fort to wait for the monks to come to their senses. But they became worse. One night, the monks snuck out and went to the village. They kidnapped young women and dragged them to the monastery."

Amalric spoke again, providing more details. Knut translated, occasionally asking for clarification on a point. "They could hear the women screaming inside the monastery."

Amalric interjected something and then stared down at his feet. Knut's face blanched, and he met Asgrim's gaze.

"He says these monks opened a door to the underworld, that they let the spirits of the dead out."

"*Draugrs*," whispered Gorm.

Asgrim shivered, despite the heat from the firepit. The men whispered among themselves within the longhouse.

"Why did the soldiers attack?" Asgrim asked.

Knut posed the question, then listened to Amalric's excited reply. "Village elders came to see this Cuthbert, pleaded with him for help. Cuthbert and six others, including this one, went to talk sense to the abbot, make him return the prisoners. But when they arrived, the monks attacked them, throwing stones from the walls. Two of the soldiers were hurt."

Amalric spoke again. Knut listened, then translated. "Says the monks were taken, possessed by this Lucifer. Seems this Cuthbert was very upset, so he went back to the fort and roused the rest of his men. He led them out against the monastery, carrying a felled tree to ram the doors open."

Asgrim rubbed his bearded chin and considered the prisoner. "Why wasn't this one with them?"

When Knut asked the Frank, the man stared morosely at the ground for some time. When he answered, Asgrim could hear the shame in his voice, even if he didn't speak his tongue.

"He was too frightened," answered Knut. "He says he saw a demon in one of the windows of the monastery, watching them, grinning at them. So he ran into the woods and hid. Then we found him."

"What's a demon?" asked Gorm.

Asgrim exhaled. "Like a *draugr*."

Gorm fingered his Thor's hammer.

"What did it look like, this… demon?" asked Asgrim.

"Green skin," translated Knut. "All-black eyes, pointed ears."

Asgrim nodded, feeling queasy, seeing once again the same hideous face in the crypt. "Ask about the treasure," he ordered. "Where is the monk's treasure?"

Knut repeated the question, but Asgrim didn't need to speak Frankish to recognize the confusion on the prisoner's face. Knut listened carefully to his answer before translating. "There's no treasure. The monks made salt for trade, but they were poor. Cuthbert said that coming here was beneath him. The only thing of value the monks possessed were the holy bones of this Saint Philibert."

Asgrim bent over and ran his hands over the back of his head, concentrating on his breathing, fighting to control his rage. No treasure. Of course there was no treasure. Gods damn the crones!

"Pass the word to the men," he said. "In the morning, we sail away. There's nothing here but death."

FOUR

The Soldiers' Fort,
August 2, 799,
Evening

The Franks had built two guard towers, which were little more than platforms, into the wooden wall surrounding their fort. Ladders led up to each platform, and from them, standing sentries could see over the wall and watch the surrounding countryside. Asgrim stood at the bottom of one platform, staring up at the dark shape of his brother, who had been up there, unmoving, for hours.

Bjorn had been silent and moody since leaving the monastery. Like all men, Bjorn could have his dark moments, but this prolonged gloom was uncharacteristic. Asgrim had shamed Bjorn into entering the monks' crypt when he hadn't wanted to. Even worse, Bjorn had been right. There was something evil down there. Was he still angry with Asgrim, or was it something else?

The men's mood had improved when Asgrim announced they would be leaving in the morning, but Bjorn's gloom had not lifted. He had become even more withdrawn. Now, the men avoided him, terrified they might anger him.

Usually, Bjorn was the one who tempered Asgrim's mood. He hadn't realized before how much he depended on his younger brother's support. He wiped his sweaty palms against his wool trousers and began to climb the ladder. The platform sagged and creaked under his weight, but Bjorn didn't turn to see who had joined him. Instead, he kept staring out at the dark woods.

Asgrim leaned against the railing of the platform next to his brother. A half-moon peered out from behind clouds, providing just enough light to make out the dark bulk of the monastery. A light wind caressed his face, providing a welcome relief from the day's heat.

"Well…" Asgrim broke the silence. "Will you talk to me?"

When Bjorn answered, his voice sounded raw, as if talking was difficult. "We never should have come here. You've led us to ruin."

Feeling like he had been punched in the gut, Asgrim stared at the dark profile of his brother's face. He needed Bjorn's support. He had no one else to turn to, not since that red night when he had been so drunk and filled with rage. Bjorn had found him, covered in blood, senseless with alcohol, and mad with guilt. Bjorn had dragged him away, gathered the men, and oversaw their escape on *Sea Eel*. If not for Bjorn, Asgrim would have died that night. Perhaps he should have. Asgrim deserved death for what he had done; he saw it in the faces of his men when they didn't think he was looking. Only Bjorn had stood by him, but if his brother was turning against him…

"We had no choice," said Asgrim. "We had to try, to take a chance here. I'm sorry. I shouldn't have listened to that damned Saracen. I wanted to believe him too much." Asgrim reached out and gripped his brother's forearm. "I'll make this right, bring you home again."

"I don't feel… *right*," said his brother, almost whispering.

"You should sleep. You'll feel better in the morning. We all will."

His brother turned and stared at him in the darkness. "Do you hear the voice? Does it call to you, as well?"

"Voice? What voice?"

His brother turned away again, putting his back to Asgrim. "I feel… as if… someone or something is pushing me out… pushing me away from myself." Bjorn chuckled, but it sounded half like a cry.

Asgrim reached out for his brother's shoulder, then hesitated, not quite touching him. "Brother, what do you mean?"

"Go away!" Bjorn hissed. "Leave me."

Menace tainted his brother's voice. Asgrim recognized Bjorn was moments from violence. He nodded and lowered his hand, then turned away. A deep sense of unease welled up within him as he climbed down the ladder. *Sleep. That's all he needs. In the morning, he'll be himself again.*

* * *

When the last of the raiders had left the monastery, heading in the direction of the soldiers' fort, Alda wanted to rush in and check it, to immediately search for her sister. Instead, she forced herself to wait and to remain calm, not to do something hasty and foolish. It would be safer if she waited, she told herself. There might still be Vikings within the monastery. That thought sent chills down her spine. Would they pretend to march away, to the fort, yet leave men behind in ambush?

So she waited until late in the night. Once, she actually fell asleep for a bit, before startling herself awake again, angry at her weakness. She couldn't sleep. She was exhausted, but she couldn't give in to her body. If she did, she might doze away until morning, and the foreigners would probably come back in the daylight. Then, she would no longer have the opportunity to save Celsa.

Save Celsa? Who was she kidding?

She knew she could never save her sister now. That chance was long gone, and Celsa had to be dead. The prisoner the northmen had led to the fort had been a soldier, not a woman. Even from where she was hiding, she was close enough to tell a man from a woman. Earlier, she had watched the raiders drag the bodies out and pile them just beyond the monastery's walls into an obscene mound of the dead. She had gotten as close as she could, but she had been too frightened to get too close and risk being discovered. She had been too far away to see if any of the corpses had been women, but she was still certain Celsa had never left the monastery, and the northmen would never free a beautiful woman like her sister.

Alda had failed Celsa.

But she had to do something, had to make sure. So when she was certain that anyone still within the monastery—if there was anyone still within the monastery—must be asleep, she rose from her hiding place and began to slip silently toward the complex, sweat pouring from her flushed skin, her senses hyperaware. She was ready to bolt at a moment's notice.

Within a hundred paces of the walls, the smell struck her, forcing her to stagger to a stop and clutch a hand over her mouth and nose. Sweet Jesus, the stench! How could the raiders have stood it for the entire day they were within the monastery? No wonder they left for the fort.

Shaking her head, feeling like she was going to vomit, she forced herself to keep going. When she got closer, she heard the buzzing of flies. Their droning became louder with every step she took, sounding as if every single fly that had ever been hatched was buzzing about her ears. Even in the darkness, she saw the mound of corpses and pieces of corpses in the field near the monastery's gate. The monks and the soldiers were all dead—a rotting pile of dead flesh. She stood back, staring at the obscene mound. She cursed the northmen, but they probably had not killed these men. There had been no sound of battle, and no screams of the dying, when they attacked the monastery. Whatever had happened here had started with those damned monks.

She had been right when she was a child. Some dark, malignant rot had been within that damned monastery and always had been. Eyes reflected in the moonlight among the dead, and she heard the skitter of tiny paws. Rats and other creatures had found the dead. As she stared at the obscene mound, her world seemed to spin about her. Someone should bury them. It was the Christian thing to do. But she also knew no one would approach the monastery until the raiders had sailed away. Was Celsa in that pile? Could she bring herself to look closer?

She took a step toward the pile, and then another. The rats didn't even acknowledge her presence. Alda jumped when a rat ran over her foot, then leapt back into the feast with the others. She moaned softly, and her hands trembled, but she forced herself to go closer. She had to look for Celsa. She had to.

How many dead men had been piled up outside the monastery? How many priests had there been? Twenty? How many soldiers? Just then, the clouds that had been blocking the moon drifted away, and the moon's full light fell upon the pile of dead. She staggered to a stop, gasping, her hand reaching for her throat. The head of every single corpse in the pile was somehow staring directly at her.

She turned and fled, hating herself for her weakness.

* * *

Asgrim lunged at Hrolf the Elder, stepping in to jab the edge of his shield against the other man's, trying shove it aside as he moved from the high guard to simultaneously slash at the taller man's helmeted head. But Hrolf managed to keep his shield in place, so Asgrim altered his strike, moving instead to slash against Hrolf's neck. Hrolf was far too good for such a feeble attack, and the large man's blade met Asgrim's in a bind. Sparks flew through the air as the men applied pressure, subtly seeking weakness in the other's position. Slightly off balance, but still trying to stay on the offensive, Asgrim was the first to move from the bind, coming over Hrolf's blade to slash down at his front thigh. But the other man—making sure his feet didn't leave the blanket—simply pulled his foot back while simultaneously lashing out at Asgrim's face with his sword, so fast that Asgrim only just managed to catch it with his shield. Sweat poured into Asgrim's eyes. His breathing was wild, rushed. Having no other choice, he attacked again, hoping to score a lucky hit by overwhelming the older man.

Usually, in combat, all men followed a cycle: attack, counter-attack, withdrawal. Then the cycle would begin again—until someone found an opening. But this was different. This was a duel, and both men had to stay on the blanket upon which they stood. They couldn't pull back to catch their breath and look for their opponent's weaknesses, so instead, they hammered at one another, again and again, from so close they could each hear the other's strained breathing and see the pain in his face from constant exertion. Duels rarely lasted more than extended moments, a minute at best. Asgrim had no idea how long he and his captain had been fighting, but it was well past a minute. Any moment now, thought Asgrim, any moment now. He's too old for this. He'll make a mistake and drop his guard. Asgrim would get his chance.

Hrolf struck out, changing from a middle guard to low guard as he slashed out at Asgrim's leg beneath his shield. Unable to step out of the way and still remain on the blanket, Asgrim dropped his shield, catching the blade just in time. Hrolf, however, had overextended himself, exposing his own lead leg. Seizing the moment, Asgrim slashed down at it. His blade scraped against Hrolf's thigh, and his face twisted in pain.

Yes! Asgrim's heart surged with joy. And then he realized his mistake. He had leaned forward too far, too quickly, and despite cutting Hrolf, he was now off balance—with his shield dropped. In horror, Asgrim realized Hrolf's attack had been nothing more than a trap, a feint. The real attack came from Hrolf's shield, which was rushing toward Asgrim's exposed face.

In the moment before the metal boss of the shield smashed into his face, Asgrim, seemingly standing outside himself and watching the duel dispassionately, noted his own surprise that the older man had been that good, that tricky. When had old men ever been that skilled with a blade? Asgrim had thought him fat and slow, but Hrolf had been neither.

Crack!

A bright light filled his head. The blow lifted him from his feet and sent him flying. The world spun about him, and he became aware he was on the ground, on his back.

But he was still on the blanket.

He tried to focus his vision, seeing a blurred Hrolf standing above him. He shook his head, surprised at the absence of pain and unable to focus, but still somehow, he was aware of what went on around him. All around them, men stared, some shaking their heads. Above him, Hrolf looked down upon him. The older man's eyes were calm, angry but calm.

"You're done, boy. It's over," Hrolf's voice boomed through the ringing in his ears.

Asgrim shook his head, tasting the blood flowing into his mouth. "No. Not done."

His sword lay nearby, and he grasped at it, somehow wrapping his fingers around its hilt. He stabbed with the blade from where he lay on the ground, but the attack had no force. With a howl of outrage, Hrolf brought his sword blade down upon Asgrim's, and the metal snapped in two. Asgrim stared stupidly at the ruin of his sword. He pulled himself up onto his knees and glared at Hrolf before lunging up at him with his broken blade. The older man shook his head and then hit him in the face again with his metal shield boss. This time, it came from above, with his full weight behind it.

This time, he was pounded by pain, oceans of agony.

And then Asgrim's dreams shifted and changed. He was no longer the boy he had been. Now he was the man, the famous war band leader: Asgrim Wood-Nose, the Wolf from the Northern Sea—the fool who couldn't keep his own woman. Once again, he saw Freya's beautiful freckled face covered in blood, her dead eyes staring at Asgrim from beneath the corpse of Frodi—who had been almost the same age as Asgrim was when he had fought Hrolf. And what had young Frodi ever done to Asgrim to deserve death? He had been a good lad, always ready with a smile or a friendly word. There would be no Valhalla for Frodi, no drinking and fighting among the other warriors. To get into Valhalla, a man needed to die with a weapon in his hand, not his manhood inside a woman.

Inside Asgrim's woman.

Men had died for far less. What had the boy been thinking? He was the son of the earl. He could have had any woman in Hedeby. Why had he wanted Asgrim's?

No, that wasn't correct. She may have been his wife, but when had Freya ever truly been Asgrim's woman? Never. Lovemaking had always been nothing but tears and shame, tears and shame. Her tears, his shame.

No children, no future.

Now, in his dream, the corpse of Frodi moved again, turned and rolled off Freya's naked, blood-soaked body to stare at Asgrim. Frodi scowled accusingly at Asgrim, who stared in horror as Freya's corpse also moved, sitting up to point at Asgrim. Her mouth opened to speak, to condemn him, but instead of words, a dog's pitiful whine came from her lips.

Asgrim bolted awake.

Hopp cried out beside him again. The vallhund was whining in terror as it tried to bury its large head beneath Asgrim's arm. The night air felt cool on his sweaty skin, and he glanced about, trying to find his bearings. He pulled Hopp's head in close, then put his arm around the dog and hugged him, rubbing his flank.

He was within the darkened longhouse. The rest of the men were asleep, dark shadows outlined by the smoldering firepit. He listened for a while, hearing only their snores and heavy breathing. But something *felt* wrong. Long ago, he had learned to trust his instincts, and this night, his instincts screamed of danger. Something was out there in the dark, something malignant and filled with hate. The night air practically throbbed with menace. Asgrim climbed unsteadily to his feet, almost tripping over the sleeping form of another man. Behind him, Hopp buried himself in Asgrim's discarded blanket. His weapons and chain mail armor lay near his feet, always within reach, and he drew *Heart-Ripper* from its sealskin scabbard before walking out the doorway into the night. Looking about, he saw the two sentries standing near the fort's entrance.

Asgrim glanced up at the stars. It was early morning yet, he guessed, probably an hour or two before sunrise. Although the sky was still dark, he could just make out the faces of the two sentries: Sigmund Sigmundson and Gjuki Horse-Dick. Both were good men, two of the more experienced of the crew. Asgrim could see the concern on their faces as he approached. Whatever it was he felt, they must have picked up on it, as well.

"Have you seen something?" Asgrim whispered.

Both men shook their heads.

"Not a damned thing," said Sigmund. "But a few minutes ago, we began to *feel* something."

Gjuki nodded, fear in his eyes. "Something is out there, a *dra*—"

"Don't name it, you damned fool," said Sigmund. "You'll draw its attention."

Asgrim leaned past them and looked beyond the fort's entrance. He saw nothing but the dark bulk of the monastery in the distance and the trees surrounding them. "Whatever it is, I think we already have its attention," he whispered.

"You feel it, too, Captain?" Gjuki whispered. "There, in the trees?"

Asgrim nodded. There was *something* there, watching them. He was certain of it. The air was becoming moist, and a fog was settling around them, obscuring his vision. Once again, he smelled the sea.

"Should we wake the others?" asked Sigmund.

In the daylight, Asgrim might have felt differently and told himself it was his imagination, just as he had in the courtyard when he had been absolutely certain someone was sneaking up on him. But as he stared out into the dark woods, he had no doubts. His breathing was rushed, as were his thoughts; this time he was certain someone or something was watching them. And so, apparently, was Hopp. "Yes," he said. "Quietly. If there are men out there, they'll wait for the sun to rise before attacking, but let's not take that chance."

As the two sentries left to rouse the men, Asgrim remained behind, watching the woods. His crew made some noise as they woke up, as all men do, but overall, they seemed to quickly grasp the seriousness of the situation and quietly moved to take up positions along the wall. Gorm joined Asgrim, but Bjorn was nowhere to be seen. When Asgrim asked Gorm if he had seen him, Gorm nodded.

"He's near the other side," he said, "sitting alone in the dark. I asked him if he was all right. He told me to go fuck myself."

Asgrim felt a sinking sensation in his stomach. "Has he slept?"

"I don't know."

It's this damned island, Asgrim thought. His brother would be better again once they were out to sea, far from the island.

"Leave him, then," said Asgrim. "He knows his business. If we're attacked, he'll fight."

"I wouldn't want to run up against him in the mood he's in," said Gorm.

Putting his concern for his brother aside, Asgrim forced his attention to the dark woods outside the fort, looking for a sign that an attack was imminent. The men huddled silently against the wall. Any attempt at whispered conversation was quickly put to an end by Asgrim or Gorm. Time advanced slowly, turning from night to early morning. In the east, the first red glow of the rising sun appeared over the trees, and Asgrim and Gorm could see more of the forest.

Asgrim glanced at Gorm. "Anything?"

Without taking his eyes from the forest, Gorm shook his head and whispered, "No."

But the feeling that they were being watched remained. Then, still staring intently into the darkness, Gorm reached out and gripped Asgrim's forearm. "There," he whispered excitedly. "The trees near the far edge of the closest salt field. About three fingers in, there's a man."

For several moments, Asgrim saw nothing. Then his eyes locked onto the form of a man standing beside a mimosa tree. At first, his gaze had passed right over him, as if he wasn't there, which was odd, because he didn't seem to be trying to hide. Instead, he stood in plain sight. Asgrim squinted in the early morning light. He had no doubt in his mind that the presence he felt came from this man. Even from this far away, Asgrim could see that the man's face was shaved, in the manner of Frankish warriors, but that was about all he could make of him.

"Go get the prisoner," he whispered, keeping his eyes locked on the man.

With a soft rustle of movement, Gorm slipped away. Asgrim saw no one else out there. If there were other warriors, they were very well hidden.

No. No one was that good at hiding. This man was alone.

Asgrim heard footsteps coming up on him from behind. Glancing over his shoulder, he saw Gorm, Knut, and Amalric. All three men knelt beside him. Gorm pointed out the man in the woods to Amalric, with Knut softly translating in a hushed whisper. When Amalric's gaze locked on the man, he inhaled sharply.

Asgrim glanced at the prisoner and saw the fear on his face.

He recognized him.

"Ask him who it is," Asgrim ordered.

Knut translated the question, then listened to Amalric's reply, but Asgrim had heard the name himself from Amalric's whispers: Cuthbert, the Frankish knight sent by his king to bring the monks to the mainland. So this Cuthbert had somehow survived the battle with the monks. And now he was watching them. Why?

"I think he's alone, Captain," whispered Gorm. "Should we… try to capture him?"

Asgrim turned to Gorm and shook his head. "Something's not right here."

Gorm nodded quickly, clearly not really wanting to go out after this man.

"He's gone," said Knut.

Asgrim's gaze snapped back to the trees. The man was indeed no longer there. He seemed to have simply vanished. The malignant presence they had all felt disappeared with the Frankish knight. Even Hopp reappeared to sniff at his master, looking sad. Asgrim, still staring into the woods, reached down and scratched behind Hopp's ears.

They remained like that, kneeling and watching the woods as the sun rose, chasing away the mist and shadows. No attack came.

Asgrim rose to his feet. "Stand the men down. Prepare something hot to eat. We're leaving."

FIVE

The Island of Noirmoutier,
August 2, 799,
Morning

Asgrim led his men away from the fort. During the night, a thick mist had rolled in from the sea, and the last vestiges of it still blanketed the ground, reaching their shins. Asgrim rode above it, on one of the horses they had found; he had sent the other three horses forward with scouts.

Gorm walked beside him. "Why do you suppose the Saracen lied to us?"

Asgrim glanced down at his first mate and shook his head. "I was wondering the same thing. Why tell us about the monastery at all?"

"No great love between the Saracens and Franks. They're always fighting."

"Not recently. Not for years," said Asgrim. "Now they trade, profit. Everyone gets rich."

"Aye," muttered Gorm, scratching beneath his beard. "There's the life. No risk, no blood. A man could settle, make a real living."

Despite his foul mood, Asgrim raised an eyebrow and smiled. "You'd become a merchant, the infamous Gorm Louse-Beard? The man who stood his ground against Tallman's brothers at High Crossing Bridge—and chased those killers off."

Gorm snorted. "Killed one of 'em, I did. Finehair, I think. Least, no one's spoken of him since that day."

Still smiling, Asgrim shook his head. "The poets should sing songs of *you*. You're no merchant, Gorm, no more than I am."

"I do enjoy a spot of battle." Gorm glanced toward the monastery walls across the salt fields, and his smile vanished. "Still, some days, such a life does have its shine."

Asgrim adjusted the scabbard of *Heart-Ripper* from where it hung across his back. "It does at that… some days."

They walked along in silence for a few moments, but when Asgrim took the path leading back to the monastery, Gorm stopped in place behind him. Asgrim felt the other man's eyes on his back. Then he felt all their eyes as conversation among the men died abruptly.

"Captain…" said Gorm.

Fear hid in the other man's voice. Asgrim could tell without looking that that same fear would be reflected in the eyes of his men.

Without turning, Asgrim said, "I have a promise to keep to a dead man."

Asgrim glared at the stone walls of the monastery before him. When he spoke again, it was only a whisper and only to himself. "I may already be damned for what I did, but I'm not leaving this place standing."

Staring at the monastery before him, he felt his heartbeat quicken, and he kicked his horse into a trot before he lost his courage and changed his mind.

"We burn it!" he yelled.

* * *

The main buildings were stone and tile, but the framework, floors, and much of the furnishings of the monastery were wood. Within minutes, great sheets of flames and black smoke poured from the windows. The men cheered—except for Bjorn, who was as morose and sullen as ever. While the men had set the fire, Asgrim had tried once again to talk to his brother, but Bjorn had simply scowled and walked away.

His face grey, Gorm approached Asgrim. “Well, Captain?”

Asgrim stared at the flames and nodded, satisfied. He then pointed to the west, toward their ship and the sea. “We sail.”

The men needed no other motivation.

As they marched through the woods, Asgrim wondered where they would go next. This raid had been a waste of time, but at least he hadn’t lost anyone. They still had time to raid somewhere else, perhaps even farther south. He could sack the island’s small village, but he saw little point in bothering. As soon as the locals realized Asgrim and his men had landed, they would have almost certainly fled into the surrounding woods to hide out until after the raiders sailed away, taking or hiding anything worth stealing.

Many captains raided for slaves, either taking them home to Denmark or selling them elsewhere, but Asgrim had no stomach for that and hadn’t since his first raid, so many years before. Being a slaver meant slaughtering the enemy’s men first and then those too old or infirm to sell. Then came the inevitable raping, often in front of the children. Once again, in his memory, he saw flames pour from that church, so many years ago, and heard the screams of those who had chosen to burn rather than become slaves. No. He would not attack a defenseless village. He wasn’t much of a man, but at least he wasn’t a slaver.

Hopp walked alongside Asgrim's mount, stopping occasionally to sniff whatever interested him. As they approached the edge of a large copse of trees, Hopp stopped. The dog's tail rose, as did the fur on his back, and the animal began to growl. Asgrim reined in his horse and raised his hand for the others to stop. He stared into the bushes, but couldn't see what was bothering Hopp.

"Go!" Asgrim pointed.

Hopp disappeared into the woods, a blur of light brown fur.

"What is it?" asked Gorm from beside him.

Raising his hand to silence the other man, Asgrim rose in his stirrups until he was standing. He tried to peer farther into the thick woods, but saw nothing. The men began to nervously look about themselves, obviously worried they were about to be ambushed. They began to edge closer together, to make sure they weren't strung out. Then, from somewhere within the trees, Hopp began barking ferociously.

That was all Asgrim needed. In one motion, he was off the horse and slipping his shield off his back. He drew *Heart-Ripper* as he dashed into the trees.

"To the captain, sluggards!" Gorm called out from behind him. A moment later, he heard the men following after him.

Branches and bushes pulled at him, catching against his shield and slowing him down. Cursing to himself, he turned his shield to the side, turned his shoulder forward, and barreled through the underbrush. Hopp's barking grew louder. The animal was just ahead of him, at the top of a small, gradual rise that overlooked the path his men had been traveling. The spot was perfect for ambushers, especially if they were armed with bows.

Expecting arrows in his face at any moment, Asgrim angled his shield to his front, assumed a mid-guard ward with his sword, and dashed up the incline ahead of him. Sometimes in battle, it was best to be bold; too much caution accomplishes nothing. His men crashed through the brush just behind him. Gorm yelled at them to hurry.

His knees pushed him over the top of the rise, and he peered over the wooden edge of his shield. Whatever he found, man or spirit, he was going to attack straight on. Ready for anything, he was still surprised by what he saw. Just ahead of him, fangs bared, Hopp stood, growling, cornering a young woman. She had her back to a tree, and her eyes darted about, looking for a way to escape the animal, but Hopp was well trained and more than a little vicious. Whenever the woman moved or prepared to move, Hopp barked threateningly and repositioned himself to cut her off, pushing her back against the tree. She was lucky she hadn't tried to flee in terror. The slightest wrong move would have provoked an attack.

She must have been hiding on the hilltop, spying on him and his men. What a stupid, stupid thing to do, spying on armed men.

His eyes scanned the surroundings, but he saw no one else. She must have been alone.

He stalked forward. "Back, Hopp, back."

Overexcited, the hunting dog was reluctant to give up his prey. If Hopp bit her and tasted blood, he would be nearly impossible to pull off her. Asgrim stood next to the dog, nudging him aside with his thigh. "Down, Hopp. I have it."

Although still clearly hesitant to give up his cornered quarry, Hopp stopped barking, growled once, and grudgingly moved aside, giving Asgrim the space. The woman's eyes darted from the animal to Asgrim. When she saw his face, though, her own went pale, turning snowy white, and she seemed to shrink in upon herself, trying to push her back through the tree Hopp had cornered her against.

It was, sadly, a far too common reaction from women when they saw his face. Sighing, Asgrim looked about but saw no one else, which didn't mean there was no threat. Any man who thought women were no danger was a fool.

“Search the woods,” he ordered his men as they came up behind him. “Look for others.”

While some of his men fanned out to search the area, others, drawn by the woman’s presence, crowded around Asgrim and his captive. Hopp, still excited, came back, rubbed up next to Asgrim’s thigh, and began to growl again.

“Sit, Hopp,” he ordered. “Sit.”

The animal dropped his rump to the ground and did as he was commanded.

Asgrim breathed deeply and examined the woman in front of him. She wore peasant garb—a blue cloth cap and a green dress splattered with mud. She was a bit plain, not much of a beauty at all, but there was something captivating about her blue eyes that were almost the color of the sea. Obviously, she came from the island’s sole village. The village, though, was to the south. Why would she come all this way to spy on them? This was an unbelievably stupid thing to do—especially for a woman. She should have been hiding as far from him and his men as someone could get on an island.

Gorm appeared at his side. “No one else about.”

Asgrim nodded and sheathed his sword before hanging his shield by its strap over his shoulder, all the time keeping an eye on the woman to his front. She trembled like a frightened doe, her eyes darting about at him and his men, but there was no escape now. Even in her shock, she must have known this.

His breathing was still rushed from the prospect of battle, but it now appeared that there would be no fight. He ran a hand through his hair and looked about the faces of his men. “Where’s Knut?”

Two men, Gjuki Horse-Dick and Erp, moved up against her, and each man grabbed one of her arms, holding her tightly in place. Tears ran down her cheeks, and she looked as though she would collapse had the men not been holding her. The rest of his men came closer, smirking. They had not had a woman in weeks.

The stupid woman shouldn't be here. What happened next was her fault, not Asgrim's. She should have been hiding with the rest of her people, not trailing killers.

Her fault.

Knut pushed forward. When he saw the girl, his face lit up.

"Find out why she's spying on us," Asgrim ordered.

Knut had to repeat the question several times before she managed a halting reply, her voice shaking. Knut listened carefully, asked several more questions, and then turned to Asgrim.

"She's from the village, all right," said Knut. He scratched his beard. "Says her little sister was taken by the monks two nights ago, and she came looking for her, but then she saw us. She saw the other Frank, the soldier, with us and wanted to make sure we didn't have her sister, as well."

The image of the desecrated corpses of the women in the upper church flashed through Asgrim's mind. This one had courage, more than the sheep from her village. And as a reward for her courage, she was about to be used and dishonored by scores of Danish Vikings.

Her one god was cruel, as cruel as his many gods.

"Captain?" one of the men asked, indicating the woman with his head, an expectant look on his face.

She'll live through this, Asgrim told himself. Probably.

Frowning, he nodded. "Go ahead, but be quick about it. We need to get back to the ship."

The men swarmed her, and this time, she did scream, quickly, before a harsh slap smashed her head back, silencing her. Gjuki and Erp held her in place while another of the men, Johan Horse-Gelder, started roughly massaging her breasts through her dress, spit running down the side of his mouth and into his beard. She glared at him in hatred and struggled briefly, but the men only grew more excited and laughed. Johan grabbed the side of her face in both hands, cupping it roughly, and yanked her face toward him, kissing her savagely on the lips. The men cheered and pulled closer, making a ring around her. She tried to knee him in the groin, but he was ready for her and turned his thigh so that her feeble strike only hit his leg.

"Go on," yelled Gorm, grabbing the closest of the men and pulling them back, clearing some space. "You'll all get your turn. Everybody wants to see."

Johan pulled his hand back and slapped her two more times. The fight disappeared from her, and she hung by her arms. He gripped the top of her dress with both hands and yanked it down, ripping it and exposing a grey under-tunic. The men cheered and yelled encouragement, and Johan yanked away the rest of her dress, tearing and discarding it on the ground behind him. Then he gripped her under-tunic and yanked it down and off; it fell around her ankles. She was now almost completely naked, wearing only her hair cap. Despite his disdain for taking women by force, Asgrim's lips parted, and he felt himself becoming hard as he looked at her. How long had it been since he'd had a woman? Months. Freya had been the last, but there had been damn few before that. The woman's skin was flushed red. Her breasts were small, but firm, with nipples like cherries. She was thin—thinner than he liked—and had small hips, but her thighs were firm and muscular. Through the jostling of the men around her, he saw Johan step closer and rub his palm against her crotch. She shuddered and looked away, closing her eyes as the man put his lips around one of her nipples and began to suck at it. Another man came up behind her and began to rub himself up against her backside.

Asgrim looked away. Her fault, not his.

Gorm was staring at him, waiting for something.

"What?" Asgrim asked.

"I asked if you want me to put out sentries while the men have their fun."

"Gods yes, man, I want sentries put out. I'm surprised you'd even ask," Asgrim snapped, surprising himself with his anger.

Suddenly, the men cheered again, and Asgrim glanced over just in time to see them begin to lower her to the ground. But his eyes were drawn to the source of the men's cheer—her hair. Someone had pulled away her cap, exposing her striking long red hair. He gasped, and the ground seemed to sway beneath him, as if he were drunk. Her hair was the exact same color as Freya's had been. His heart hammered wildly, the blood thundering in his ears. Once again, he saw Freya's dead eyes staring up at him, accusing him.

He had loved Freya; for all his other crimes, he had loved her.

He had killed her.

And now this woman—with the exact same hair…

Johan stood at her feet, unfastening the string holding his hose. Men yelled at him to hurry up; they wanted their turn.

"No," Asgrim said, almost inaudibly. Then he repeated the word with more force, stabbing it at the men's backs. "No!"

They paused, turning toward him in confusion. A frightening silence descended upon the woods.

"There's no time for this shit!" thundered Asgrim, glaring at them.

Then they all began to talk at once, creating a low, angry buzzing. Someone mentioned the word "prize." Most stared stupidly at Asgrim, their faces reflecting their sense of betrayal, as if he had just taken away something that belonged to them—and he had. When warriors went Viking, women were prizes. That was how life was and always would be. Some men went on raids just for that reason. While he never raided specifically for slaves, Asgrim had never before begrudged the men their right to have any woman they came across. Only a fool stood between men with their blood on fire and their rightful prize.

But he did so now.

"Leave her be!" he ordered, grabbing Johan by the scruff of his neck and yanking him away. Off-balance, with his hose around his ankles, Johan fell forward into the dirt.

The others, too surprised to do anything else, cleared a space around her. The naked woman sat up, pulled her knees against her chest, and hugged her legs.

"Are you going first, then, Captain?" the new lad Ham asked with an uncertain smile on his freckled face.

Asgrim ignored him. "Where's the damned prisoner?" he said as he reached for the girl.

She tried to shrink from him, but he gripped her upper arm and angrily yanked her to her feet, holding her in place with an iron grip. Tears ran down her cheeks, and her eyes were wild, as if she didn't believe what was happening. No doubt she expected him to take her first before handing her off to the rest of his men.

He let go of her just long enough to grab her ripped shift from the ground and thrust it at her. "Gods damn it, woman. Cover yourself before I have to kill someone."

She may not have understood Danish, but she grasped at her shift and quickly pulled it on. The men continued their angry muttering, but he glared at them, matching their fury, and they stepped back, clearing more space around him and the woman. Out of the corner of his eye, he noted the massive bulk of his brother Bjorn, and Asgrim immediately felt relief. No matter what was up his brother's ass, he knew he could count on him.

"I said, where's the Frank?"

"Here, Captain." Gorm pushed the man forward.

Asgrim had intended to release the Frank as soon as they reached *Sea Eel.* Instead, he would let him go now—him *and* the woman. He would get them as far from his men as he could.

So far, this raid had been nothing but shit. Never in his life had Asgrim even heard of a captain who denied men their rights to captured women.

Stupid, stupid, stupid woman.

With far more force than he needed, he shoved her at the prisoner. Asgrim saw the surprise in the man's eyes as he caught her. She peered through her loose red hair hanging over her face, confusion in her eyes.

He pointed away from them, angrily stabbing a finger into the woods. "Get out of here!" he bellowed.

Even though the man did not speak his tongue, Asgrim's intent was clear, but the Frank still hesitated, looking about himself warily, perhaps suspecting a trick. Asgrim stalked forward, spun them both around, and shoved them toward the trees.

His trepidation gone, the Frank put his arm around the woman's shoulders and guided her from the raiders. His men stared sullenly, disbelief still etched on their faces. The resentment would follow. It would simmer and build; they would hate him for this. Some would never, not ever, forgive him, while others back home, when they heard this tale, would shake their heads in wonder at his stupidity and his unfair treatment of the lads.

They could hate him all they wanted. He would kill any man who challenged him.

And then Bjorn rushed forward and buried his two-handed ax in the back of Amalric's skull, splitting it to his shoulder blades.

The Frank's body dropped. The woman, tangled up with him, also fell. Bjorn put his boot on the Frank's corpse and yanked his ax free. As he did, the man's glistening brains spilled out in a rush. Bjorn turned, and Asgrim's breath caught in his throat. His brother's eyes had turned completely black, like the creature he had seen in the crypt. For several moments, Asgrim couldn't move and only stared in bewilderment.

Then the girl screamed, and Bjorn turned back to her, standing over her, blood from his ax dripping on her face. Planting his feet on either side of her prostrate form, Bjorn hefted his ax and then raised it up above his head. Asgrim snapped; rushing forward, he hit Bjorn from behind, ramming his shoulder into his brother's massive bulk. He felt as though he'd run into a tree. Asgrim rebounded and fell onto his back, but he had managed to stagger the larger man and send him stumbling off balance, away from the girl.

Asgrim jumped to his feet, watching as his brother spun on him.

"Bjorn," said Asgrim, raising his hands, palms exposed. "What are you doing?"

Bjorn lurched forward, striking Asgrim in the chest with the top of his ax. He flew back, his entire body numb with pain. He felt as if he had been struck with a battering ram. When the initial wave of agony passed, he became aware that he was lying on his back, staring up stupidly at Bjorn.

And in Bjorn's hate-filled face, Asgrim saw no hint of the brother who had grown up with him, who had played with him as a small child, and who had always followed him as a man. This black-eyed creature was going to kill him.

His brother stepped forward, raising his Dane ax above his head in both hands. But before Bjorn's foot hit the ground, Asgrim hooked his brother's ankle with his own foot and swept it to the side, throwing him off balance. At the same time, Asgrim rolled to his right, away from the descending ax. The ax head buried itself a half foot into the soft earth. As Bjorn freed his ax, Asgrim jumped to his feet.

Bjorn snarled in rage with a growl that sounded more animal than man. Spit flew from his mouth as he spun back on his brother. In a blur *Heart-Ripper* was in Asgrim's hand. His own anger flared, and he fought to control it, to stay calm. Bjorn's ax whistled as it swept through the air. Asgrim stepped back out of the way. Only a fool attempted to block a two-handed ax with a sword. Then he darted in, slashing at Bjorn's arms. His sword's blade connected but slid off Bjorn's chain mail sleeve without causing any injury. Swords—even *Ulfberht* blades—couldn't cut through chain mail. He would need to stab the point through the links to do any damage, but there was no way he was going to kill his own brother. The two men faced off again, slowly stepping to the side as they circled one another. Someone yelled encouragement, but Asgrim couldn't tell whom it was directed at.

His brother panted, looking like a crazed animal. Blood and spit dribbled into Bjorn's blond beard from his mouth. He must have bit his own tongue, Asgrim realized.

Bjorn lunged again, and this time, Asgrim couldn't step out of the way quickly enough and had to block with his sword. Sparks flew from the impact, and Asgrim's sword was wrenched from his hands, winging off into the air. His arm went numb from the force of the blow.

Asgrim's back hit a tree, and he stumbled to a halt. Most of the men stood back watching, too stunned to intervene, but Gorm and one other, Steiner Ghost-Foot, rushed forward, each grabbing one of Bjorn's arms. He shrugged them both off as if they were nothing more than children, sending them reeling backward without even loosening his grip on his ax. Bjorn then turned back to Asgrim and swung his weapon at him, but the distraction provided by Gorm and Steiner was just enough to allow Asgrim to dodge out of the way. Bjorn followed him, swinging wildly as he tried to take his head off with his ax. Asgrim saw *Heart-Ripper* gleaming in the dirt, but couldn't reach it. Screaming in senseless, animalistic rage, Bjorn advanced, his black eyes practically glowing with fury, his ax swinging in wild, uncontrolled arcs, as if he were trying to chop down a tree, not fight a man. Asgrim should have been dead already, he knew; his brother was just that good with an ax. But Bjorn's fighting was all rage and no skill. The other man seemed to have forgotten all his countless hours of training in favor of using his ax like a club. Eventually, though, his brother would connect. His brother was going to kill him unless he did something. He pulled his hand ax from his belt and tossed it toward his brother, not intending to hit him, but merely distract him. As Bjorn swung wildly to deflect the hand ax, he opened himself up, exposing his midsection. Asgrim, seeing his chance, rushed forward to tackle his brother at his knees. If he could knock him down, he and the others could hold him in place long enough to subdue him. He smashed into the other man, staggering him, but his aim had been slightly off, and instead of knocking his brother down, he only sent him stumbling back several steps. Then Asgrim's vision exploded into bright light as Bjorn hammered the side of his head with the end of his ax handle, smashing him down onto his back in the dirt. He shook his head, and through his now-blurry vision, he saw Bjorn rushing at him again.

No!

He moved instinctively, pushing up off the ground and into his advancing brother. Somehow, his knife was now in his hand. He hadn't even realized he had drawn it. Bjorn's eyes opened wide as Asgrim's knife slipped beneath the bottom of his chain mail, ripping into his flesh. Blood drenched the hand holding his knife, and he let go of it, as if it burned him, but he knew it was already too late.

Bjorn dropped his ax, and his fingers reached for Asgrim's throat, then closed around it. Lights popped in Asgrim's vision as his brother choked him. He was vaguely aware of his brother's hoarse breathing in his face and the stupefied expression on his features. Asgrim brought his arms up and down, dropping his weight and twisting to the side as he smashed his elbows into his brother's arms at the elbow. Releasing Asgrim's throat, Bjorn fell to the ground in one direction as Asgrim collapsed in the other.

Asgrim coughed and hacked as air flowed back into his pain-filled throat. As his vision cleared, he saw his brother lying on the ground, a foot of glistening intestine hanging from beneath the hem of his chain mail coat. He crawled to his brother over ground already soaked with blood. Bjorn stared at him stupidly, with black eyes still filled with hatred.

Blood bubbled from his lips, and he mumbled something incomprehensible, something in a language other than Danish.

Asgrim grasped for the handle of Bjorn's ax, then thrust it into his brother's fingers. At first, Bjorn couldn't hold the weapon, but Asgrim wrapped his brother's fingers around the shaft and held them in place with his own.

"I'm sorry, brother," Asgrim croaked, finding it hard to talk. "I'm sorry."

Bjorn didn't answer. In death, his eyes had returned to their deep blue, but they stared accusingly at Asgrim.

He pulled his brother's head to his chest, hugged him hard. "Wait for me in Valhalla, little brother."

Despite his pain, Asgrim lifted his head and cried out. His scream echoed through the woods, startling birds.

* * *

It felt the destruction of its servant and paused where it stood in the woods. Somehow, his ghul had been sent back to its own realm. Unfortunate perhaps, but failure wasn't unexpected with lesser servants such as ghuls.

This man, though, the leader of the raiders, this Asgrim Wood-Nose, he was interesting.

So was his ship.

SIX

The Island of Noirmoutier,
August 3, 799,
Morning

The men loitered nearby, talking quietly among themselves, casting nervous glances at Asgrim. Bjorn lay on his back, holding his ax on his massive chest. Asgrim knelt beside him, stuffing his intestines back under his armor.

Gorm crouched beside him and handed him a wineskin. The other man's face reflected his sorrow. "Captain, we can't stay here."

Asgrim shook his head and tried to drink a mouthful of wine, but ended up coughing it back up and rubbing his throat.

Kinslayer. He was a kinslayer. First his wife, now his brother. He had killed his own brother—over a Frankish woman he would never see again. Freya, Frodi, now Bjorn. Had there ever been a man more cursed by the gods? He laughed, really wanting to cry. Gorm stared at him with concern in his eyes. Asgrim drank again, this time getting some of the wine down his throat.

"Your weapons, Captain." Gorm handed *Heart-Ripper,* Asgrim's hand ax, and his long-knife to him.

Woodenly, Asgrim took them, then sheathed them. He stared down at his brother's dead face, which was now unnaturally white.

"Wasn't your fault. You had no choice, him or you. No one could blame—"

"We're not burying him here," said Asgrim. "Not here."

"What… what, then, Captain?" asked Gorm.

"I won't have Franks digging him up, stealing his armor and weapons, desecrating his body. Have the men build a fire. We'll burn him."

"Captain… if we light a fire, we'll draw more attention to ourselves. There may be Frankish soldiers. They would know where—"

Asgrim glared over his shoulder at the other man. "We've just burned their monastery. Look at the smoke in the air. One more bonfire now won't make a difference. Besides, I don't care. We're going to send my brother to Valhalla—and right now!"

"Aye, Captain." Gorm walked away.

Asgrim searched his brother's corpse, rooting through his belongings. First, he discarded the small coins and pieces of silver he found in his brother's coin pouch, letting them plop from his palm onto the wet ground. Then he upended the pouch, letting the rest of the contents spill out, looking for something to keep as a memento of his brother. Instead, his breath caught in his throat when he saw a yellowed fragment among the coins and other spilled knickknacks.

It was the fragment of bone from the monastery's crypt.

His brother had taken it with him. Why?

Asgrim drew his hand ax and picked up the bone with its blade. He carried it to a nearby moss-covered boulder and set it atop it. This cursed thing had driven his brother mad. He was certain of it. It still carried the taint of the monks' damned Saint Philibert. The rot of his evil was so strong that it had stayed in his bones, infecting his brother. That had to be what had happened.

Feeling nauseated, Asgrim glared at the sliver of bone. He hefted his hand ax and then smashed it down on the bone, shattering it. The shock of the impact ran up his arm, but he struck the bone again and again, crushing the pieces into powder, not caring that he would dull his ax blade. When he was done, the bone was nothing more than yellow crumbs cascading down the side of the boulder.

Feeling empty inside, he stepped back and let the ax hang next to his leg.

* * *

The flames of Bjorn's pyre roared and cracked, their heat washing over Asgrim's face. It was midday, but the men had taken that long to gather the wood for Bjorn's pyre. They had built a four-poster timber platform for his brother's corpse that was high enough to pile three feet of wood beneath it. The flames were intense, and Bjorn's body blazed along with them.

Gorm joined him. "We should get moving, Captain. Bjorn's gone now, well on his way to Valhalla—if he isn't there already."

The fire popped, and sparks flew out as some pieces of wood shifted and fell.

Asgrim nodded. If ever a man deserved to drink among the heroes in Odin's mead hall, it was his brother. What a pathetic end for such a man. Gods damn the crones and their destiny. For the first time ever, he was happy his parents were both dead and couldn't see what he had become. But Bjorn had a family, a large family. Who would take care of them now? He had an obligation—even though they would hate him for what he had done—but he couldn't return home yet, not until he raised the wergild for Frodi's death.

Asgrim closed his eyes and fought to maintain control over his emotions. He was a captain; he still had a crew he was responsible for, and he had made a promise of plunder to them. Despite what had happened on the island, he needed to keep his word, his ship, and his men.

It was all he had left.

Most of the men stood some distance away, watching him with dark expressions. Asgrim sighed. There would be trouble over this. They would curse his foul luck, curse this damned raid, and curse him. Harald Skull-Splitter stood among a knot of men and glared at him. Asgrim stared back until the other man hawked, spit on the ground, and turned away.

Definitely trouble.

He grabbed the reins of his horse and climbed into the saddle. Once they were away from this place, the men would regain their cheer. He would find another settlement to raid, someplace that actually had something to steal. He told himself everything would be fine, all the while knowing it wouldn't.

What kind of a man kills his own brother? The three crones had to be giggling with glee.

Asgrim led his men away from his brother's pyre. The happy chatter among the men had disappeared. Asgrim could feel their stares on his back. He looked up at the red dragon, now almost completely gone from the sky. Bjorn had been so wrong about it. Odin and Thor weren't here and had never been watching over them. He prayed Bjorn was in Valhalla, that the Valkyries had somehow managed to find him, even in the land of the Franks and their bizarre one god and black monks.

His thoughts swirled in his head as they marched to the sea. The sea—escape from this cursed island. Soon, he heard waves crashing against the beach and knew they were almost back at the longship and freedom. The men picked up the pace, anxious to be gone, but when he heard the pounding of horses' hooves to their front and saw the two scouts with grim faces riding out of the trees, he knew something else had gone very wrong. His hands clenched into fists, and he forced himself to take deep breaths.

What had the crones woven for him now?

The scouts pulled up on their reins; their horses danced in place, eyes wild with terror. The two riders looked much the same.

"They're dead," said one of the men.

Asgrim exhaled, feeling his world crash in upon him. "The longship?"

The other scout shook his head and opened his mouth, but then closed it again.

The men began to yell out questions and push forward. With a sharp yell, Asgrim lashed his horse into a run, darting between the two scouts.

He broke through the screen of trees, coming out on the beach, and stared in disbelief at *Sea Eel*. The vessel had been dragged up all the way onto the sand and sat there, leaning over on its side. Its mast had been broken off at the base and was now impaled through the hull.

How was that possible?

Asgrim almost fell while climbing down from his mount. His legs trembled as he approached his prized vessel, noticing for the first time the low droning of the flies and the stench of rot. Lying before him on the sand, mocking him, were the corpses of the five men he had left behind.

Someone had carefully laid them out together, one beside the other, their arms linked around the neck of the man on either side, as if they were the greatest of friends and had reposed for a nap together. The horror on their dead faces, however, betrayed that lie. And this charade was only the beginning of the abuse heaped upon the dead. Someone had skinned the men, leaving their heads still intact but their bodies nothing more than empty husks of skin, deflated and obscene. Asgrim remembered the skinned monk Gorm had found within the monastery and trembled in rage, barely believing what he was seeing. It seemed impossible, a cruel joke. From where Asgrim stood, the empty husks of these men looked intact, like deflated wineskins. But when he turned them over and looked beneath, he found the gaping hole in their backs where everything had been scraped out. The discarded remains lay only paces away in a stinking, glistening pile of bones, guts, muscle, and internal organs, crawling with a skin of flies. A cold sweat drenched Asgrim's skin.

Who could do such a thing? Why?

He heard the sudden pounding of hooves, then turned to watch his horse galloping away down the beach. Even Hopp whined, hiding behind his legs.

Gorm and the rest of the men followed him out onto the beach. At first, not a man said a word. Each just stared in horror at the sight before him. Then several vomited, and not just the young ones. Others called upon the mercy of the gods. Still more bellowed in outrage, stomping up and down the beach, trying to vent their fury.

Far too many glared at Asgrim.

Several moments passed before he noticed Gorm standing beside him. The two men considered the mast shoved through the hull of *Sea Eel*.

"What do we do?" Gorm asked.

"What choice do we have?" Asgrim said. "We fix her, then sail away."

Gorm reached out and ran his fingers over the broken edge of one of the planks. "It will take days, maybe weeks."

"Maybe," said Asgrim.

"The Franks. They'll come in force."

Asgrim nodded. "Aye. So first, we build a log wall around her. Once we have a wall to fight behind, we hold fast and fix her. If the Franks come against us, we kill them until they stop coming. Once *Sea Eel's* seaworthy again, we go."

Gorm snorted. "That seems simple enough."

Ignoring the sarcasm, Asgrim replied, "No, it won't be, but it's our only option."

Asgrim heard a commotion behind him. He turned to find the men gathering nearby, arguing with one another, their voices getting louder. There seemed to be two groups of men forming, one far larger than the other. The larger group had Harald at its core, with all of the younger men. The second, much smaller group, comprised the steadiest of the old hands, men like Steiner and Snorri. Asgrim approached the men just in time to hear Harald speaking.

"Can't let 'em get away with this, with killing our friends." Harald looked about himself as he spoke, clearly talking for the benefit of the forming mob.

"We follow the captain's orders, not yours, Skull-Splitter. No one swore an oath to you," Steiner answered, his voice much lower and calmer, his eyes thin slits.

There's going to be blood, Asgrim thought.

Steiner's posture was that of a man ready to fight. His hands edged near his knife, and his feet were set for balance and action. Harald, on the other hand, seemed too preoccupied with the attention that the others were paying him to react to what was about to happen.

Steiner was a thin man, nowhere near the size of Harald, but anyone who underestimated him was taking his life in his own hands. The warrior was one of the hardest men Asgrim had ever sailed with. Not only could he track a mouse for days across fresh snow, but he could also put an arrow into the creature's anus from two hundred paces away. As well, he was a particularly nasty hand with a knife. If Harald was too poor a judge of men to see that Steiner was moments away from violence, then the young blowhard would never command his own men, at least not for long. A good captain understood men.

Asgrim pushed himself between the two men, interrupting their argument. "What's this nonsense, then?" He looked about himself at the gathering men, willing steel into his face.

Red-faced, Harald glared at Asgrim. "Fucking villagers have murdered our mates, and we want blood." Harald paused for a moment before adding, "Captain."

"Villagers?" Asgrim let his face and voice show his disdain and incredulity. He shook his head and turned, letting his gaze fall across all of the men. "Is this what you think, that villagers did this? That snot-nosed Frankish farmers captured five warriors and then had the skill and time to spare to skin them?" He paused, and some of the men looked down, to stare at their feet.

Hopp moved up just past Asgrim, bared his fangs, and growled. Several of the men stepped back. Others—including Harald—didn't.

"Villagers didn't do this," said Asgrim. "There's no gods-damned way, and you men know this to be true. This wasn't peasants. This was the same horror that killed the monks, the same spirit that possessed my brother."

"No," someone muttered. "Those bastards did it, all right."

Others shook their heads in denial. Harald finally seemed to grasp the danger he was in, or perhaps he just didn't want to take on Asgrim, because he looked about himself and stepped back, letting others talk.

"We should kill a bunch of them, just in case," said Ham. "It'll show them not to mess with killers like us."

Asgrim cocked his head and glared at the young man. "We should, should we? And how many battles have you been in, you pimple-faced git?"

The young man's face blanched, and he shut up, disappearing back into the throng, muttering beneath his breath.

Asgrim jabbed a finger at the corpses. "I've killed more men than I can count, and I tell you this: men don't do things like this."

They stared at the gutted corpses in silence.

"Captain's right," yelled Gorm, who now stood beside Asgrim. "There's evil here, but the captain'll bring us out of it, take us home."

"We can fix *Sea Eel*," said Asgrim. "It'll take time, and we may have to kill some Franks whether we want to or not, but we can do this. We are the wolves of the northern seas. Nothing is beyond us."

Some of the men stared at the ground, uncertainty on their faces. Others, though, still glared in rage. One of them, a normally good-natured young man named Hæfnir, stepped forward and spat on the ground near Asgrim's feet. "This is your fault, kinslayer."

Gorm kicked him in the balls, and he dropped like an anchor. Several of the men stepped back, but others pushed forward, tensing.

"Enough!" yelled Asgrim. "We don't have time for this. We have work to do if you ever want to go home again. But first, we build another fire and send our friends on to Valhalla."

"Listen to him, you fucking idiots." Gorm grabbed the closest man by the shoulders, spun him about, and shoved him toward the forest. "Go gather some fucking wood, or I will beat you all to fucking death right fucking now!"

Some of the men turned and stalked off, but others stayed in place, still glaring. Asgrim's hand drifted over the head of his hand ax on his belt. *Heart-Ripper* hung from its sheath on his back, beneath his shield. If it came to violence, he could draw the hand ax first, with barely a thought.

And then the moment of danger was gone. As more men drifted away, following orders, the others lost their courage. Those who remained cast nervous glances at Asgrim and Gorm, then at each other. And just like that, they all began to stalk off, some still muttering curses and shaking their heads. The last two picked up Hæfnir and led him away.

"And somebody get out on sentry right gods-damned now!" Asgrim yelled at their backs. "Before the Franks come on us for real."

Asgrim sighed and wiped his sweaty palms on his trousers. That had been a near thing. And the problem wasn't going away anytime soon. Mutiny was like rot; once it started, it needed constant checking and scouring.

They needed to get away from here, soon, and to get out to sea again. He stared into the trees. But something out there didn't want them to go.

SEVEN

The Island of Noirmoutier,
August 3, 799,
Afternoon

Steiner Ghost-Foot leaned against the trunk of a tree, watching the path he and the other raiders had taken from the fort to the shoreline. Asgrim had demanded a sentry position, and this was as good a spot as any other. He could climb a tree to see better, but if he had to get down fast and get back to the others, he would be in a spot. He would be… well, up a tree. He was out of sight of the beach and the ship, but it was only a short dash back to the men if he saw something.

He wasn't entirely sure he wanted to be out here by himself while the others worked on the camp. The land spirits on the island were angry and hostile. For all he or anyone else knew, they had somehow angered whatever made this place its home. There were many spirits here, or one great one. Whatever it was, it was angry, terribly angry, and strong enough to kill men.

Behind him, in the direction of the beach, seagulls cried incessantly. He wanted to be back at sea and to be gone from this cursed place.

Steiner knew he was as brave as any other man, but this place scared him shitless, and he didn't mind admitting that. He could fight a man, but the supernatural? No mortal man could do anything against the spirit world. It they were just gone from this place, they would be far better off. But whatever haunted this island, whatever murdered those priests and soldiers… it didn't want them to leave. Whatever it was, it had damaged the ship to keep them here. Why?

To his front, a pair of thrushes broke from the trees at the same moment. Startled by something, the birds flew off toward the shoreline. Slowly, without drawing attention to himself by any sudden movement, he eased an iron-tipped arrow from his quiver and nocked it behind his bowstring. His eyes scanned the tree line, searching for any signs of movement. It was probably nothing, but he would be damned if he would take a chance here.

Then he heard a branch snap behind him and the sound of someone approaching from the beach. He removed his arrow from his string and slipped it back into his quiver. Looking over his shoulder, he saw two men walking toward him: Harald Skull-Splitter and Koll. Gorm must have decided to send two men to replace him rather than just one, which was a good call. He could have made a better choice, though. Steiner had thought he was going to have to kill Harald earlier. Asgrim shouldn't trust this one. He was nothing but trouble, always trying to stir shit up. It was too bad Bjorn hadn't finished what he had started in the monastery.

Both men looked about, obviously trying to find Steiner.

He stepped out from behind the tree. "Here," he said.

The heads of both men spun about in surprise. Clearly, they hadn't expected him to be so close.

"Have you seen anything?" Harald asked.

Steiner shook his head. "No, but a moment ago, something startled a pair of thrushes from over that way." He indicated inland with his bow.

All three men stared off toward the trees. They remained like that for some minutes.

Finally, Koll broke the silence. "Could be nothing."

Steiner nodded. "Keep an eye open, anyhow. A man can't be too careful here."

"Aye," said Harald. "That's why I wanted to talk to you."

Steiner's eyes narrowed, and he watched the other man's face carefully as he released the tension on his bowstring and removed the string.

"Talk to me about what?" Steiner asked. "You're not going to bring this same shit up again, are you? You're wasting your time. You're wasting my time—and you're beginning to really piss me off."

Harald sat down on a large moss-covered stone. His eyes considered Steiner, and he raised his hands, palms toward the other man. "I don't want a fight. I just want to talk. That's all."

"That's dangerous enough when the talk is about mutiny," said Steiner.

Steiner had never liked Harald. The man thought himself far more clever than he really was. And he was always trying to push the others about, particularly the younger men.

"It's not mutiny," Harald said. "It's about this place."

Steiner shook his head. Dumb shit wouldn't let it go. He was going to get himself killed. He had no idea how close he had come to dying on the beach earlier. "Harald," said Steiner. "What do you want?"

"I want to go home," said Harald. "To Hedeby. But first, I want to make some profit. So far, this trip has been a complete waste of time."

"The captain will—"

"Nothing. The captain will do nothing. He's no captain, not no more. His luck is gone. The gods have deserted him—if they were ever even with him."

"He's always brought us through every bit of trouble. He'll do it again."

"He's a kinslayer. First his own woman, now his brother. You'd serve a man like that?"

"He had no choice, you damned idiot! I liked Bjorn as well as any other man, but he was crazed. He wouldn't stop."

Steiner prided himself on always keeping his anger in check, but now, despite his control, he felt it rising. This loudmouthed fool was going to get men killed. Worse, he was trying to convince Steiner to join him and to forsake his vow.

"Any man can't keep his own woman, who'd kill his own brother, doesn't deserve to be captain," Harald hissed.

"Listen carefully, Harald. You've sworn an oath, an oath! You'd damn yourself forever if you break it now."

"No!" Harald jumped to his feet, his face red. "He broke his oath to us first. He promised us plunder and fame. Instead, we've traveled halfway around the world, and for what? Nothing! There's nothing here but death and the fucking otherworld."

"You need to trust him," Steiner said, his fingers once again drifting near the hilt of his long-knife. "Asgrim Wood-Nose is the best damned captain I've ever seen. He'll bring us out of this."

Looking away, Koll nonchalantly stepped to the side of Steiner.

"Harald," Steiner said very slowly, "If that fucking idiot friend of yours moves one more step, I'll cut his balls off. Then I'll gut you."

Harald's eye's locked on his, and they remained like that for long moments. Finally, Harald looked away first, shaking his head in resignation.

"Fine, stay loyal to that ugly bastard," Harald said. "But he'll kill us all."

Steiner stepped to the side, away from both men. He glanced at the other man, who was leaning against a tree, trying to feign innocence.

"You have the watch," Steiner said.

"Aye," muttered Harald.

Damned stupid fools. Steiner walked away from both of them. They would keep causing trouble, he knew. Harald was going to keep stirring up the others until he decided he had enough of the men to challenge Asgrim. And then he would die for the attempt. Asgrim would kill him; Steiner had no doubt of this. But it would cause more trouble. And they would need every man if the Franks came against them while they were stuck here.

His thoughts swirled about his head as he walked away. He would need to talk to the captain about this. Harald had gone too far. If he had the courage to try to convince Steiner, a man he knew to be loyal to the captain, to break his oaths, then he was almost certainly already convinced the others would do so. Harald had sealed his own fate. Asgrim would need to kill him now. There was no other option.

So be it. If this was Harald's fate, it wasn't Steiner's fault.

"Hey, Steiner!" Harald called out from behind him.

What now?

Steiner's eyes narrowed as he turned back to the two men who were too far away now to pose a threat.

"You had your chance, fucker," Harald said, a smug look on his face.

Steiner's eyes narrowed. And then he sensed movement from right behind him and heard the sound of a man stepping out from behind a tree where he had been hiding. Steiner spun about, dropping his bow and going for his long-knife. But he was too slow, and something smashed into the side of his head. His legs gave out, and he dropped to the ground. His fingers still fumbled for his long-knife as Mar advanced toward him, a club in his hand. The club descended once more, and Steiner's world went black.

* * *

For the second time in a single day, Asgrim and his men lit a fire and burned their dead. Asgrim stood apart from the others; even Hopp, who rarely left his side, had found somewhere else to be. They had set the weapons of the dead men on top of their mangled remains, hoping the spirits of the men would find their way to Valhalla. None of the weapons showed signs of use. If these men had fought back, they had accomplished nothing. Still, Asgrim prayed for their sake that they had died with their weapons in hand, as Bjorn had.

There was evil on this island. And somehow, it was connected to the man the monks had entombed in the crypt: Saint Philibert, the founder of their monastery. First, this evil had possessed the monks, turning them against each other, then the villagers, and finally against the soldiers sent to protect them. It had taken his brother Bjorn, as well, but only after Asgrim had forced him to go down into that cursed crypt.

It was Asgrim's fault his brother was dead.

All his fault.

Now this same evil had trapped them here. How long did they have until Frankish soldiers from the mainland arrived? A day or two at best, maybe not even that long. They needed to build a wall right away.

But their situation, although grave, wasn't completely hopeless. They had the provisions they had taken from the fort, which would last them at least a week or two. And eighty Danish warriors was a formidable force, each man a killer. If Asgrim put them behind a log wall, they would hold against anyone foolish enough to challenge them. What other choice did they have? Besides, they only needed to make temporary repairs here and put the mast back up. After they sailed away, they could hole up in some small, deserted inlet somewhere and fix *Sea Eel* properly. This would work. He would make it work.

Asgrim turned away from the bonfire and left the men to their grief and fear. He needed to get them working, to take their minds off the murder of their friends and their situation. He circled his beached ship, examining the ground, picking the best place to build the log wall. He felt the eyes of his men on him and sensed their anger and resentment.

They had a right to be angry, he knew. It was his fault they were here. He had brought them all this way seeking plunder to pay *his* wergild, which had been fairly levied upon him. If only he hadn't been so drunk that night and so full of self-pity, so taken by rage and jealousy…

He forced his thoughts back to the task at hand. Once they repaired *Sea Eel*, they could leave this damned place. They could find some other place to plunder. He could still make this work.

Pacing a perimeter around *Sea Eel*, he counted his steps and measured where the wall needed to go. Fresh water would be a problem, especially if they were besieged by the Franks, which was likely. He should send Gorm out with a party of men to find a stream. It would have to be a large party, considering whoever—or whatever—had killed five of his men was still out there. Twenty men should be safe.

Several of his men were approaching, carrying more driftwood to the funeral pyre. Gorm too was walking over to join him. He wore a worried look on his face, as well he should; he had much to be concerned about.

Asgrim faced his ship, considering the hole in *Sea Eel's* hull. The damage was extensive, but they could fix it. They would have to cut and shape replacement planks, but there were no good trees here, not the oak he needed. Any repairs would only be temporary, lasting just long enough to find a better source of wood. The mast, in particular, would be an issue, but even if they couldn't replace the mast here, they could row their way along the coast to someplace where they could. He touched the jagged edges of the broken planks in his hull, marveling at the force it had taken to shove the mast through them.

He leaned forward and rested his forearms on the slanted edge of the hull. So far, all of his decisions had turned out badly, but he could still get away from the island. That much he could do…

Then his thoughts halted abruptly as he stared in confusion at the fresh blood spots on the deck of *Sea Eel* leading to something shoved under one of the benches. Squinting, Asgrim saw glistening wet fur in the shadows beneath the bench, then the long pink tongue hanging out of a dog's mouth.

Hopp? It was Hopp.

His muscles went rigid as he straightened, turning away from the boat. A sudden coldness swept through him. Someone had killed his dog.

Spinning about, Asgrim saw the three men now closing in on Gorm from behind with weapons in hand. Two of them were Harald Skull-Splitter's mates, Koll and Mar.

"Gorm, look out—"

His warning came too late. Gorm paused mid-step and glanced toward Asgrim—just as Koll shoved a spear through Gorm's back so hard that the weapon's head jutted out of his chest. Asgrim heard the pounding of boots on either side of him and saw a flash of movement.

The men carrying driftwood!

He threw himself forward, scrambling through the hole in the side of *Sea Eel*, just as an ax struck the wood behind him. Three men had rushed him. One of them was Harald Skull-Splitter, his face twisted in rage. Another, the young man Glum, reached through the hole after Asgrim, grasping at his legs with one hand while stabbing at him with a long-knife in the other. Asgrim kicked back hard, smashing Glum in the face and hearing the satisfying snap of cartilage. Glum fell back, but Harald and the third mutineer, Glum's buddy Ham, pulled themselves over the side of *Sea Eel*. Asgrim scrambled to his feet and backed up toward the prow of his ship, drawing *Heart-Ripper* from its sheath over his back. He didn't have his shield.

"Gods-damned oath-breakers," he snarled. "I'll kill you!"

A quick glance showed him that a fight had broken out among the rest of his men. Most of the men stood watching, but others wrestled on the sand. No one moved to come help Asgrim. Worse, the three men who had killed Gorm were now rushing to join Harald. Bastard was well prepared for this, Asgrim realized. Harald and Ham stalked forward down the slanted ship; both men held hand axes.

Ham struck first, but clumsily. Asgrim knocked the attack aside, while at the same time extending his parry down the wooden ax handle, cutting into the hand holding the ax. The young man shrieked, dropping both ax and fingers. Asgrim stepped in, putting Ham between himself and Harald. He gripped the young man's long hair in one hand and spun him about before slashing open his throat.

Blood sprayed into Harald's face, and Asgrim threw the dying Ham into him, entangling him. If he'd had the time, he would have killed Harald, as well, but he didn't because the other men were almost on him. A spear flew toward him, and he nearly slipped on the bloody deck as he knocked it aside with his sword. He turned and leapt off the opposite side of *Sea Eel*, landing on the sand.

"Kill him, you idiots!" Harald Skull-Splitter yelled.

The men ran around *Sea Eel's* prow in an attempt to cut him off, and Asgrim tossed *Heart-Ripper* to his other hand as he pulled his hand ax from his belt. As the first man, Koll, rounded the prow of the ship, Asgrim threw the ax, catching him square in the face. Gorm's killer fell onto his back, and the handle of Asgrim's ax vibrated as it stood straight up.

The other two men paused, probably realizing Asgrim was not the easy prey they had hoped he would be. Seizing their indecision, Asgrim spun and ran for the trees. Immediately, he heard them running after him. He was almost at the trees when something slammed into him from behind, sending him stumbling and almost falling. *Heart-Ripper* slipped from his fingers as intense pain coursed through his left shoulder, stabbing down his arm. His shield arm felt wrong, then went numb. He gasped for air and saw the spear that had hit him lying in the dirt just behind him. His chain mail must have stopped it from penetrating his flesh, but he felt as if the impact had broken something just the same.

He bent over and grasped at the hilt of *Heart-Ripper* as his pursuers closed in on him. If he was to die, he would do it with his sword in his hand. Despite pain numbing the left side of his body, he fumbled for his weapon, only just managing to pick it up. He stumbled into the foliage without looking back. Branches snapped behind him as Asgrim ran stumbling through the trees. His breath came in ragged pain-filled gulps, and the numbness in his arm and shoulder started to spread throughout the left side of his body. Was he bleeding? Had the spear point penetrated, after all? His vision began to grow dim.

He heard the gurgling of a stream just before he burst out onto its banks. He slipped on the mud and tumbled down the embankment, then splashed into the water. As he hit, white-hot fire lanced through his body. Somehow, he staggered to his feet and splashed down the stream. He no longer heard his pursuers, but they couldn't be very far behind; Harald couldn't let him go. If he did, some of the men might suddenly remember their oaths.

He considered making a stand, but he knew he was too badly hurt to do more than die—and he wanted to live, to get revenge on the oath-breakers and take back his ship. If he fought back now, they'd defeat him easily. He needed to get away first, to recover his strength.

Dizziness rushed in on him, and he almost fell. He stopped running, bent over, and waited for the disorientation to pass, using the respite to try to catch his breath. A cold sweat drenched him, and he knew he was spent, unable to run much farther. He had to hide while he still could.

Lush green vegetation grew wild along the muddy banks of the stream, and Asgrim stumbled into a thick patch of bushes. He crawled into the bushes as deeply as he could, using his right arm to drag himself along. It was a poor hiding spot, but he didn't have any other choice. Once again, vertigo swept through him.

They would find him here, he knew. They would drag him out and finish him, and they would laugh as they did it. This was where he would die, not like a man, but like a wounded animal. Desperate to hold on to the weapon, he squeezed *Heart-Ripper's* hilt. Once he was dead, the sword would belong to Harald—the gods-damned oath-breaker—Skull-Splitter. But perhaps it was no more than he deserved, punishment for Freya, for Frodi, the fate the crones had spun for him.

No man could avoid his fate.

Still, he wished he had let Bjorn kill Harald when he had the chance.

Drowsiness drifted through his body, and he had to fight to stay awake. Birds sang overhead, and beams of sunlight streamed through the bushes. It was a perfect summer day, as good a day as any to die. Farther down the stream, boots splashed through water.

"Here they come."

He tried to control his breathing, to slow it down, but it was no good. He was too exhausted, and they would hear him for sure. How could they miss him? Had he left boot prints in the wet mud leading to his hiding spot? Probably. He bit his lip, knowing he needed to stay conscious just a little longer. He couldn't die in his sleep, helpless.

And then the air seemed to throb with the exact same malignancy he had felt in the crypt and in the fort when the Frankish knight had spied on them. His blood began to pound in his ears, and he shivered uncontrollably. The smell of sea air washed over him, as if he were surrounded by waves. Then he saw the legs of a man standing in front of his hiding spot, facing him. Cuthbert, the Frankish knight, bent down and regarded Asgrim with a look of amusement on his face. The Frank sported a long, drooping moustache over a beardless chin. His face was pale, and his veins were visible under the skin. He looked like a dead fish left to rot in the sun.

"What do you here, man of the north, hiding like a squirrel?" he asked in perfect Danish. *"I thought you a wolf, a predator."*

The Frank's voice seemed to throb within Asgrim's skull. He opened his mouth to answer, but the words wouldn't come. The air felt heavy, like water.

Cuthbert's eyes glanced away, toward the noise of the approaching traitors hunting Asgrim. He looked back and then nodded, smiling as if he had just understood the punch line of a joke. *"This is no fitting end for a killer like you. Sleep, northman. We shall speak again soon."*

He straightened and disappeared without another word. Asgrim couldn't keep his eyes open any longer, but just before he drifted into sleep, he heard men screaming.

EIGHT

An unknown shoreline,
An unknown time.

Tendrils of fog clung to Asgrim's legs, and thick walls of mist blanketed the world around him, turning it grey. It was unearthly quiet, a complete absence of sound, like a becalmed sea. He stood barefoot on a pebbled beach, and paces away, the oncoming tide soaked the shoreline, depositing clumps of seaweed and froth. The air was dense with the smell of the sea, thick and cloying, almost overpowering. And it was cold, too cold to be Frankia. It felt more like autumn in Denmark, but the shoreline looked nothing like home.

He didn't know where he was, but he knew this was not a place of men.

"Asgrim Wood-Nose," called a voice from the sea.

He turned and stared. A young man stood in the water, paces from the shore, watching him. The air around Asgrim seemed to throb and push in on him.

It was Frodi, but Frodi was dead. This could only be a *draugr*, a spirit. Did this mean Asgrim was dead, as well? The last thing he remembered was looking into the eyes of the Frankish knight, the Frankish spirit. Was this the afterlife?

Asgrim stared in horror, and his throat constricted. When he spoke, the words came out like a croak. "Frodi? Why are you here?"

The young man's skin was so pale that it looked blue and bloodless. Water drenched his long blond hair, soaking it to his skull.

"She wants to see you," said Frodi. "She has a message."

"Who has a message?" Asgrim asked.

"I can't stay. I can't see her. It isn't permitted."

"See who?" asked Asgrim, already knowing.

Freya. He meant Freya.

Pink blood dripped from the ends of Frodi's hair and stained his shirt. Had the blood been there before? He didn't think so. One long rivulet of red suddenly ran down Frodi's forehead, along his nose, and into his mouth.

"I liked you," Frodi said. He cocked his head as he regarded Asgrim. His eyes tightened. "You know, I asked my father if I could sail with you, to go to Ireland. He told me to wait until I was a year older. Said there'd still be time for plunder."

"I… I…" Asgrim's skin burned, yet for some reason, he shivered.

"I'm sorry we did it, dishonored you. But I loved her, and she loved me," said Frodi, his face clearly pained. "We had no choice. No choice."

"I… I…"

"She never loved you, you know, never."

"I… know," answered Asgrim.

Their marriage had been arranged, bought and paid for. In truth, Freya had been nothing more than another possession, despite Asgrim's feelings for her. She had been beautiful, so beautiful. Tears and shame.

"We had to do it," said Frodi. "I'm sorry, but we had no choice. None."

Breathing the humid, heavy air became harder. "I'm… sorry also, Frodi. I was angry, drunk."

"Sorry?" mumbled Frodi, sounding as though he didn't understand the word. He turned away, facing out to sea, and began to walk. Each step sank deeper into the water. Blood drenched the entire back of his shirt.

"I didn't realize what I was doing," Asgrim called after him.

A wave of dizziness overcame him, and he squeezed his eyes shut, bending over at the waist and covering his face with his palms. He had recognized the lie on his lips the moment he had spoken it. He *had* known exactly what he was doing, and the moment of rage had felt good, pure, and *right*. The alcohol had only made it easier.

He opened his eyes and found himself standing deep within a forest. The fog was gone, but it was still a cloudy, grey day. The leaves on the trees were turning red and falling, blanketing the forest floor. In the darkening sky above, clouds roiled and churned. Lightning struck nearby, burning away the shadows.

"Hello, husband," a woman said from behind.

He turned, his heart sinking. Freya sat on a fallen tree trunk, her small hands clasped over her knees. She was as beautiful as she had always been. She wore a simple green dress, and her striking red hair was pulled back and tied in a ponytail over her shoulder. Her skin was white, like snow, with a sprinkling of freckles over her tiny nose. She looked like the young bride she had been, the perfect companion with whom he would raise children. But she was dead, and there was a chill in her eyes that hadn't been there in life. As she regarded Asgrim, this coldness seemed to seep into him, freezing him.

Lightning flashed again, and for a moment, she was naked and covered in blood.

He moaned, shutting his eyes. "I'm so sorry. So sorry."

"It is too late for sorry, husband," she said. "You of all men should know this." Her voice carried no warmth. It was the voice of the dead, devoid of all joy, all happiness.

When he found the courage to open his eyes again, she was as she had been before, unhurt, as if she were alive. But she wasn't.

"If not for you, we would have been together. He would have married me—as he should have—and I would have had Frodi's children, beautiful little girls and handsome boys. The boys would have grown up to be leaders of men, perhaps even kings someday." She looked away, deep into the shadows of the forest. "I can't even cry now. Even that's been taken from me."

"Are you… are you… at peace?"

She gave him a look of pure hatred. He stared at the ground, shivering, knowing he could never atone for this act. He would have no redemption.

"Another sent me to speak to you." She laughed abruptly without any joy. "I am among only women now, forever separated from my true love. This other begged me to speak to you, to warn you. I have become a herald for the woman's afterlife."

"Who begged you?" asked Asgrim.

"It has to be me," she continued, "because of the link between us, a link forged by your violence." She shook her head and then looked away again. "What a cruel joke."

"I don't understand."

"There is another, one who resides with me here. She believes you are a human being. She's wrong, I think, Asgrim Wood-Nose, killer of young lovers, kinslayer. You can never really know a man until you lie with him, and there is nothing good within your black heart."

"Another?"

"A woman who loved you once, if such a thing is possible. One who gave you life." Freya glared at Asgrim. "Better for all, I think, had she smothered you as a babe."

Lightning struck, again and again. The hair on his arms stood straight as a sword blade, and the air throbbed with energy.

"There is little time," said Freya. "And I have made a promise. So listen well then to my warning. You face a great evil, one even fouler than you, if such a thing is possible. The Saracens have tricked you, and an eastern evil has been released."

"The bones," whispered Asgrim.

She nodded. "The *Saracens* call this spirit a *djinn,* and for years, the spirit was bound away within the tomb of Philibert, the first of the black monks. Now it is free again, free to torture and slaughter—and these acts give it joy. It will butcher every man, woman, and child with whom it comes into contact, for as long as it is free upon the earth, killing and killing and killing. And somehow, *you* must stop it, husband. This is your burden now. If it escapes the island—"

"The gods take this spirit!" said Asgrim. "The Frankish monks released it, and the damned *Saracens* tricked me into coming here. I will take back my men *and* my ship—and I will leave."

She glared at him, slowly shaking her head in disgust. "I told her. I told her what kind of a man you were, but she didn't believe it, didn't want to." Freya looked away and snorted in disgust. "A mother's love is blind."

Asgrim's flesh burned, and he stared at her feet. "This isn't my burden to bear, not my responsibility. I'm sorry for what I did to you and Frodi, but—"

"Stop! Just stop talking, you fiend! Your soul is as scarred as your face. You knew I loved him. I told you before we married. I begged you to take back your money, to cancel your deal with my father. You forced me to marry you anyway! Forced me to lie with you."

Her rage rolled off her in waves, and he staggered back, holding his hands in front of his face. When he looked up again, she was gone.

"Sorry," he mumbled, knowing his apology would never be enough. "I… thought you could grow to… love me."

The fog had returned, all at once, and it rolled in on him, surrounding him.

"I'm sorry."

And he was.

And it didn't matter.

* * *

Crack!

Searing pain coursed through him as his shoulder popped back into its joint. He screamed, arching his back. Hands pushed down on his shoulders, forcing him to lie back again. The worst of the agony began to pass. His eyelids were sticky and didn't want to open. Everything around him was blurry and dark, but he could just make out a woman's face, one he recognized, staring down at him.

"Freya," he mumbled. "I'm sorry…"

Something wet dribbled on his face and into his mouth, and he realized how parched he was. He swallowed greedily but then began coughing as pain wracked his body all over again.

Freya said something, but he couldn't understand her words, only her tone, smooth, soothing, like a mother, like his mother.

He drifted back to sleep, returning to a world where he hadn't murdered two young lovers.

But that world was only a dream.

* * *

When he awoke again, he saw her more clearly and recognized the truth. He had already suspected as much: it wasn't Freya who nursed him but the Frankish woman, the villager with Freya's bright-red hair.

He lay on a soft bed in the corner of a round hut that looked as if it was ready to fall down. Blankets covered him, and he shivered despite the summer air. His shield arm was tied to his chest and held tightly in place. He flexed it, just to test it, and was rewarded for his stupidity with a vertigo-inducing white-hot wave of pain that ran up his arm and into his jaw. He closed his eyes and waited until the throbbing began to lessen.

Was his shoulder broken?

When he opened his eyes again, he considered the hut in which he lay. Beams of sunlight stabbed down through the many holes in the rush-covered roof. A small, smoky fire burned in a firepit, and the smoke escaped through the ceiling. A small fish sizzled and dripped over the fire. He should have been hungry, but instead, the smell made him feel nauseated and dizzy.

The peasant woman sat on a stump of wood several feet from him, watching him with a bold arrogance that Asgrim had rarely seen in women. He snorted, rose to the challenge, and stared back at her, considering her carefully. If she were intimidated by his ugliness, she didn't show it.

She wasn't afraid of him. Why not?

Despite the hair, she looked nothing like Freya. She was older than he had first thought, past the age when she should have had a husband and many children. Freya had been much younger, still in her teens. This woman looked to be in her late twenties or early thirties, closer to his age. She didn't have Freya's freckles; this one's skin was as white and smooth as a bowl of cream. Her hair was the same bright-red color as Freya's, but hers shimmered with long, flowing curls that fell to her waist. She was no beauty; in truth, she was plain. Her eyes, though, were the most intense blue he had ever seen and clearly masked a keen intellect. She regarded him with these eyes, staring at him as if she could see right through him to the evil that resided within him.

He looked away first.

"Alda," she said, speaking just that word and pointing a long narrow finger between her breasts.

When he looked back, the slightest hint of a smile was on her lips.

He nodded and used his good hand to pat his chest. "As… Asgrim."

"Asgrim," she repeated, letting his name roll off her lips.

He liked the way she said it.

NINE

Alda's Hut,
August 4, 799,
Midday

Alda watched the northman sleep; he was snoring softly. She had managed to get him to drink some broth and eat a little, although he had only managed a few bites. His shoulder had been dislocated, and she'd needed considerable effort to pop it back into place. The tendons and muscles around it had been damaged, but she was certain he would recover his full strength, which she could tell was considerable. This man was built like a knight, with wide shoulders and heavily muscled arms. He looked far stronger than her husband Marellus had been. Of course, Marellus had been a farmer, not a warrior; he was used to pushing a plow, not swinging a sword.

For a while longer, Alda sat beside him, watching his chest rise and fall. What kind of man was this? What had she done?

He was a Viking, this Asgrim, a ravager, a heathen. But the monks who had murdered her sister Celsa had been Christians. Good, pious men of God.

At the thought of her little sister, who had never hurt anyone, the grief swept over her again, like a tide, threatening to wash her away. The torment Celsa must have gone through before dying… it was too much for Alda to think about. She closed her eyes and whispered a prayer for Celsa. Could her sister be in heaven if she had been murdered by holy men? Would God have taken her? And what of the monks who had murdered her? Were they in heaven, laughing with Jesus, or in hell, screaming for all eternity?

The latter, please, Jesus, the latter.

Not for the first time, Alda wondered if the monks had taken her sister because of her. Had it been her fault? But if so, why had they taken the other women, as well?

She would never know.

For two months, she had lived alone in the woods, as an outcast from the village. Only Celsa had visited her regularly. Alda had no doubt that her sister's cowardly husband punished her each time she did. Others from the village would come see her only when they had to, when they wanted her help. Some within the village, especially her former mother-in-law, whispered lies about Alda, accusing her of prostitution. She would not have put it past the wicked old crone to accuse Alda of being a witch, as well. In fact, it was likely. She snorted. If anyone was a witch, it was the mother of her dead husband.

Her mother-in-law hadn't always been so evil; once, she had been kind. How different Alda's life would have been had she had children. Then, after Marellus had died of the Black Death, her husband's family might not have blamed her. How quickly they had turned on her. Within days of Marellus's passing, the lies and whispering had started. 'Alda was a healer,' they said, 'so why hadn't she healed Marellus?' She had tried, Jesus only knew, but nothing had worked, and he passed so quickly—leaving Alda alone, a twenty-nine-year-old widow with no children and no future. And as bad as her mother-in-law was, her brother-in-law was far worse.

When Marellus died, he came to visit her, making a secret offer. She would have sooner have taken a pig to bed.

So the whispers started. Alda had no family within the village; they were almost strangers. Alda had no brothers to defend her. Her father had been an elderly widower, but he had tried. Jesus bless him, he had tried. And for his courage, her brother-in-law had beaten him nearly to death in the village square, an abject lesson to others who dared challenge him. Then, that night, when all were asleep, he had come to pay his first nocturnal visit to Alda, kicking open her door and catching her in her bed.

No one helped her, although everyone must have heard her screams. Her father died soon after, heartbroken. Alda fled into the woods, finding refuge in an abandoned hut that had been used to store hunting supplies.

She hated the lying hypocrites—and not just her brother-in-law and his mother, but all the others who had done nothing to help her. She felt trapped. But where could she go? What could she do? If she moved back to the city, she would be forced into prostitution in days. She had absolutely no doubt of that. And then she would become what they whispered she already was.

She wanted revenge—revenge for Celsa, revenge for her father, and revenge for herself. But what could a woman do?

Nothing.

She considered the sleeping Dane.

This one, though, was a warrior—a man of violence and death. There was little this one couldn't do.

Is that why she had saved him when she found him beside the stream, why she made a litter and dragged him through the woods to her hut? So that he could take vengeance on her enemies? What kind of a Christian was she?

What did she want from him?

He had saved her from his men. They would have taken her, one after another, but he stopped them. He had even fought for her, battling that black-eyed giant with the ax who would have killed her. And he had set fire to that damned black monastery. Surely that had been the act of a good man, cleansing that foul place with fire. But he didn't look like a good man. Never before had she seen such a face. His nose had been caved in and mangled, and it had healed badly, so it was more hardened scar tissue than flesh. And the skin surrounding his left eye and all the way down to his cheekbone was discolored and misshapen. The bone around his eye socket had been crushed, she knew. He had the visage of the devil. But she could tell that before these injuries, he had been handsome. Her brother-in-law was a handsome man, but his soul was black and weak. She no longer trusted how a man looked. Only naïve little girls made that mistake. She felt there was good in this man—as well as evil. He was of two sides, like a coin.

But which side was stronger?

She bent forward and placed the back of her hand against his cheek. It was still warm to the touch and feverish.

"Why did I save you?" she asked aloud. "Did I do it for you or for me?"

* * *

Asgrim's dreams troubled him. In them, he was half-frantic with some uncertain fear, convinced he was being pursued by a dark force. But whenever he turned around or looked over his shoulder, nothing was there. He was certain, though, that if he stayed in place, he would die.

So he ran, struggling and panting through dark forests. Twisted branches snagged at him, slowing him down.

And then, just like that, as dreams do, his changed abruptly.

Now, he dreamed of Bjorn, not Bjorn the giant warrior, but Bjorn the little boy, not yet five, with loose locks of curly blond hair and bright blue eyes as he chased after his older brother through the woods behind their farm.

Annoyed, Asgrim waited for Bjorn to catch up. The adult Asgrim stood invisible, watching himself as a little boy waiting for his younger brother. He remembered this day perfectly, although he had not thought of it in decades. He had snuck out of the farmhouse early to hunt rabbit with his new bow, wanting to shoot something for his mother to put in a stew. Bjorn, ever hounding his footsteps, had seen him leaving the house and had chased after him. A flush of shame burned Asgrim's skin as he remembered how he had treated his younger brother that day, becoming angry with him and chasing him away with harsh words.

"Wait, wait," hollered Bjorn, stumbling over moss-covered rocks.

Asgrim frowned, annoyed with the little boy. He made too much noise, and he would scare the rabbits. Asgrim was ten, almost a man, really, far too old to play with little boys, but Bjorn never seemed to understand that. Always, he trailed after Asgrim, following him wherever he went, spying on him and his friends, and getting in the way. The young boy caught up to him with a huge, eager smile on his face, and Asgrim's temper simmered again, as it had that day. He would spend his entire life looking after Bjorn, he knew. It wasn't fair.

Asgrim shook his head. "No, Bjorn. Go home. You're too little."

Bjorn paused, his eyes reflecting his hurt. "No. I want to go with you. I'll be good. I promise."

The boy Asgrim's anger flared, and the adult Asgrim remembered with mounting shame what came next. He would shove Bjorn, push him down, and yell at him, and Bjorn would stare up at him with eyes filled with tears of betrayal. Then Asgrim would slap him hard, and the little boy would run crying back to the farmhouse.

No. Not this dream. He didn't want to remember this dream anymore. It was worse than being chased by an unknown foe.

Asgrim the boy advanced on his brother, getting ready to shove him. "Go home, Bjorn!"

Then Bjorn looked up at Asgrim with all-black eyes.

"Brother," he said with Bjorn the man's voice. "Help me. I'm damned."

Asgrim bolted upright, suddenly awake, breathing wildly. His eyes darted about the darkened room, and several moments passed before he remembered where he was: the woman's hut, Alda's hut. A small fire still burned in the firepit, and sunlight poured through cracks in the wattle-and-daub walls. He was alone. Where had she gone?

A dull ache throbbed in his shoulder, and just for a moment, the darkened room seemed to spin and wobble. He lay back again, closing his eyes, and waited for his disorientation to pass. But then, from just outside the hut, he heard the sound of flesh striking flesh, followed by the laughter of men. His eyes flashed open again, and his pulse quickened as adrenaline coursed through his blood. Had Harald and the others found him? If so, Asgrim would soon be dead. He was far too weak to defend himself.

He heard a woman's voice, pleading in Frankish, then more laughter. It was Alda.

Weakly, he stood up, setting his bare feet upon the rush-covered dirt floor of the hut before staggering unsteadily toward his sword, which lay nearby, atop his chain mail coat. As a sudden wave of nausea gripped him, he had to reach out to the wall and steady himself. He heard Alda pleading again, followed by more harsh laughter. Gritting his teeth, he focused on his weapon and staggered toward it. His legs didn't move properly, and he suddenly pitched forward, falling against the wall where his gear had been stacked. Pain lanced through his shoulder and back, and he almost cried out. Gasping and heaving with the effort, Asgrim's fingers closed on the hilt of *Heart-Ripper,* and he yanked the weapon free of its sheath.

He heard the sound of an open hand striking flesh again outside. Forcing himself to move, Asgrim staggered toward the door, his sword in hand. His left arm and shoulder were bandaged. His arm was held tightly in place across his chest, but at least he could still move his sword arm, not that he could do much with it. When a man fought, he fought with his entire body, not just the arm holding the weapon.

Panting, he paused at the door, trying to catch his breath and focus. He was still too badly hurt to fight, but he had no choice. So be it. His fate was already written by the *Nornar* anyhow, and he could do nothing to change it. He put his shoulder against the door and pushed it open before staggering out into the bright, blinding sunlight.

Three men surrounded Alda. Two of the men held her arms, and the third stood in front of her, pulling at her ripped dress. Rage distorted her features, and she struggled against them, trying futilely to kick out at the one in front, but her efforts just seemed to encourage them. Just for a moment, his mind flashed back to the woods, where his crew had been about to take her. What kind of life did this woman live? Where were her relatives, the men who were supposed to protect her honor? And who in the name of the gods were these men?

They weren't warriors, neither Frankish soldiers, nor his crew. All three wore peasant garb: poor dirty brown tunics and hose. They were locals, more villagers, but why were they attacking one of their own? The men had been talking and laughing, but at the sight of Asgrim, their grins disappeared and were replaced by confusion. All three stared at the naked sword blade in his hand. The rage in Alda's face was replaced by fear, and

Asgrim realized suddenly that she feared for him and for what these men would do to him. That was why she hadn't screamed when they attacked her. She was trying to protect him.

He exhaled, trying to stand as steady as he could. She was brave, this one, too brave to be abused by these dirt-eating shitbags.

"I don't know who you are, and I don't really care," he said, "but if you don't let her go and leave, I'm going to kill all three of you."

The men stared at him in confusion, their faces blank. One mumbled something, and Asgrim thought he heard the word "Viking." He scowled, trying to appear as threatening as he could, thankful for once for his frightening visage. Their eyes went from his sword to the bandages pinning his left arm to his chest, then to his face. He saw the fear in their eyes and knew what they were thinking: here was a warrior, armed with a long sword, who was more than a match for any three farmers. But as he stepped away from the doorway, he stumbled and swayed, only just catching himself before falling down.

Gods damn it!

Two of the men looked to the third, the one who had been trying to disrobe Alda. A tall handsome fellow with a trimmed beard and large ears, he was obviously the ringleader, because he began giving orders to the other two, watching Asgrim with uncertainty. Even without speaking Frankish, Asgrim understood the man's intent as all three stepped away from Alda, letting her go as they drew knives and spread out around him.

Asgrim closed his eyes and staggered backward. Seeing his chance, one of the men rushed forward—exactly as Asgrim had hoped. He pivoted on his back leg, moving out of the way of the man's clumsy attack at the same time as he lashed out with his blade against the side of the man's neck. The moment his sword made contact, he yanked it back, cutting deeply. The man's shriek was cut off almost instantly as he fell forward, spraying blood from the lethal wound. But Asgrim, off balance now, collapsed forward onto his knees, his shoulder throbbing in agony, his vision going black. Another of the men rushed forward, but Asgrim managed to thrust out with *Heart-Ripper,* stabbing the sword point into his groin. It was a clumsy attack and would have failed had the man not practically thrown himself onto the weapon in his rush to get at Asgrim. Even though Asgrim skewered the man's balls, he still collided into Asgrim, entangling them both and sending Asgrim to his back. He savagely twisted his blade deeper into the man. Blood drenched his sword hand, and the man began screaming and thrashing. Something popped in his shoulder, and the agony that ripped through him was far worse than before. Unable to hold on to his sword any longer, he let go of the weapon. With a yell of pure agony, he shoved the wounded man away with his good arm, disentangling himself.

Asgrim lay on his back, gasping for air, his vision fading. The last man, the leader, scrambled forward and plopped down atop Asgrim, pinning his arms with his legs. His face was filled with rage as he leaned forward with his knife to cut Asgrim's throat.

So this would be his fate, to die at the hands of some dirty peasant, a man he would have cut open in a moment had he not been injured. The *Nornar* must have been laughing.

Just for a moment, Asgrim felt the cold touch of steel at his throat. If the blade was sharp, he would barely feel the cut, just the gush of his blood pouring out. Then he saw Alda's fingers yank back on the man's hair, pulling his head back. The man's eyes registered his surprise as Alda cut his throat open with a knife. Hot blood sprayed into Asgrim's face, and the man fell away from him.

Asgrim rolled over onto his uninjured side, gasping and heaving with the effort of breathing. The pain throbbed and pulsed in his shoulder, but he lived. He wouldn't die today, after all.

Fate.

He closed his eyes and laughed through his agony.

Alda helped him up and led him back into her hut, where she put him to bed again. He fell asleep in a moment, but this time, he didn't remember his dreams.

* * *

Alda dragged the corpses of her brother-in-law and his friends into the woods and buried them, praying no one would ever find them. It took her the better part of a day, and when she finished packing the last of the dirt over the unmarked graves, she leaned against her shovel and wiped her arm against her sweaty forehead. It was late in the evening, already dark. She felt strangely empty of emotion, as if nothing that had happened was real. Certainly, she felt no pity or remorse for the deaths of the three men. They were worse than animals. They would have dishonored her, just as her brother-in-law had after Marellus had died. All three of them would have taken turns, and after… would they have left her alive when they were done? Or, fearing she might tell their wives, would they have killed her? Alda closed her eyes and shivered.

She knew what was most likely.

Asgrim had saved her life. And she herself had killed her brother-in-law. She was a murderer now. Would God forgive her sins? Perhaps if she confessed, but there was no priest in the village. The monks had filled that role, and now the monks were all dead.

She whispered a short prayer, asking God for forgiveness. She then added a short prayer for the souls of the men she had just buried. Then she turned and walked back through the woods to her hut, carrying her shovel over her shoulder.

What now? Would others come looking for the men, or would they assume the northmen had killed them? Would they think to come here and blame her? If they did, they would kill Asgrim and her, as well. He had saved her, but he was a Viking, the terror of good Christians everywhere. No one would forgive her for tending his wounds. They would kill him on the spot and then kill her, as well, for hiding him. But she had saved his life, making her responsible for him. And twice now, he had fought for her. It was all so convoluted, so complex. She didn't know what to do. She couldn't stay here anymore; she had no place among these people, not with her husband dead. Celsa had been her last connection with them, and now she was gone, as well. Had Alda had children, they would have bonded her more firmly with the villagers, but that path was gone. It had died with Marellus. The villagers wouldn't accept her, not ever. She just wasn't a member of their extended family. Without a husband to take her in, she was nothing more than a curiosity, a nonexistent person to be used and abused whenever they wanted.

But if she had no place here among them, what then? On her own, she would get nowhere, but she would never survive the winter, not without help. How long before other men came to attack her—the lone woman living in the woods?

Alda had put herself in grave danger by taking in Asgrim. Often, women from the village would come to see her, seeking help such as poultices, herbal teas, and other remedies she had learned from her father. In fact, one young woman was supposed to drop by within days, seeking a draught to help her conceive. Of course, with the northmen on the island, she almost certainly wouldn't come now; the trip was far too dangerous. But if she were to arrive suddenly and see Asgrim, she would tell the others about him, for sure.

Her hut was dark when she got there. Asgrim was likely still asleep, which was good. His shoulder would heal better with rest. She placed her shovel against the wall of her hut and slipped inside. Asgrim's snores met her, making her smile. Marellus had snored much like that. She curled up on the floor with an old blanket. Despite her exhaustion, sleep was a long time coming. And when she did sleep, she relived the day's attack again. Only this time, Asgrim wasn't there to stop them.

And the eyes of the men were all-black.

TEN

Alda's Hut,
August 5, 799,
Morning

The next day, Asgrim woke feeling more like himself. His shoulder still pained him, but the throbbing had mostly ceased. Alda wasn't there. However, a cracked gourd filled with water sat on a small tree stump that served as her table, as well as an apple and some cold porridge in a bowl next to it.

He swung his feet over the bed and stood, pleased to find his disorientation gone. Ravenous, he devoured the contents of the bowl, then licked it clean. He crunched into the apple, savoring its juices, wondering when the last time he had eaten fruit had been. His face and beard were now clean of blood, which was clearly Alda's doing. *Heart-Ripper* sat in its scabbard next to the bed. He drew the weapon and was pleased to see the bright crucible steel had been cleaned. Blood rotted metal quickly if left unattended. He slid the blade back into its scabbard and then hung the weapon over his shoulder, its familiar weight comforting him immediately. Even at home, Danes did not go about unarmed; there were far too many blood feuds and too many enemies that could strike out from a hiding spot. And clearly, this island was far more dangerous than home.

He stepped outside, looking for Alda. The sun beat down on him through the canopy of trees, and he shaded his eyes with his forearm. No one was about. She had removed the corpses and swept the ground, covering the blood spilled there.

All around him, birds sang from their perches in the trees. As he finished his apple, he examined her home. The hut was less impressive from the outside than it had been from inside, which really wasn't saying much. It was just a simple round hut made from wattle and daub, and clearly, it had seen better times. It needed repairs, desperately. It reminded Asgrim of communal hunting lodges back home, temporary structures that everyone used when they needed them. He chewed his bottom lip as he examined the hut's threadbare walls. Maybe winters were much milder on the island, but she would never survive the cold in such a hut back home in Denmark. He suspected she hadn't been there long, nor did he think she wished to be here. This was the home of an outcast, he knew. There was a story here, a sad one.

Turning, he examined her garden. While the hut was sad, her garden was impressive. She obviously knew what she was doing. Carrots and other vegetables he recognized grew beside plants he had never seen before. Most were tall and healthy. Some looked delicious, but others looked bizarre. He ripped a long leaf from one of the strange-looking plants and gazed at it. No one grew such plants in Denmark.

Dropping the leaf, he wondered where she had gone and why she was living here alone in the first place. And who had those men been? They were almost certainly peasants from the village. But why had they been attacking one of their own? Alda had obviously tried to cover up what had happened here. Did that mean more would come?

Not far away, a stream gurgled, probably the same one where he had tried to hide from Harald and the other oath-breakers. A trail led through the woods, in the direction of the stream, and hitching his sword belt up around his shoulder, he followed it. After he'd walked for only a few minutes, the trail came out on top of a small rise. He heard the water below and stopped abruptly when he heard a woman singing in Frankish. Dropping down on one knee, he peered over the top of the rise, through the tall grass. Below, Alda stood to her thighs in the stream. His breath caught in his throat when he saw she was naked.

She bathed herself in the water, using a cloth to scrub at her arms and hands. Her long wet hair hung over her shoulders, almost reaching the small of her back. His gaze drifted from her small breasts to the wet patch of red pubic hair between her legs, and he bit his lower lip, straining forward through the grass on the hilltop. She had to be near his age, but her body was lean and fit, without scars from childbirth. Freya had been a far more beautiful woman, yet she had never taken Asgrim's breath away, not like this. His erection pushed against his inner thigh as he leaned closer. At that moment, a branch snapped beneath his knee, and Alda glanced up with alarm in her eyes. She saw him right away, locking eyes with him. Her eyes narrowed, and the fear that had been in her gaze disappeared and was replaced by a look of challenge. They stayed like that, frozen in place, for long moments, neither moving. She made no effort to cover herself and showed no sign that she was embarrassed. The back of his neck become hot, and Asgrim stood and turned away, stumbling back to Alda's hut.

Even on his wedding night to Freya, his erection hadn't been like this, like petrified wood. He shook his head, trying to get the memory of the naked woman from his mind. What sort of a man spies on the woman who saved his life?

But by the gods, he wanted her. He wanted her so badly.

He sighed and pushed through the trees.

* * *

Two days later, Asgrim trailed Alda through the woods. He was breathing heavily, but unlike the day before, at least this time, he was able to keep up with her. They were checking snares she had set along a game trail, and already, Alda carried a small rabbit over her shoulder.

Asgrim flexed the fingers of his left hand, then made a fist, happy there was no longer pain shooting through his arm. Thankfully, his shoulder had been dislocated, not broken. The tissue surrounding the shoulder joint was still tender, but he knew it was healing. When he checked his chain mail coat, he had noticed several of the rings over his left shoulder were badly dented; two had even been snapped in half. He had been exceptionally lucky. Most chain mail links weren't strong enough to withstand a spear point; instead, they were designed to prevent cutting wounds from edged weapons, like swords and knives, not blunt trauma. The oath-breakers had almost had him. Thank the gods his luck had held out.

Asgrim's mood darkened. He had so many good reasons to pay back those traitorous, ship-stealing sons of whores. But that would come later. For now, he needed to get his strength back.

And where were his ship and his men now? In the days following the mutiny, had Harald enough time to repair *Sea Eel*? Perhaps. If so, his ship and his men could already be gone—or dead by Frankish hands. And where did that leave Asgrim? Abandoned here, surrounded by enemies.

If so, he would never make his way home again, not that far.

He ducked beneath a low-hanging branch and paused to wipe sweat from his eyes. He needed to do something soon, before it was too late—if it wasn't already.

Ahead, Alda paused, as well, then turned and raised an eyebrow inquisitively. Asgrim nodded at her and patted his chest, wishing for the hundredth time in the last three days that he spoke her tongue. She got the message though and came back. Standing in front of him, she watched him. Then she put both hands on his shoulders and pushed him down on the forest floor. He put his back against a large tree trunk and sighed. She joined him, pulling her knees up to her chest and leaning against his uninjured shoulder. Heat rushed through Asgrim, and he felt an erection growing.

She untied a waterskin hanging from her waist and handed it to him. The contents sloshed as he upended it into his mouth. Satiated, he handed it back to her, and she drank, as well. He watched her profile as she drank, the line of her throat, her deep blue eyes. She had covered her hair again with her linen cap, but several scarlet locks stuck out haphazardly. She smelled so good. He had been around only warriors for so long that he had forgotten what women smelled like: herbs, flowers, and clean flesh. He knew she had washed him, as well, when he had been feverish; he could feel his fresh-scrubbed skin. Back home, he had bathed once a week, like most other men. At sea, though, there was never enough water for washing, so the men shared the same washing water and made do. It had been weeks since his last bath.

What a strange woman. She saves a Dane, the enemy of her people, brings him back to her hut, where she lives alone, without a guardian or any family, then she not only tends to his injuries—and damned well, as good as any skald could have done—but also bathes him.

And what would his people have to say about a woman who lived alone in the woods and healed others?

Witch.

It began to rain, just light drops that were a welcome relief from the muggy heat.

Damn what others thought. She had saved his life.

The rain began to fall faster, and they glanced at one another. She said something he didn't understand.

"If you're saying we should go back, then, I agree," he said.

She smiled; her eyes seemed to sparkle, and he couldn't help but smile back. And when was the last time the hideous Asgrim Wood-Nose had smiled at anyone? He indicated the way they had come with a toss of his head, and she nodded.

They were about to climb to their feet when Asgrim abruptly felt the same cold presence he had within the crypt and when the Frankish knight Cuthbert had found him hiding by the stream. The spirit was close by.

She felt it too; he could see it in her expression. Her already pale skin drained of all color, and her blue eyes grew wide.

He put a hand on her shoulder and pushed her back down so they were hidden behind the tree trunk. He lay almost on top of her, covering her protectively. His heart pounded, and he had to force himself to control his breathing. Very carefully, he peered around the tree trunk. At first, he saw and heard nothing, but it was unnaturally quiet, and he was reminded of his dream, where the dead had spoken to him. The rain had soaked him entirely, washing away his sweat. He shivered. Beneath him, Alda trembled, as well.

What was this damned Eastern spirit? He didn't remember everything from his dream, but Freya had called it a *djinn*, claiming it was an entity of unspeakable malevolence. He believed her.

Then he saw it, or rather he saw the Frankish knight, less than a hundred paces away. The Frank appeared suddenly among the trees, heading in another direction. Even from far away, Asgrim could see that the man looked even more cadaverous than he had before, as if his body were wearing out. The Frank abruptly stopped, pausing next to a giant mimosa tree, before turning and staring right where Asgrim and Alda hid. Asgrim drew his head back in sudden fear, hoping he hadn't moved too quickly and given away their hiding place. He hadn't been able to help himself. His terror had been too strong.

His feeling of dread increased. He could hear his own heart pounding. Slowly, he reached up to his shoulder, where he had slung his weapon, and gripped the pommel of *Heart-Ripper*. As he began to draw the weapon from its elaborately carved scabbard of leather and sealskin, Alda's breath caught in her throat. She reached out and placed her hand over his and shook her head. Her eyes were begging; the message was clear. He closed his eyes and nodded, then slid the weapon back in.

They stayed like that for some time, lying against one another, shivering and wet, their hearts pounding in sync. Then the evil presence just disappeared, gone in a moment, as if it had never been there, and they exhaled in relief. Asgrim peered around the tree trunk again, but saw nothing. The spirit had gone. The rain stopped as abruptly as it had begun, and the sun beamed down upon them, warming them again.

They lay curled up together, sharing heat and relief. Before long, he realized his erection had grown again and was now as stiff as a sword blade. There was no way she couldn't help but feel it pressing against her. His face flushed with heat, he began to rise, to pull away, but then she grabbed him and pushed him back against the ground, onto his back, and straddled him. Putting both hands on either side of his scarred face, she bent over and kissed him deeply, hungrily, as if she needed to devour him. They were both panting, and his need was unstoppable. His hands grabbed at her, pulling her so hard against him that his erection felt as if it would burst. She yanked his breeches down and cupped him, stroking him. He moaned loudly, not caring if the spirit was still around.

His emotions surged within him, and his eyes watered. Since the day of his injury, no woman had ever demonstrated the slightest bit of longing for him. Freya had come to their marriage bed in tears and as seldom as possible. Every other woman who had lain with him had done so for money. Each had closed her eyes and suffered through the act. But this woman, this Frankish peasant, wanted him, hungered for him.

And he needed her, as well.

Grabbing her dress, he yanked it up past her hips. She was naked, hot, and wet against him, and he slipped into her, gasping and marveling at how good—no *perfect*—the penetration felt. This is where he needed to be all the time, he realized, inside her, thrusting against her, again and again, and—

He cried out in sudden ecstasy.

She collapsed against him, panting and crying, her ivory skin flushing. The act was so fast because he had been so hungry. It had been so long that he felt like a young boy again.

They rushed back to her hut, where they undressed one another and made love again, this time slower, their pleasure growing in intensity until they both cried out in joy. They were voracious in their need for one another, as if they would have starved without the other's touch.

* * *

Asgrim drifted through his large manor house in Hedeby. His hands were covered in fresh blood, but he couldn't understand why. He wasn't injured, nor was he wearing armor. Instead, he wore his finest clothing, as if he were expecting important guests. Then, as though for the first time, he heard the loud, boisterous singing coming from the mead hall. There was a party—no, a celebration.

His.

Asgrim forgot the blood on his hands and strolled into the mead hall. A fire blazed in the central hearth, and men and women sat about on stools and benches, drinking beer and filling the large smoky room with song and laughter. Engaged in some important debate, Bjorn and Gorm sat together near the central firepit. Bjorn's argument required him to gesticulate broadly with his hands as he spoke, spilling his beer. On the table at which they sat were several wooden pitchers of beer. Feeling a surge of warmth and contentment, Asgrim walked over to join them.

Gorm nodded up at him in greeting. "Captain."

Bjorn smiled broadly and shoved a half-empty pitcher of beer at his older brother. "Come, drink with us. Celebrate your luck."

His luck? What luck?

Then he remembered. He had just been chosen to lead a large raid on the land of the Irish. Twenty ships would sail under his command, more than had ever sailed together in one raid from Hedeby. In fact, men and ships would come from as far away as Trondheim just to join the massive attack. Unlike previous raids, where they hit swiftly from the sea and then sailed away again just as quickly, this time, they were going to move inland and capture entire villages and towns. Asgrim was going to lead a Danish army to pillage and burn to their heart's content. And if the Irish mongrels didn't like it, they would send those dogs scurrying with their tails between their legs.

He took the beer from Bjorn and drank deeply, letting some of it pour over his chin and soak his trimmed beard. He dropped onto a stool in front of Bjorn and Gorm and wiped his mouth with the back of his hand, smearing away some of the blood.

Bjorn pointed with his beer mug at Asgrim's hands. "So you've killed Freya already, have you?"

"Of course," Asgrim answered. "She was unfaithful."

Gorm snorted. "Unfaithful? Gods, man, she rutted with all of us, even me."

"S'truth," said Bjorn. Then he paused, frowning. "Still, she was your wife."

Bjorn's wife, Dalla, appeared and dropped onto Bjorn's lap. She scowled at her husband, gripped his blond beard and shook his head. "No, you're wrong, you great big lout. She was as faithful to this ugly freak as she could be. She only ever cheated on him once, and Frodi is very, very good looking."

"Was," answered Asgrim. "Was."

"Was," repeated Gorm solemnly.

Dalla shook her head. "You've blood on your hands, Asgrim Wood-Nose."

"Blood on your hands," said Bjorn.

"Blood on your hands," repeated Gorm.

Dalla snuggled closer into Bjorn's lap and nuzzled her nose against his neck. She was small, plump, and dark-haired—nothing at all like Bjorn. His brother doted on her and always had, even as children. Everyone had just known they would be a pair. It hadn't been that way with him and Freya. In truth, Freya hadn't been much more than a child when Asgrim married her. Her father had thought it a wonderful arrangement at the time, but that had been before Asgrim had killed her. Asgrim noticed Freya's widower father, Engli, sitting alone in a corner of the hall, drinking beer and staring at his feet. Had Asgrim invited Engli to his home? He didn't remember.

At that moment, as if he were suddenly aware that Asgrim was watching him, the old man stood and glared at him. "You're a murderer, Wood-Nose," he called out across the mead hall, interrupting conversations. "You've slaughtered my baby. First you took her innocence, then you took her life."

"Shut up, old man," Gorm called out. "Asgrim's a great captain. He's lucky."

"No, he's not," answered Engli. "He's cursed, and you're going to die following him."

Gorm scowled and turned away from the old man. But a pool of glistening blood was now spreading out over his chest, soaking through his woolen over-tunic.

Asgrim pointed to it with his beer pitcher. "You're bleeding, Gorm."

Gorm glanced down at his chest. He seemed puzzled by the blood. "So I am. I hope the beer doesn't get out."

They all laughed at this, including Asgrim, who had already forgotten Engli. He watched their faces, enjoying the camaraderie. Then he noticed Bjorn's eyes, and the laughter died in his throat. "Brother," he said. "Your eyes are black."

Dalla sat back and looked at her husband, who now sat silent and staring. He could have been a corpse sitting upright. She shook her head and glanced back at Asgrim. "He's damned."

"I know," answered Asgrim. "We're all damned."

"He's not in Valhalla," Dalla whispered. "It's not right that a man like my Bjorn didn't get to go to Valhalla."

"Damned," whispered Asgrim.

"You have no luck," yelled Freya's father. "You're a kinslayer, a murderer. The gods have deserted you. Even your own men have turned on you."

An eerie silence dropped like a sail over the mead hall. Every single man and women turned and stared at Asgrim. When they spoke, they spoke with a single voice, throbbing and powerful.

"Kinslayer. Murderer. Damned."

Asgrim turned on his stool and glared at his guests. But they were no longer his guests. Now, the only people within the mead hall were his crew, the men who had betrayed him. Clearly in charge, Harald Skull-Splitter stood in front of them.

With a grimace on his lips, Asgrim jumped up and threw his half-empty beer pitcher at Harald, spraying beer. “To Niflheim with all of you. Odin curse you. You are oath-breakers. Every one of you.”

“Kinslayer. Murderer. Damned,” they all chanted in unison.

All of their eyes were black and accusing.

“It’s watching you,” Harald said. “It’s always been watching you. It wants *you*, Asgrim Wood-Nose.”

“Watching you. Wants you,” the men chanted.

Asgrim’s temper flared as white-hot as the sun, and he stormed out of the mead hall. He would be damned if he would drink with oath-breakers. The door of his mansion slammed behind him as he stomped out into the Danish winter.

Cuthbert stood waiting for him, with all-black eyes.

Asgrim bolted upright, panting in the dark of Alda’s hut, his heart hammering against his naked chest, sweat drenching his skin.

Alda mumbled something in her sleep in her Frankish tongue. Asgrim barely heard it. Instead, he heard the voices from his dream once more: Kinslayer. Murderer. Damned.

And he was.

* * *

It sat cross-legged on the ocean’s floor, not far from the island’s shoreline, perhaps only a hundred paces into the water. No fish swam near it, none ever did. As soon as it had entered the water, all life had fled from its presence, just as the birds and the animals of the woods had.

It was searching, seeking, using the waves to advance its awareness out past the terrestrial limits of the island. And, with no surface distractions and only the gentle rocking of the ocean’s current, it brooded over its choices. The flesh of the knight Cuthbert was rotting. Soon, it would have to take another host or risk entrapment. Leaving this island would be simple enough. It now had both the means and power to take what it needed—and it had already identified a new strong host in the northerner. In fact, it had nearly taken the warrior earlier that day when it had stumbled across him and his female. Only one reason had stopped it: the easterners.

They were still out there somewhere, waiting, hatching their miserable little plots, preparing to force their will upon it again.

Never! That would never happen again.

If it took the warrior before dealing with them, his body might begin to rot too soon, and it wanted the warrior for after it left the island, not before. No, it was best to wait, to keep the warrior fresh until it needed him. Once it had dealt with the easterners, nothing could stop it. Nothing. Then, when it was safe, it would inflict such delightful pain and misery upon every mortal it came across. Thousands and thousands would suffer.

The thought was such a pleasant one.

It closed Cuthbert's eyes, sending its awareness out further, pushed by the waves and the undersea current.

And then it found them. They were coming.

It smiled.

ELEVEN

Alda's Hut,
August 6, 799,
Just before dawn

Further sleep eluded Asgrim that night, and he lay on his back on Alda's sad little bed, staring up at the thatched roof. Alda turned in her sleep, and her flesh, sticky and hot, pressed up against his. She moved her head, resting it across his chest, her hair near his face, her breath wet against his skin.

There was no future here with Alda, only momentary joy, an all-too-brief respite from the misery that was his life. Somehow, this woman had looked past his ruined face, accepting him as a lover, giving him the joy of another's touch. He was grateful, and he was happy, happier than he had been in years. But it couldn't last. Soon, very soon, his men would fix his ship and sail away, stranding him here. When that happened, he was as good as dead. He had no doubt that, together, he and Alda could survive in the wilderness, but they wouldn't be left alone. The island was too small. Soon, the Frankish villagers would find out about the Dane living with Alda, and then they would send soldiers for him. There was no way they would live with a northern raider among them. They would be fools if they did. If he had silver, perhaps he and Alda could head inland to find a city where they could lose themselves among the population… but not on the island. They could never stay. He watched the dark shadow of her face lying against his chest. Did she realize that?

He was torn by his need to stay with her, with the only woman who had ever looked past his visage and accepted him as a man, and his need to get his ship back. He wanted—needed—to stay here with her, but there was just no way he could. It was impossible. He truly was damned. He had lost his brother, his best friend, and his ship. Then he'd found a woman who could love him—only to have to leave her behind, perhaps to her death.

Gods damn the Nornar. Gods damn his fate. It was bitterly unfair.

No. No, it wasn't. It was all that he deserved… and earned.

His fingers gripped the wooden Thor's hammer on the leather thong about his neck. Freya and Frodi had been in the throes of passion when Asgrim had found them, when he had murdered them. They had loved one another; he knew this to be true. Freya had never loved Asgrim. How could he take their happiness away and then expect to have that same joy? Alda was a special woman, a kind person, but he did not deserve her. He was a monster, on the inside as well as the outside. The gods didn't want Asgrim Wood-Nose to put down roots and raise a family with a Frankish woman on a foreign shore. He was a sword-Dane, a war band leader, and a Viking. His fate was to kill and take what he wanted; that was all he knew. And what man could change his fate?

No man.

And even if, by some bizarre turn of fate, the Franks chose to leave him and Alda be, how long could they last with the eastern spirit on the loose? They had almost run right into it earlier that day in the woods. It seemed unlikely they could continue to avoid it. He wanted to die with his sword in his hand, so he could reach Valhalla, not to be skinned alive by a spirit. No man should die like that.

But Freya's words, unbidden and unwelcome, rang out in his memory: *Somehow, you must stop it, Asgrim Wood-Nose. This is your burden now.*

He shook his head. No man could fight the dead. The gods take this *djinn!* It was a Saracen spirit and not his concern. He had already lost his brother to it. That was enough. He chased away Freya's words, banishing them, finding strength in his anger and need for revenge. He knew his anger was self-destructive. But what could he do? That was how the gods had made him and how the crones had woven his life's thread. No man took advantage of him and lived. Many had tried, and they were all dead now. He had been tricked into coming here by those damned Saracens—and there would be an accounting for that. Even if he never found the same damned merchant again, he would take out his anger on any easterner he did come across. Or better yet, he would destroy one of their settlements. How far south would he have to sail to find Saracen lands? He felt his blood heat. By the gods, someone would pay for tricking him. He had killed his own brother—his own brother! And Harald fucking Skull-Splitter had murdered his friend Gorm and stolen his ship! His hands clenched into fists, and his body went rigid.

No one could take his ship. He would kill them all, the traitorous pricks. He would feed Harald his own stinking guts!

He knew then that he couldn't stay with Alda. That wasn't his fate.

TWELVE

Alda's Hut,
August 6, 799,
Early morning

In disbelief, Alda watched Asgrim pull his chain mail coat over his shoulders, then adjust his sword belt over his shoulder. While he did this, he refused to look her in the eyes. He was leaving her. But why? What had she done?

She told herself she would be strong and that she wouldn't cry, but she couldn't help it. Tears flowed down her cheeks, which flushed with shame and anger. She turned from him, unwilling to let him see her weakness and how he had hurt her. With her back to him, she stood in front of the fire and poked the embers with a stick. Why was God so cruel? She would be alone again, all alone, and the demon that possessed the knight was still out there somewhere. She would die alone and terrified.

Why did she care if he left? She had only saved him because she needed help with her brother-in-law. Hadn't she? And he had certainly helped her. Neither that pig nor his friends would ever force themselves on another woman again. She was a mature woman, not some simple girl who was infatuated with a man simply because she had lain with him. But there was more to Asgrim than she had first thought; there was good in him. He had been kind to her. Despite that they had only been together for a short time, she had grown to care for him… if only a little. So what was wrong with her? Why was he leaving?

She closed her eyes and exhaled, trying to find her calm.

There was nothing wrong with her, she realized. It was just God's will, that was all. Asgrim had saved her from her brother-in-law, but he couldn't stay with her. She saw that, too, even if she didn't want to admit it. They had no future together, not here in Frankia. There was no way the villagers would permit his presence on their island. Eventually, men would come to kill him and to kill her, as well. Asgrim was only doing what he had to do. He had to go, but she wanted—no, needed—him to stay with her, to help her survive. She didn't want to be alone any more. Everyone she loved had left her, and she was so lonely. She understood there was no love between them. It had been too soon for love. But she thought, perhaps, a spark had been kindled into an ember that could grow in time into something stronger, something real.

But it wouldn't.

She felt his presence behind her, watching her. He placed his calloused hand on her shoulder, but she pulled away without turning to look at him. He stayed there for a while longer, but then she heard him leave.

Alone again, perhaps forever this time, she bent over and sobbed.

* * *

Asgrim headed toward the shore, finding his way back to the stream where he had hidden from the mutineers. His shoulder wasn't completely healed, but he could move his arm, and if necessary, he could fight. What he couldn't do was wait any longer. If he did, his ship would be gone… if it weren't already.

A cool breeze caressed his skin, a welcome relief from the near-constant muggy heat. All too soon, summer would be over, and they needed to be gone before the winter storms made sea travel treacherous. At best, he had only two to three weeks to fix *Sea Eel* and put to sea.

He needed to take back his ship. And abandon Alda.

He forced away his guilt and replaced it with anger. He was a Dane, a war band leader. He couldn't be responsible for every foolish woman he came across.

As he got closer to the beach, he began to consider what he would do next. He had no plan and did not know how he would take on Harald Skull-Splitter and his cronies. By now, any man who had been loyal to Asgrim would have given him up for dead and transferred that loyalty to Harald. But Harald should have made sure he had killed Asgrim. Leaving him alive was stupid.

He would pay for that mistake—if he was even still here. *Sea Eel* could be halfway home.

However, the moment Asgrim stepped out onto the beach, he saw *Sea Eel* still sitting where he had left her, with the mast still impaling her hull. Harald had built no log palisade and made no repairs. In fact, there was no camp, and there were no Danes.

Sea Eel sat abandoned.

"What foolishness is this?" Asgrim asked himself.

His vision narrowed on the ship. He shook his head and exhaled, then wiped his sweaty palms against his legs before drawing *Heart-Ripper.* With sword in hand, he stalked toward his ship. The incoming waves cast cold spray into the air. Gulls shrieked as they climbed and dived along the shoreline.

Why would Harald abandon his only way home? It made no sense.

The ship was exactly as he had left it the day Harald and the others had attacked him. He climbed over the hull and saw that animals had been all over the ship, making a mess. He plopped down on a bench and considered his options. With a crew, he could still repair the hull. But without his men to help him, this ship would never leave this beach again. He could never fix it by himself, and there was no way he could sail it alone. He needed help. Where would Harald have taken the men? Had the *djinn* attacked them? If so, where were the bodies? Even the corpses of the men Asgrim had killed were not here. Harald must have buried or burned them.

His gaze darted about, searching for signs of his men. His stomach churned, and restlessness settled over his dark thoughts. These were good lads, most of them. And he had promised to look after them, to bring them back home. So far, he had failed, and this was all his fault. If he hadn't brought his men to the island, none of this would have happened. Bjorn would still be alive, and so would Gorm. Harald may have led the mutiny, but Asgrim had set the conditions in which the men would feel they had no other choice.

He should have sailed away as soon as he realized the monastery was cursed, when he still had time to escape.

So where were his men?

Some of the men had wanted to raid the village, to get revenge for the slaughter of the men he had left behind to defend the ship. Asgrim had seen little profit in stealing from villagers, but Harald likely did. And there were women in the village. Many of the men would find that alone worth a fight—especially after he had denied them Alda.

He searched the ship, but found little worth taking. An empty waterskin, a small roll of walrus-hide rope, an old wool blanket, and a small skinning knife had been left behind. All the shields and weapons were gone, reinforcing his suspicions that Harald had led the men to the village.

But if they had raided the village, why had they not returned to the ship? Those people were farmers and fishermen, not warriors. Had Harald decided to stay there? If so, why? Could he have gone somewhere else? Asgrim had nothing but questions, and no answers were to be found on the ship. The village lay to the south, near the long spit of land that almost reached the mainland.

He dropped back down over the hull of *Sea Eel*. That was when he first saw the Frankish knight watching him from about five paces away, standing like a statue. Instantly, Asgrim's skin turned clammy, and he froze, rooted to the spot.

It was Cuthbert, the one possessed by the eastern spirit. He had not felt the spirit's unearthly presence this time.

Why not?

As if someone had suddenly poured water into a cup, he felt the spirit's presence. It hit him all at once, staggering him with its enormity. The two men stared at one another, neither moving. The omnipresent cries of the gulls sounded faraway and distorted, almost as if he were hearing them from underwater. His muscles trembled, almost vibrating, and he knew he should do something, but he just couldn't bring himself to move.

How long had the knight been standing there watching him?

He was as tall as Asgrim, with a knight's wide shoulders. But he also looked gaunt, as if he had lost much weight. His fine coat of Frankish chain mail looked too large for him. His hair was cut short in the Frankish style, but his face with pale, bloodshot skin and all-black eyes looked more as though it belonged on a corpse. He carried a sword in a scabbard around his waist, but had not drawn it. Even without a weapon in his hand, this… *thing* radiated power and menace. This was no man, Asgrim knew, not anymore.

Pain coursed through Asgrim's jaw from grinding his teeth, and his knees began to shake violently.

Don't collapse, damn it. Don't collapse!

Finally, the spirit spoke: "*What are you, northman?*"

Asgrim's mouth opened and then closed again wordlessly. He couldn't bring himself to form words. At the same time, he couldn't tear his gaze away from the Frank's black eyes.

"At first, I thought you a kindred spirit, a predator like me, but now, I feel the taint of another realm on you, a realm I've never touched before. You've spoken with the dead, haven't you? Why?"

"I… you…" Asgrim's chest hurt, and breathing was a chore. He felt suffocated, as if there weren't enough air left in the world.

"But I can still smell the blood of innocents on you, the delicious aroma of wanton slaughter. You're no hero. You're one of mine." The man smiled, sending shivers through Asgrim's heart.

"Tell me, northman," the Frank continued, "why did your own men turn on you, cast you out?"

"I…" Asgrim's vision blurred, and his body swayed in place, like a sail filling and emptying with wind.

"Were they disappointed in you, in your leadership?"

Asgrim's vision began to darken around the edges, and he heard the buzzing of thousands and thousands of flies, building in intensity, coming from everywhere.

"Stop… you." The droning of the flies became a storm, yet still, the spirit's words reached him and vibrated within his skull.

"I can't be *stopped. Didn't your dead explain that to you? You can't kill what was never alive."*

"You..." Asgrim's fingers finally began to move, drifting over the hilt of *Heart-Ripper* across his back.

The spirit's eyes narrowed, and then it nodded, still smiling. *"All right, northman, we'll play this game out to the end. Just know, I could have taken you now—without your even being aware of my presence. Soon, but not yet. For now, know that I will not permit you to remain with the woman. Such frivolities are unbecoming for killers like us... and I do so wish to skin something."*

It turned away and walked into the trees, disappearing almost immediately, leaving Asgrim alone again. The cacophony of the flies abruptly disappeared, and Asgrim's legs gave out. He fell to the sand, gasping for air, seeing bright spots in his vision. He ran his hand over his face, and his palm came away bloody, leaving a smear from his nose.

He couldn't fight that thing. It was impossible.

He rolled over onto his back and closed his eyes, trying to regain control over his racing heart, feeling as if he had just fought all day long.

His eyes flashed open. Alda!

* * *

Alda knelt in her garden, tending her herbs, still feeling sorry for herself. She knew she had to get over her self-pity. She needed to be strong to survive the coming winter alone. For now, though, she just couldn't help it. She realized she barely knew Asgrim and couldn't even speak his language. What future could they have had together? None. At least her brother-in-law was dead and wouldn't ever hurt her again. With all that had occurred on the island—the evil at the monastery, the battle between the soldiers and the monks, and the presence of the Vikings—Alda doubted anyone would ever connect her to the disappearance of the three men. She yanked some weeds out and wiped sweat from her forehead with the back of her arm.

She would have to keep going, to survive.

Alone.

She had no other choice.

She paused, feeling as though she were being watched. Standing slowly, she picked up a wooden ax lying nearby and looked about the trees around her. The forest was silent and still. Even the birds had stopped singing.

Everything felt so very, very wrong.

When a branch snapped in the direction of the trail that led to her hut, Alda's head spun about, and she gasped. Holding the ax in front of her, she slowly backed away toward the front door of her hut.

Someone was coming.

THIRTEEN

Alda's Hut,
August 6, 799,
Late morning

Asgrim ran through the trees, desperation and fear spurring him on. How long had it taken him to reach the beach from Alda's hut? He couldn't remember, but it hadn't been that far; nothing was very far on such a small island. Then, sooner than he would have thought, he burst out of the trees and arrived back at her hut.

"Alda, where are you, woman?" he called out as he stuck his head through her door.

The hut was empty. Everything was exactly as he had left it, as he had left her. It looked as though she had just that moment stepped away. His gaze darted about, settling on the still-smoldering fire. She wouldn't have left a fire burning.

He stepped outside again, feeling chills run down his spine. He began to stalk through the nearby woods, looking for signs of her. Starting near her garden, he searched the ground for her tracks, slowly moving in an ever-increasing spiral around her hut. With each pass, he moved deeper into the woods.

The spirit had been here; he was certain of it. After mocking him, it had left him and come here for Alda. Why? And why after he had already left her? It could have killed them both at any point over the last couple of days. It didn't seem to want him dead. But what was it—

He staggered in place, staring at the blood-soaked ground near the base of an elm tree. So much blood. Flies settled over the wet ground, droning madly. In horror, his gaze drifted up, seeking the blood's source. When he saw her, he dropped to his knees and moaned. Hanging by the arms, which were literally tied around a tree branch, was Alda's bloody skin. The gods-damned *djinn* had skinned her, and the empty husk slowly dripped blood. Her head hung forward, and her long hair, now dark with matted blood, mud, and leaves hung down, obscuring her face, which was a small mercy, because he couldn't stand to look into her dead eyes anyway. On the other side of the elm tree lay the obscene, gleaming pile of her internal organs, tissue, and bones.

His fault, all his fault.

Shaking his head, he closed his eyes and swayed in place, kneeling on the forest floor. He couldn't go any closer. He could do nothing more for her.

No. There was vengeance. He could *kill* the damned *djinn*.

Kill a spirit?

He rose to his feet and turned away, staggering back to the empty hut. Nothing. He could do nothing. What man could fight the dead?

He leaned against a tree trunk beside her garden and gripped it with both hands, certain he would collapse if he didn't hold himself up. He settled his forehead against the rough bark and closed his eyes, staying like that for some time, breathing deeply, knowing that he had betrayed

Alda and left her defenseless. She had saved his life, and he had let the spirit take her.

A twig broke nearby. Turning, he glared into the forest and saw a flash of movement as someone darted behind the trunk of a large tree. The forest was silent; pink blossoms drifted through the air, landing on the ground.

Grinding his teeth, Asgrim reached above his shoulder and drew *Heart-Ripper*. Maybe he couldn't kill this thing, but he would die trying.

"Come out, damn you, spirit!"

The figure that stepped out from behind the tree was a man, but not the *djinn*. Haggard and filthy, with twigs and leaves stuck in his blond hair and beard, he looked as though he had been sleeping in bushes—and not well. He wore leather armor and carried a battle-ax in both hands. With a wild, crazed look in his eyes, Harald Skull-Splitter glared hatred at Asgrim.

"Harald," Asgrim said, a dangerous smile playing on his lips, "Where're my men?"

Stepping closer, Asgrim made sure he had room to fight, quickly scanning his surroundings and making sure Harald was alone. He felt the familiar rush of excitement, the dry mouth, and the racing pulse.

The other man assumed a fighting stance and glared at Asgrim. "Not *your* men. Not no more."

He looked half-starved. Good.

Harald's eyes took in the hut behind Asgrim. "So this is where you crawled away to hide, coward."

Asgrim stepped to the side, slowly closing the distance. He assumed a high guard position, both hands gripping the sword hilt near his ear. He would have preferred to have a shield, but a man made do with what he had.

"I should have let Bjorn kill you."

Harald's eye twitched in a spasm. "You can try it yourself, you ugly bastard!" He lunged, swinging his ax up from the middle guard position, trying to catch Asgrim under the chin with its edge. But Asgrim stepped back, easily knocking the ax head aside with the flat of his blade before darting forward in an attempt to cut the underside of Harald's exposed arm. Yet for all his other faults, Harald was an experienced fighter, and he stepped back out of range of Asgrim's sword.

Harald swung an overhead blow aimed at the side of Asgrim's neck, missing, but following almost immediately with a reverse stroke that was the real attack. Asgrim countered, giving only a foot of ground before launching his own attack. He faked a high slash at Harald's face before altering his strike and coming down instead at Harald's front thigh. This time, Harald only just managed to back away.

Harald screamed, using both hands on the battle-ax this time in another overhead strike that would have split Asgrim's skull—had he not stepped in at exactly the same moment, catching the ax head with his blade and pushing it aside. Harald's eyes, only inches from Asgrim's, widened in surprise as Asgrim, drawing power from his hips, brought his elbow up and smashed it into Harald's jaw. Harald fell onto his back, letting his battle-ax fall beside him.

Asgrim dropped onto Harald's chest, pinning his arms with his knees. Harald's face twisted into a mixture of rage and fear as he bucked wildly, trying to dislodge Asgrim. He dropped his sword, then grabbed Harald's ears in both hands and head-butted him. The resounding crack made Asgrim see spots, but Harald's eyes rolled up into the back of his head.

Asgrim picked up *Heart-Ripper* again and climbed to his feet, standing over the half-conscious man.

"Skull-Splitter, my ass," Asgrim said. "Where're my men?"

* * *

Watching Harald, Asgrim sat with his back resting against a tree trunk. He had used the rope he had found on *Sea Eel* to tie the other man's hands behind his back. Harald glared at him. Glistening blood ran from his nose into his mustache and beard.

"Just do it, you ugly bastard. Kill me, and get it over with," Harald said.

Asgrim hefted the waterskin in his hands, letting the fluid slosh about. He pulled the wooden stopper with his teeth, then drank deeply, noting the sudden flash of desire in Harald's eyes.

"I'll kill you when I want to kill you," Asgrim said.

He approached Harald, and the other man jerked back in fear, but Asgrim gripped his hair with one hand, holding him in place while he poured water into his mouth. Harald coughed and gagged, but still managed to drink.

Asgrim sat back again, drew his long-knife, and began to cut into an apple. "Where are my men, Harald? What are you doing out here skulking about in the woods by yourself?" Asgrim bit into a slice of apple.

Harald stared at his own feet. "Dead, I expect."

"Dead?"

"Or worse."

Asgrim felt a sinking sensation in his gut. Everything on this island turned to shit.

"How is it you found me here?" Asgrim asked.

"Saw you at the beach. Saw you talking to the Frank knight, the *draugr*. I was hiding."

Asgrim cut off another piece of apple, popped it in his mouth, and chewed it as he watched the other man. "You took the men to the village, yes?"

This time, Harald met Asgrim's eyes, if only briefly, and he nodded. "The men wanted revenge. I wanted slaves."

"Slaves?" Asgrim practically spit the word.

"I thought we could sell them."

"Women and children, I expect, right?"

Harald nodded. "The men are too much—"

"Too much trouble for the voyage," Asgrim finished. He paused, watching Harald. "Tell me, Harald Skull-Splitter, great war band leader, how exactly would you have kept these slaves alive on the voyage home? Even with our losses, we still had almost a full crew. That's a lot of mouths to feed—and very little provisions."

"I…"

"Wait. Don't bother answering. There's still a hole in *Sea Eel* big enough for a frost giant to stick its cock through—and no mast. How did you plan on getting home at all?"

"It's a fishing village. They have ships."

Asgrim groaned and ran his hands over his face, then back through his hair. He sighed and shook his head. "Fishing boats? You were going to sail into northern waters in fishing boats?"

"Just… just along the coast, close to the shoreline."

"You and all your slaves? In an armada of small fishing boats?"

"It seemed like a good plan," said Harald in a small voice.

Asgrim shook his head again, cut off another chunk of apple, and popped it into his mouth. He chewed as he spoke. "You're too fucking stupid to be in charge, Harald. You know that now, right?"

The other man stared at his feet again, and they sat there in silence for a few moments.

"So what happened to this grand plan of yours to sail your fishing fleet and all your slaves?"

The color drained from Harald's face. "*Everything.* Frankish soldiers were waiting for us at the village, a war party—with horses. We stumbled right into them, came out of the woods expecting to find farmers and fishermen… and women to plow. Instead, we ran into warriors. They were even already in a shield wall, with archers on the roofs of the village huts. We tried to form our own wall, but the men on horseback kept hitting us from behind. We… *I* couldn't get the men organized. They wouldn't give us a chance."

Heat rushed into Asgrim's face, and he forced himself to breathe deeply. No scouts? They had sent no scouts forward first? Had his crew wanted to die? Asgrim could understand the young, inexperienced ones being that stupid, but the others should have said something.

"Where were your scouts? What happened to Steiner?" He ground his teeth, tensing, fighting to control his anger. Steiner was a good man. "Did you kill him, too?"

"No. He's alive." Harald paused. His eyes met Asgrim's for only a moment before looking away again. "At least he *was*. He tried to talk me out of going to the village, but I… wouldn't listen to him. I thought he was still loyal to you, not me. I told him to shut it, or I'd kill him."

Embarrassment filled Harald's voice. He closed his eyes and nodded. So they had walked right into an ambush set by Frankish soldiers, not peasants.

"The young ones broke first," continued Harald. "Then it all just went to shit, with everyone running to save their own skin. We just… fell apart… all at once."

Asgrim shook his head. He had fought in enough shield walls to understand exactly what had happened. If cohesion and discipline held, the fighting could go on and on, with neither side suffering too badly—*until* one side broke. Then it became a slaughter. The hairs on his skin stood straight, and a chill ran through him just thinking about it. They may have betrayed him, but they were still his men. He had brought them to this. And besides, not all of them had participated in the mutiny.

"And you?" he asked.

"In the confusion, I… I managed to reach the trees. Hid."

"The others?"

Harald's face went scarlet with shame. "I don't think so. The horses."

"Prisoners?"

"Some… maybe most. I saw them with their hands in the air. But I don't know if—"

Asgrim jabbed his knife at him. "You know you really screwed up, Harald. You get that, right?"

Harald's silence was answer enough.

Asgrim finished the apple and threw the core away from him.

"I… I didn't mean for this…" Harald said. "What do you think the Franks will do with them? Slaves?"

Asgrim snorted. "I don't know, Harald. Probably. Or they'll kill them for sport. Whatever does happen, that's on you now."

Harald, still staring at his feet, nodded slowly. Asgrim suspected he had already come to that realization. At least he had the good sense to feel badly about what he had done.

Asgrim looked away into the trees, considering his options. Really only one choice was left to him. His mind made up, he rose and came at Harald, his long-knife in hand. Harald's eyes widened in fear, and he tried to crawl away, but didn't get anywhere before Asgrim grabbed him and threw him onto his belly, putting his knee on his back to hold him in place.

"Please," Harald said. "Not like this. At least put a weapon in my hand."

"No," said Asgrim. "No easy way out for you, oath-breaker."

Harald closed his eyes, and Asgrim slashed the bonds over his wrists. Then he got up and sat down again, his back against a tree, watching Harald. The other man rolled over, sat up, and rubbed his wrists, staring at Asgrim in confusion.

"There's some food in the hut, not much, but enough," said Asgrim. "The woman who lived here was alone." He glanced away, not wishing to let Harald see his face. "Take whatever you find. You'll need your strength."

"Why?" Harald asked.

"Because we have some Franks to kill."

FOURTEEN

The village,
August 7, 799,
Near midnight

A dark, moonless night blanketed the countryside as Asgrim and Harald silently slipped toward the village. They moved slowly, cautiously, approaching the village from the woods and making sure they avoided the outlying farms, which would have dogs. They had to leave the darkness of the forest and make for a series of hills and ridges along the seaward side of the village, where the hills would provide cover from winter storms.

Asgrim glanced at Harald, now just a dark shadow beside him, and then moved on toward the higher ground from which he intended to reconnoiter the village. They were very close to the village. Asgrim could smell the farm animals on the wind and see where the land had been cleared by human hands. And then, from nearby, he heard a horse snort, and both men froze in place. Asgrim could just make out Harald's white eyes in the darkness, and he slowly reached out, placed a hand on the other man's shoulder, and guided him down toward the dirt. Both men dropped to their bellies just as two Franks on horseback appeared from the direction of the village, coming straight toward them. The sound of the riders' laughter and conversation drifted down to where the two men hid. Asgrim slowly drew his long-knife. The riders came closer, still chatting away in Frankish. Their horses' hooves thumped against the stony ground, echoing in the night. Asgrim tensed, ready to rise and go for the closest rider if need be. But both riders passed by without noticing them, coming so close that Asgrim could have reached out and gripped a hoof had he wished to.

Thank the gods for dark nights. Had there been a moon, they would have been seen for certain.

The riders were Frankish soldiers. Even in the darkness, he had made out their weapons: spears, swords, and shields. He had no doubt they also wore leather armor. Such men wouldn't break easily in a shield wall. These two were almost certainly a mounted patrol. On the other hand, instead of watching their surroundings carefully and doing their job, they had ridden right past the two men while chatting like women. Perhaps they felt that with the main force of Vikings defeated, they no longer had anything to fear on this island.

He shook his head in wonder. There was nothing *but* danger on the island. That type of arrogance would cost them this night.

When they were certain the patrol was well past, Asgrim and Harald climbed back to their feet and quickly covered the remaining ground toward the rocky slope of the hills that surrounded the village. As they moved up the incline, the ground became uneven, treacherous, and dotted by rugged bushes. Several times, they slipped on loose rocks, sending pebbles cascading down the slope behind them, and each time, Asgrim was certain they would be heard by someone, a hidden sentry or dog. But their luck held out, and they continued undetected. After a few minutes, they reached a suitable vantage point and sat down to catch their breath and observe the darkened village below them.

At first, it was too black to make out anything but the rough outline of several buildings, but then the clouds drifted away, momentarily letting the moon's weak glow reveal the village. No one moved about below, and most of the village was dark and silent. This was to be expected, especially so late at night. Only the rich had enough silver to buy candles and torches for light at night. Farmers went to sleep when the sun went down. To the south, where the hills abruptly dropped off, Asgrim could just make out a long smooth beach that held the villagers' collection of little fishing boats, the largest only several ells in length, with a single, pathetic mast.

This sad little fleet had been Harald's great plan? Asgrim turned and glared at Harald, who quickly looked away in embarrassment. Sighing, Asgrim turned back to examine the village. It was smattered with some larger wattle-and-daub longhouses, and most of the thirty or so dwellings that comprised the village were poor, earthen-walled sunken huts; however, one of the homes near the center of the village stood apart from the others. It was a large, two-storied building with a thatched roof—obviously the manor house of the local authority or tribal leader. Next to this home, the Frankish soldiers had established their camp. Tents and smoldering campfires sat in tight lines in a nearby field. Around each campfire, men sat, talking and laughing. The Franks' horses, twenty or so, were penned near the camp. What drew Asgrim's attention, however, was the large barn beside the manor house.

Two soldiers stood guard in front of this building. If his men were still alive, that was where they would be.

"I count ten fires," Harald whispered.

Asgrim nodded. "Let's say eight to ten Franks for each fire, maybe a hundred soldiers."

"And their leaders in the manor house."

"Aye," said Asgrim.

"The farmers might join in, as well."

"They might."

"We can't do this thing. It's impossible," Harald said with a slight tremor in his voice.

"Courage, oath-breaker. The gods are watching." Asgrim reached over and squeezed Harald's forearm as he pointed toward the barn beside the manor house. "Look there."

The two guards stepped aside as the barn's double doors swung open, allowing beams of light to escape from inside. Two Frankish soldiers with bare chests dragged a man out of the barn. The man's naked feet trailed along the dirt. His head hung down, unmoving. A third Frankish soldier holding a torch followed them.

"Who is that?" whispered Harald.

Asgrim shook his head. "Whoever it is, he's dead now."

"How can you be sure?"

The soldiers threw the man's body into a ditch beside the barn. It rolled to a stop atop other corpses. The ditch was filled with corpses.

Asgrim closed his eyes and concentrated on taking deep breaths. His men, his men. He had sworn to protect them. When he felt he could speak again, he whispered, "I'm sure."

The men turned and went back into the barn, closing the door behind them. The screams coming from inside the barn cut across the dark night.

Asgrim put his head closer to Harald's. "I don't care if it's impossible. I don't care how many of them there are. We're going to go down there and free our friends. Then we're going to kill those Frankish soldiers. We're going to keep killing them until they break and run. If the farmers join in, we'll kill them, too. In fact, anything or anyone that gets in our way dies."

Their eyes locked, and Harald nodded. "Aye."

"Okay," said Asgrim, "here's what we're going to do."

* * *

Hours later, when the village and camp were fast asleep, the two men made their move. As if by the providence of the gods, a light fog had drifted in from the sea, providing cover for them. They approached the village from the seaward side, avoiding the farms and the inevitable dogs. Asgrim had grown up hunting and fishing, often for days at a time. When he wanted to, he could move as silently as a forest animal, and he did so this night, drifting from brush to tree like a shadow. Together, they silently slipped into the village.

They made for the barn. Asgrim didn't know how many of his men had survived the battle and been taken prisoner by the Franks, but he would save whomever he could. He hoped only two men still guarded the barn.

They slipped past the manor house, coming up on the barn from behind. At the rear of the structure, they split up, slipping around it on either side. Trying to peer through a crack, Asgrim paused next to the barn's wall. The interior was too dark for him see anything, but he heard the snores and rustling of numerous men.

He made his way to the front of the building, forcing himself to move slowly, carefully rolling his weight onto the outer edge of his foot. And, with each step, he paused and listened for any indication the guards had heard him. Closing in on the sentries seemed to take forever, but speed was the death of silence.

At the corner of the barn, he lowered himself into a crouch and peered around the wall. This close, he could just make out the guards in the mist. One man sat on a stump of wood, holding his spear against his bobbing head. The other sat in the dirt, leaning against the wall of the barn; his chin rested against his chest, he snored softly. His spear lay on the ground beside him.

Thank the gods for morons.

A light rain began to drizzle, and the guard who was awake shifted slightly, trying to draw his cloak tighter around him.

Now!

With his long-knife in hand, Asgrim came around the corner. The guard's head swung toward him, but he only stared stupidly as Asgrim rushed him. Asgrim fell upon him, shoving his hand over the man's mouth in an iron grip while yanking his head away to the side.

"Mmmrrr," the Frank mumbled, widening his eyes in alarm and slapping at Asgrim's arm with empty hands.

The point of Asgrim's knife slid into the back of the man's neck, piercing his brain. Asgrim twisted the blade, then yanked it out. Though he was already dead, the man's legs jerked as Asgrim let the corpse fall to the ground. He spun toward the other guard, half expecting a spear in his back, but Harald was already at the other man. After a flutter of movement, the sound of a knife cutting flesh, a wet gasp of air escaped from a cut throat. Harald stepped away, leaving a weakly moving lump against the barn wall. A moment later, the shape fell over onto its side.

The night was too dark for Asgrim to make out Harald's face, but he saw his shining eyes. Then Harald slipped off into the darkness, heading away from the barn.

Asgrim removed the wooden bar holding the barn doors closed and slipped inside. The sudden stench of blood, sweat, and human feces almost made him gag. Complete darkness met him inside, and Asgrim had to carefully edge his way forward toward the sound of the sleeping men.

Almost right away, his foot came up against a man's body, stopping him. The sleeping man grunted, mumbled, and rolled away. Asgrim dropped and felt for his face. Placing his hand over the man's mouth, he shook his shoulder.

"Wake up, sluggard," whispered Asgrim. "But keep quiet."

The man thrashed about, and Asgrim tightened his grip over his mouth and leaned in closer. "It's me, Asgrim Wood-Nose, your fucking captain, you traitorous prick… whichever one of you whoresons this is. Quit making a fuss if you ever want to get out of here alive."

At the sound of Asgrim's voice, the man quit thrashing about. Asgrim could just make out the shine of his eyes. He took his hand off the man's mouth.

"Captain, thank Odin," the other man whispered.

"Fuck Odin. *I'm* the one freeing you." Asgrim pushed him onto his side and felt for his bonds. He cut the straps holding his arms bound, then reached down and cut the ones on his ankles. The man sighed in relief, rubbing his wrists.

How long have they been trussed up like that?

"Who is this?" he asked.

"Snorri."

Asgrim clapped a hand over the man's shoulder. "Can you *fight*, Snorri?"

"Gods damned right I can fight, Captain. We'll *all* fucking fight."

Asgrim snorted, drew another knife, and handed it hilt first to Snorri. "Hurry. Cut the others loose. But keep 'em quiet. If the Franks wake, we're all dead."

"Aye, Captain." The man paused, and Asgrim heard him inhale deeply. "Captain… on the beach—"

Asgrim grabbed him and pushed him toward the others. "Go. I'll kick your traitorous ass later."

Some of the others began to wake and quietly ask questions in the dark. Asgrim hissed at them to shut up and then went from man to man, cutting each one's bonds. As the men woke, each one helped free the others. Asgrim felt their excitement rise. Hope was a powerful emotion.

As was revenge.

Asgrim needed only minutes to free forty of his men. The others were dead, killed in the battle, or tortured and executed by the Franks. The men crowded near the doors, and Asgrim had them drag the corpses of the two dead sentries inside and strip them for armor and weapons. Then he sent two men out wearing the Franks' helmets and holding spears. The men took up positions on either side of the door; from a distance, they would pass for the sentries. The remainder of the men waited silently. Their only chance was to keep the Franks sleeping, unaware of what was happening in the dark.

One of the two men pretending to be sentries opened the door a crack and whispered, "Someone's coming."

Asgrim peered past the doors and saw a figure emerge from the mist, silently creeping toward them with a bundle in its arms. Asgrim smiled and pulled the doors open.

"Let him by," he whispered.

Harald Skull-Crusher stumbled into the barn, his arms filled with spears. The others rushed him, taking the weapons from him and passing them out among themselves.

"Well?" whispered Asgrim.

Harald sighed. "There's spears and shields in front of each of the tents, as well as bows and quivers of arrows. They're probably sleeping with their swords."

"I don't care about swords. We need axes for the shield wall."

"I don't know," said Harald. "Our weapons must be in one of their tents, 'cause I couldn't find them, but there's still weapons to fight with—*if* we're quick and quiet."

"Fires?"

"The campfires are mostly out, but I managed to get one smoldering again. It should do."

"Sentries?"

"Two men roving about. I killed one, but the other is farther away, on the other side of the camp. I didn't want to take the chance."

Asgrim turned away and peered at the mass of shadows that was his men. "Steiner, you sneaky prick. You still alive?"

One of the shadows moved forward. "I think so, Captain."

Recognizing Steiner's hushed voice, Asgrim handed him his long-knife. "I want that sentry dead. Go with Harald. He'll show you where he is. Then come back here. I have something special I want you to do."

"Aye, Captain."

"Anyone or anything else you see awake and moving, you kill."

Harald whispered some directions to Steiner, and together, they slipped away. In battle, things could always go wrong, but Steiner could give a cat lessons in stalking. The Frank sentry would soon be among the dead.

"What are we going to do, Captain," one of the men asked. "Sneak away?"

Asgrim whispered just loudly enough for all of them to hear him. "No. The only way out of here is *through* the Franks. Even if we got away without raising an alarm, which is impossible in your state, they'd come after us. No. We fight them now, while they're still half-asleep."

"That's just fine, Captain," one of the men whispered, Snorri perhaps. "I got a score to settle with these pricks."

The others mumbled in agreement.

Good, thought Asgrim. Anger will give them strength.

Waiting for Steiner and Harald seemed to take forever, and Asgrim's worry began to grow. The sky was beginning to become lighter in the east. Soon, the camp would be waking. How much longer could they stay here? Should they move now, without Steiner and Harald?

Just then, two figures appeared out of the darkness, scurrying silently to the barn. Harald and Steiner slipped through the doors. Both men held a bundle of battle axes, which they handed out to the others.

"We found our weapons," said Harald. "They're in a tent not twenty ells away."

"Unguarded?" asked Asgrim.

"They are now," answered Steiner.

Asgrim exhaled, feeling his excitement grow. "All right, then, we've sat here long enough." He turned to the men and raised his voice just slightly. "Arm yourselves—silently. Ax, shield, or spear… shit, a piece of stick if that's all you can find."

Asgrim, *Heart-Ripper* in hand, led his men out of the barn. His mouth was dry, but his senses were heightened, as they always were before a fight. With the eastern sky becoming lighter and the fog beginning to lift, his night vision was superb, and he could easily make out the individual shapes of his men, as well as the camp. The camp's tents were laid out in two parallel lines. Shields and spears had been set in front of each of the ten tents in which Frankish soldiers snored. Each Dane took a shield. Those who had no weapons took spears. They moved as silently as they could, but still made some noise. And each time they did, Asgrim winced, expecting a challenge.

But none came.

Steiner led them to the tent that held their axes. The men could fight with whatever they got their hands on, but they had been training with ax in hand since childhood. A shield wall bristling with ax-armed Danes was a formidable construct.

The men beamed as they hefted their axes. Then Asgrim sent Steiner to do his special task. In minutes, the sun would begin to show. A rooster crowed.

Asgrim led the men to the first row of tents. They silently formed their shield wall, jostling one another into position three ranks deep in front of the tent. The men in the first rank locked their shields together, each man protecting the man on his right. The men with spears took up position in the second rank, so they could stab the longer weapons over the heads of the men in front of them. Those in the third rank would shove against the men in front. Most shield walls were nothing more than shoving matches between half-drunken, poorly trained conscripts, often lasting hours, with neither side moving more than a few feet. But Asgrim's father had taught him how to fight and how to drill and train the men to move as one unit, much as the Romans had done centuries before. Asgrim's shield wall was an instrument of death, of bloody ax and deadly spear. Each man, even the young ones, had trained for weeks back home in Hedeby to fight at Asgrim's command. Rather than stand in place and push and shove and hack and hope the other force broke first, Asgrim's wall could move and turn and adjust to the tempo of battle. And when the men in the front rank tired, on Asgrim's order the second rank could move up to take their place.

And the Franks slept on, oblivious to the danger forming within their very midst.

Standing in the center of the shield wall, a Frankish round shield in one hand, and *Heart-Ripper* in the other, Asgrim watched Steiner climb the wall of the manor house. Three other men watched him from below, each one holding a bow and quiver of arrows. One man also held a half-burned log, its end glowing red. When Steiner reached the thatched roof, the man passed him the burning branch. Steiner used it to set fire to the tight bundles of thatch before quickly climbing down. The flames caught instantly, sweeping over the roof of the manor house like a wave. Orange light lit up the dawn, adding to the horizon's glow.

Smoke drifted through the air as Asgrim yelled, "Forward!"

The men shouted and smashed their axes against their shields, then stepped forward as one unit. They hit the first tent, knocking it down and hacking at anything that looked like it might be a man. Screams of agony and horror cut through the night, and the bloody axes rose and fell, rose and fell. In moments, they were on to the next tent, from which men now stumbled out in confusion. They slaughtered the inhabitants of this tent, as well, and then the next.

The manor house was an inferno lighting up the camp. Unarmed, half-asleep Franks stumbled about in dazed confusion. The next two tents Asgrim and his men hit were empty of Franks, and they simply swept the tents out of their way, killing anyone who didn't run away fast enough.

Asgrim turned the shield wall toward the second line of tents. Under his direction, the men moved as one. Horses screamed in fear, running wild through the camp. Steiner had cut them loose before lighting the house afire. Several of the animals ran into the terrified Franks. But now, several of the Franks had armed themselves. Men with swords charged at the Danish shield wall. But they moved without shields, without organization, and without hope. It was a brave but foolish act, and they were hacked down almost immediately by the well-disciplined Danes. Only another shield wall could stand against them, and Asgrim had no intention of letting the Franks organize themselves.

"Kill, kill, kill," chanted the men, berserk with rage and battle lust.

Asgrim grinned, loving the battle and needing it. This! This was what the spinners had intended for him.

A Frank, his sword raised overhead in two hands, ran at Asgrim, who caught the man's clumsy attack on the rim of his shield and then brought *Heart-Ripper* down on his clavicle before yanking the weapon back, cutting through tissue and killing him.

"Forward, forward!" commanded Asgrim.

The men stomped over dead and dying Franks, sweeping them away. From the shield wall's flanks, Asgrim heard the release of bow strings, then the short whistling of arrows before they hit the Franks almost at point-blank range. Asgrim glanced over and saw that Steiner and his men, armed with their bows, had rejoined the shield wall. Franks spun away and collapsed with arrows embedded in their bodies. And the shield wall kept advancing, now more than half way down the second line of tents.

Someone among the Franks was screaming orders, and a small group of soldiers tried to form their own shield wall. Several even held shields.

"No you don't," yelled Asgrim.

He turned the shield wall again, sending it to confront the growing knot of Frankish soldiers. The men had trained in this maneuver so often even the young lads could have done it in their sleep. The men stomped toward the Franks, yelling and slamming their ax heads against the metal bosses of their shields. The wall of angry Danes hit the Franks hard, shattering them. Each time the Franks tried to organize themselves, Asgrim hit them, again and again. The ground was littered with the dead and the dying.

A group of Franks armed with spears rushed forward, thrusting at the shield wall with the longer weapons. Some of the spears got past their shields, and several Danes fell back with wounds. Asgrim saw Gjuki Horse-Dick fall back, his neck a bloody ruin. But then the shield wall swept into them, and up close—without a shield wall to provide cover for them—the Frankish spearmen were defenseless. The Danes hacked them down.

The only chance the Franks had was to put shield and spear together in their own wall and hold the Danes long enough to let their numbers give them the advantage, but Asgrim much preferred slaughter to a fair fight.

"Forward! Kill! Forward! Kill!" he screamed.

A pair of Franks on horseback rode hard for the shield wall. The men riding the horses leaned into their spears.

Idiots! Horses don't charge shield walls.

At the last moment, the horses balked, reared up, and pawed at the air with their hooves. One of the riders fell off. The other managed to gain control over his animal and turned away, intent on escape. He didn't make it far before two arrows hit him in the back and he fell off. His horse disappeared into the sunrise, its hooves pounding the earth.

A soldier rushed Asgrim, who, caught up in the excitement, leaped out past the rest of the men in the shield wall. He rammed his sword point into the man's surprised face, tearing through his cheek and into his eye socket. Two other Franks came forward, trying to get at Asgrim from either side. He braced himself, getting ready to leap into them, but then hands grabbed him from behind and dragged him back into the shield wall. The two soldiers paused, but then arrows drove into them from the flanks, sending them reeling. A moment later, the wall shoved forward, finishing them off.

Just ahead, Asgrim saw another Frank, an officer wearing chain mail and carrying a shield and sword, yelling orders and trying to overcome the confusion. Franks flocked to his side and began to form ranks. Some even held shields, which they locked together as they formed into a group. Asgrim turned the shield wall and advanced into them. Within seconds, the two forces smashed into each other with a bone-jarring shudder. Men cried out in rage, yelling incoherent curses. The axes of the men in the front rank rose and fell, beating a bloody tempo against the Frankish shield wall while the men in the second rank shoved their spears over the heads of the men in front and into the faces of the Franks they battled. Asgrim roared curses and shoved forward with his shield, knocking Franks aside in his rage to get at the Frankish officer. The officer, recognizing Asgrim as the Danish leader, also pushed to get at him. Then the two men were carried together by the press of the shield walls. Shield locked against shield, and both men were shoved up against each other.

Asgrim was close enough to spit into the face of the other man, so he did. Then, the press subsided for a moment, allowing both men the room to stab at one another. Asgrim saw the Frank's sword coming at his face, and he dropped his shoulder and turned at the same moment that he thrust at the momentary opening between the man's shield and his body. Asgrim felt a burning sensation on the side of his head, but ignored it and rammed *Heart-Ripper* into the Frank's armored chest. His blow ran right through the man, cutting through the chain mail links and coming out his back. The Frank, a gaze of profound surprise on his face, collapsed.

And then the rest of the enemy, seeing the fall of their leader, broke and fell apart.

A cheer rose among Asgrim's men as they realized the Franks were defeated, reeling, and running for their lives. Survivors fled in every direction, desperate to get away. Steiner and his bowmen kept putting arrows into them as they ran. Several of his men broke ranks and went after the fleeing Danes.

Asgrim yanked his sword from the body of the Frankish war leader. "Get back, you damned fools. Let 'em run. Let 'em go!"

Panting heavily, his injured shoulder throbbing from the effort of holding a shield all this time, Asgrim bent over and gasped for air, taking huge gulps. Stinging sweat rolled into his eyes. The sun was above the horizon, and he could see the entire village around him. Terrified peasants—men, women, and children—joined the fleeing soldiers. He couldn't tell how many warriors had gotten away, but the ground around the campsite was littered with dead Franks.

Someone clapped him on the back, and his men were cheering, yelling his name over and over.

With forty men, and in a span of only minutes, he had routed more than twice as many Frankish soldiers.

FIFTEEN

The village,
August 8, 799,
Early morning

In the quiet aftermath of the battle, Asgrim's blood lust disappeared, leaving him exhausted and sullen. The Frankish officer had cut through his scalp, and although the cut had bled badly at first, the bleeding had almost stopped. Asgrim walked the battleground, brooding, as his men plundered the camp and the village, reveling in the spoils of victory. They stripped good leather armor from the dead, and each Dane claimed his own Frankish sword, laughing as he cut the air with the finely wrought weapon. Two of the dead Franks, including the one Asgrim had killed, had worn coats of fine chain mail. Perhaps they had even been knights. Asgrim gave the one with the ruptured rings to Harald and the other to Steiner, and the two men smirked as they tried them on, taking turns slapping each other's chest and shoulders. There were axes, daggers, shields, bows, and spears—more weapons than they could ever possibly use. Such a surplus, particularly the Frankish swords, would sell for a fine price, far more than they had made raiding that damned black monastery.

They found some silver as well, not much, but again, more than they had taken from the monks. In addition, they collected several silver arm rings, necklaces, and Christian crosses; some were cast in bronze. And, in the now-deserted village, the men found some small coins of silver and copper, as well as food: meat, fish, vegetables—and best of all, beer.

It had been a one-sided victory. By Asgrim's count, more than seventy Frankish soldiers were dead. His men had quickly killed the wounded Franks, a kinder fate than they had been giving his men when they had the same chance. That meant some thirty Frankish soldiers still ran loose on the island. This was a problem. During the battle, Asgrim had lost another six men. An additional four were likely to die of their wounds. That left him only thirty-one fit men: even odds. Those Frankish soldiers were scattered, but they would regroup and perhaps even force the villagers to fight with them. If they came back, they might even outnumber his men. He would not have surprise on his side again; attacking half-asleep, half-armed men had given him an advantage that would be hard to duplicate.

Asgrim ran his eyes over the large piles of shields, spears, swords, and armor neatly piled for transport to *Sea Eel*.

Screw them! They could come back and fight if they wanted, but he had their weapons.

And it was an arsenal, to be certain. The foreign soldiers had been well-equipped and well-armored. The Franks made excellent swords; everyone knew that. They were not crucible steel, but excellent just the same. Even after sharing the armor and giving each man a sword, Asgrim still had plenty more to sell. The profit wouldn't pay his wergild, but even if he sold only half the weapons and armor, he would still have enough left over to equip a replacement crew. And while he couldn't go home, he knew of other ports along the northern coast, perhaps among the Norse, where he could find like-minded men seeking profit.

And he would continue to live by the sword, killing and killing and killing. Once more, he saw the bloody face of Freya and her dead eyes staring accusingly at him.

Was there nothing more to his existence but death? Perhaps not. No man could change his fate, and he was so very good at killing.

He turned away and forced his thoughts elsewhere. The Franks wouldn't come back, not without their weapons, not after getting their asses so thoroughly kicked. Instead, they would go for help. At low tide they would make their way over to the mainland and come back with more soldiers. They would probably claim that they were set upon by hundreds of northmen, only just escaping with their lives.

Which was half right.

At any rate, Asgrim guessed he and his men had some breathing space, perhaps only days, but more likely at least a week, if not two, which was enough time to fix *Sea Eel* and sail away.

He walked among the men, forcing himself to joke with them and see to their welfare. They worshipped him now. After all, he had saved them from torture and death and won a magnificent victory against overwhelming odds. Danes loved heroes. And once the tales of this battle spread, other men would seek him out, wergild or not.

But the *djinn* was still out there. Fear of the spirit had driven his men to mutiny. It hadn't been just the spirit; Harald had also played his part, as had the failure to find silver at the monastery and Asgrim's killing of his own brother. And the men had been very, very unhappy when Asgrim had denied them Alda. But fear of the otherworld and a belief that Asgrim's luck had run out had been pivotal in allowing Harald to spread his rot. Right now, their mood was good; they were happy, elated he had saved them and that they had beaten the Franks, paying them back for their mistreatment. And after that battle, no man could say Asgrim had lost his luck. But soon, they would remember the spirit.

Then the fear would seep back in. Men, Asgrim could fight and beat, but he could do nothing against the dead. That left him with two choices: wait for low tide and flee on foot to the mainland to try to slowly make their way back home; or hold fast, fix his ship, and sail away like men.

This was no choice at all. He was taking his ship home.

They loaded the captured goods on the Franks' horses. Some of the men wanted to burn the village to the ground behind them, and Asgrim was tempted to let them, but in the end, he chose not to. The Frankish soldiers, not the peasants, were the real enemy. Instead, Asgrim led his men away, each walking beside a horse loaded down with armor, weapons, and other supplies—including all the beer.

Leading his own animal, Harald Skull-Splitter walked beside Asgrim. At some point, and without making a conscious decision, Asgrim had begun using Harald as a first mate, passing his orders down to the men through him. He wondered at that. After all, Harald had tried to kill him and had even killed his dog, or had ordered Hopp killed. The gods knew Asgrim had killed men for far less.

Was he becoming soft?

Perhaps, but he also needed to focus on what had to be done. They had a ship to repair. And the spirit was still out there in the woods, perhaps watching them even now.

And what did it want? It could have killed Asgrim on several occasions: when he was wounded escaping the mutineers, when he was alone on the beach, and during the days he had spent in the woods with Alda. Why slaughter everyone else it encountered, including Alda, yet leave him alive? He pulled out his Thor's hammer and absentmindedly let his fingers brush it. Who could say what supernatural creatures wanted with the living? It was best to just fix his ship and sail away—the sooner, the better.

He glanced at Harald. "When we reach *Sea Eel*, I want sentries and a wooden wall built all around her."

Harald nodded, "Aye, Captain."

Asgrim noted the lack of hesitation in Harald's answer. It underscored Harald's newfound willingness to follow orders. The last time Asgrim had given that particular order, Harald had mounted a mutiny and almost killed him. Now, he kept his mouth shut and did as he was told. What a difference losing a battle—and half the men—made.

"And I don't want to see any of the men drunk, not until we're gone from here."

"Aye, Captain."

He *was* getting soft. Could he trust Harald? Should he just kill him now?

He watched Harald's face for several moments before turning away and forcing his attention onto the tasks ahead of them.

He had killed enough men for one day.

* * *

Putting up the log wall around *Sea Eel* took only a day; fear was a strong motivator. The men cut down trees, laying them lengthwise atop one another along the sand around the ship, then packing dirt, rocks, and sand against the sides. Soon, they had a chest-high barricade. It wasn't pretty, but it would work. If the Franks came against them again, the Danes would have the advantage.

But a wall wasn't going to stop the spirit; only leaving would keep them safe.

With the wall in place, the men began to search for suitable trees to cut down and shape to fix *Sea Eel*. What Asgrim really needed were oak trees, but he found none. Instead, this island held stunted and gnarled mimosa trees, which were a poor substitute for oak. They cut down the best they could find. Then, using broad axes, they split the trunks into long, thin planks that they attached to *Sea Eel*'s keel, replacing the ones the spirit had destroyed. They took several days to get the strakes right, particularly because of the poor wood, but on the fourth day, Asgrim stepped back and ran his fingers over the repaired hull. It was complete shit, but it would do until they found better wood elsewhere. They re-attached the mast the best they could, with jury-rigged pulleys and tremendous difficulty—and only after having to cut off a good five feet of its length in order to fit it back into the mast fish. The men pounded moss into the cracks between the strakes, and the crack of wood on wood resonated along the beach.

"Ass-damned wood," said one of the men standing beside Asgrim with a wooden mallet in his hand.

Asgrim noted that he was one of the young lads, a boy of about sixteen named Erp.

No, he thought. That's not fair. Erp had been in two battles so far, losing one and winning the other. He had watched his friends endure days of torture. He may have looked young, but he had become a man.

"Aye," answered Asgrim, "but it'll keep the sea water out until we can put ashore somewhere else, somewhere we can lay up for the winter and fix her right."

"Hedeby?"

Asgrim gripped Erp's elbow, squeezed it, and smiled. "No. We're not going home yet. But I have friends in Trondheim, among the Norse. Good friends, old shield mates. They'll welcome us. We can winter there."

"Trondheim," the young man repeated, sounding out the word, as if it was a strange foreign land, and not just a day's sailing to the north of Denmark.

Asgrim slapped him on the back. "There's women in Trondheim, too, you know. You can plow them all day long. Then drink yourself stupid at night."

Erp grinned, his face turning red. Some of the other men yelled out insults, accusing Erp of being a virgin. The young man opened his mouth to reply, but then the smile on his face vanished, and his eyes narrowed as he stared out to sea.

Turning, Asgrim followed his gaze and saw the sails of another vessel—one heading for their beach.

It was a Saracen ship that Asgrim had seen before. The men from that ship had sent Asgrim to this damned island of death on the false promise of plunder. His brother was dead because of those men.

He snorted as a smile spread across his ruined face. His luck *was* changing.

SIXTEEN

The shoreline,
August 13, 799,
Sunset

Asgrim watched as the Saracen vessel dropped anchor and lowered a small launch into the waves. The ship was a trading vessel, the kind the Saracens called a *dhow,* and was manned by a crew of about twenty men. It was bigger than *Sea Eel,* perhaps twenty *ells* long, and boasted two large brightly colored square sails. One by one, a small group of Saracens climbed down into the small, bobbing launch. Restless, he reached over his shoulder and pulled *Heart-Ripper* several fingers' length from the sealskin scabbard, and then shoved it back in.

The Saracens didn't pose any real threat; there weren't enough of them to challenge his men—especially the eight men on the tiny launch that began to make its way to the shore. Just the same, Asgrim noted four of the men onboard the little boat wore glittering chain mail armor and carried large curved swords in scabbards; two of the others—the ones pulling the oars—were clearly sailors, barefoot and bare chested, wearing large pantaloons. The last two Saracens were richly garbed in brilliantly colorful, voluminous robes. One was a tall thin man with a nose that would have embarrassed a hawk. The other was the same fat, smug Saracen trader who had sent Asgrim on this raid that had cost him his brother and most of his men. Asgrim clenched his hands into fists.

He waited on the sand in front of the barricade around *Sea Eel*. His men waited just behind him, anxious for a fight. Harald Skull-Splitter, wearing his new Frankish mail coat, with his round shield in hand, stood just beside Asgrim.

"This Saracen prick lied to us," said Harald bitterly.

"Aye," answered Asgrim, his gaze locked on the launch.

The hull of the boat scraped against the sand of the beach, and the two sailors leapt out, hauling the boat ashore. The skin of the bare-chested sailors was dark brown, like the trunk of a tree. The four guards, moving like a single unit, wordlessly formed a screen in front of the boat. Asgrim had never seen armor like these men wore, and despite his anger, he was impressed. On top of their magnificent scale-armor coats, each man wore round plates of solid steel that protected their chests and shoulders. The scale armor beneath had been burnished, and the sunlight glittered off each piece. On their left arms, they carried small round shields made entirely of steel, each of which was conical, rising to a point in its center and bearing intricate Saracen markings. These men casually wore an earl's ransom.

"You give the word, Captain," said Harald, "and we'll hit 'em right now, take their worm-eaten ship and everything in it."

It was tempting, but Asgrim shook his head. "No. I want to hear what he has to say first. After that… well, we'll see about after."

From beneath their conical steel helms, the Saracen warriors eyed the Danes. Asgrim could see the concern in their dark eyes. And they were right to be worried. They were outnumbered six to one by the Danes, who blamed them for their presence on this damned island. But Asgrim also noted that they weren't terrified. He was a good judge of men, and these ones would fight. These men had confidence to spare.

Just how good did they think they were?

One of the sailors extended a hand, helping the fat Saracen from the launch. The man's heavy robes were trimmed with sparkling thread. He wore a bright-green turban held in place by a silver band. Such clothing was utterly unsuitable for life at sea. Had he fallen overboard, he would have sunk like a stone. If the Saracen had dressed to impress Asgrim, he needn't have bothered. The wind carried a trace of perfume, and Asgrim shook his head.

The Saracen trader smoothed his robes and then approached, his dark eyes wary, with his guards on either side. The other man, who was likely the trader's aide, followed just behind him. They halted in front of Asgrim and his men. Harald snorted and spat on the sand. Just for a moment, the eyes of one of the guards narrowed. The Saracen trader paused, his mouth open. Then he smiled broadly, extended his hand, palm to the ground, putting the other across his chest, and bowed deeply.

"Greetings once again, noble Captain Asgrim, and may Allah's blessings be upon you," he said in perfect Danish.

"Who?" Asgrim asked, although he understood perfectly that the man referred to his one god.

The Saracen's eyes widened. "Great and merciful God," he replied.

"Which one?" asked Harald. The Danes laughed.

They would like to kill these men, Asgrim knew. So would he.

The Saracen continued, ignoring Harald's insult. "There is only one God, and Mohammad is his servant. And I, *Abid al-Rahman Sayf al-Dawla,* remain *your* humble servant, Captain Asgrim. May God's Peace be upon you."

"Peace?" Asgrim smiled, then turned and indicated his men clustered around him. "Captain… Abid? You may have noticed I have far fewer men than the last time we met—by more than half." Asgrim paused, breathed deeply, and then continued. "My own brother is dead, driven mad first by the spirit of this island. An island *you* sent us to with the promise of silver—a promise that has proven false."

The Saracen's eyes widened, and he glanced quickly at the other robed man beside him. "The spirit is loose?"

Asgrim snorted, locked eyes with the Saracen, and nodded. "Aye, the spirit is loose. This island is cursed. There was no silver at that damned black monastery, and you, Abid, *you* lied to me, tricked me into coming here. Tell me now why I shouldn't cut your lying head from your fat shoulders."

The man took an involuntary step back before stopping himself. His guards shifted their stance slightly, and their hands drifted closer to the hilts of their weapons.

"Captain Asgrim," said the Saracen, "please, I wish to talk, to… explain important issues, grave matters."

"*Grave* matters?" repeated Asgrim. "Truer words have never been spoken."

Asgrim felt his temper rise and knew he was moments from a killing rage.

Sweat glistened on the man's face, and he licked his lower lip before placing a hand over his heart. "Please, Captain, my most sincere apologies for your loss, but… but there *is* silver. There *is* treasure to be had, and you may have it all."

Asgrim exhaled. "*More* treasure, Captain Abid?"

The Saracen pointed to his *dhow* behind him. "On my own vessel, in a chest. And I will give it all to you and gladly, a thousand silver coins, from the treasury of the *Serkland Caliphate* itself."

A thousand silver coins? That amount was ten times the cost of his wergild… with enough left over to buy and equip five more longships.

On the other hand, this fat Saracen whoreson had already lied to him once.

Asgrim's glance darted to the *dhow*. If he killed these men, he would never get to the ship before it pulled anchor and sailed away, and although *Sea Eel* was almost sea-worthy, she wasn't yet ready to chase down prey.

Wearing what he knew had to be a fake-looking smile, Asgrim extended a hand toward his camp on the other side of the barricade. "Well, then, Captain Abid, perhaps we *do* have matters to discuss."

* * *

Asgrim sat on a stump of wood across the fire from Abid, who sat on a folding stool one of his sailors had set out for him. Apparently, the man didn't want to get his ass dirty. The other Saracen, the thin one with the beaked nose, sat on another folding stool just beside Abid. Harald sat on the sand next to Asgrim, drinking beer and belching. Asgrim sipped from his own beer mug and then wiped his mouth with the back of his hand. He had offered the Saracens beer, but Abid had politely refused and the beak-nosed one had looked as if Asgrim had offered him a plate of steaming offal, which was fine, because he really didn't want to share his beer with them, anyhow.

The fire cracked and spit, casting errant sparks. Asgrim smiled, secretly hoping one might burn a hole through the Saracens' expensive robes. Abid's guards sat in a tight group about ten paces away, warily eyeing both Asgrim and the other Danes.

They were right to be uncomfortable, thought Asgrim. But he had given them the safety of his camp. Nothing would happen to them—for the time being.

Asgrim cocked his head to the side and considered the Saracen trader. The other man smiled obsequiously in return.

Asgrim used his beer mug to point toward Big Nose. "Who's he, then?"

Abid's eyes flicked to the other man. "My aide, *Yusuf ibn Ayyub.*"

"Yusuf," repeated Asgrim, inclining his head and then pointing to Harald. "My new first mate, Harald Skull-Splitter."

Yusuf met Asgrim's eye, then he nodded sourly, looking as if he was pained to be in Asgrim's presence. This one made no attempt to befriend him, nor did he wear the false charm of a merchant. He was also no sailor; that was clear. So what was he, then, and why was he here?

"Okay, then," said Asgrim. "We've established the pleasantries. So tell me about the silver."

Abid smiled, exposing bright-white teeth. Several small golden beads hung from the ends of his immaculately trimmed beard. "Captain Asgrim, I most humbly apologize once again for the death of your men. Please believe, we had no idea the spirit was loose. I thought you'd only have to face the black monks, poor pathetic opponents."

"And the Frankish soldiers."

Abid paused. "Of course, those unworthies, as well, but I did warn you of them. I even described their fort."

"Aye," said Asgrim. "You did. Of course, those soldiers were already dead when we arrived, slaughtered by the evil spirit loose on this cursed island."

"Yes, the spirit." Abid glanced at Yusuf. An unspoken message passed between the two Saracens. "I am most sorry, but we had no way of knowing the damned monks had released the spirit. The fools!"

"You mean the djinn, do you not?" asked Asgrim, carefully watching his reaction.

Abid paused, clearly startled. "You know what it is? How?"

So it wasn't just a dream. The dead had spoken to him.

Yusuf leaned forward and spoke softly in the Saracen tongue. Abid answered quickly, curtly. Yusuf's eyes flickered to Asgrim.

"Speak words we can all understand, eastern man," Harald snapped.

Yusuf sat back again, glaring at Harald, but Abid quickly smiled, holding out his hand. "Yes, yes, of course. We do not mean to be rude. Sometimes, we forget ourselves. My friend is not as accustomed to your Danish tongue as I am."

"Speak of this djinn," said Asgrim. "This is an eastern spirit, yes?"

"It is so," answered Abid. "But it is far more than just a spirit, far more…"

"We've seen that," spat Harald.

"This djinn drove the black monks crazy," Asgrim said. "They tortured and murdered one another." Asgrim leaned forward and stared into Abid's eyes. "Understand this, Saracen, I'm a hard man, but even I wouldn't do the things those monks did. No sane man would. By all the gods, what is this thing?"

The sky behind Abid's head blazed with the sun's dying rays. He hung his head, looking up at Asgrim with a mournful expression. "My people know of many different spirits. Ghuls, ifrits, angels, and djinn. And among the djinn, there are many variations, some far worse than others. This one is special."

Yusuf leaned forward, reached out his hand, and grabbed Abid's robes near his knee; his eyes locked on the other man's face. Abid shook his head and firmly removed Yusuf's hand from his garments before continuing. "It is called a Marid, Captain, a demon of the sea."

"Marid," repeated Asgrim. The word sounded foul on his lips.

"This Marid is most assuredly not one of God's creatures, but a servant of Shaitan," said Abid. "It ranks among the most powerful of all djinn, arrogant and haughty, utterly hateful of men. And this one, ahead of all others of its kind, revels in destruction, in murder, and sorrow.

There is no act too despicable for it. Verily, all demons thrive on misery and fear—but this one…"

Asgrim nodded, poured the dregs of his beer out onto the fire, which sizzled and popped. "Aye, we've seen this. It… took my brother, Bjorn."

"Yes, Captain. It possesses the minds of men, drives them to acts of horror. But we had believed it to still be trapped within—"

"Within the bones of Saint Philibert, the Christian priest who built the black monastery."

Abid froze, his mouth open. "How…?" He cocked his head and then nodded slowly. "Yes, Captain Asgrim. You are exactly correct. This djinn, the Marid, possessed the body of the false Christian priest, who carried it away to this island before he died."

"Why?" asked Asgrim. "How?"

"Because we trusted him, because we believed him to be a servant of God, a holy man. He fooled us by sharing certain… secrets he had gleaned from the otherworld. But he was, in truth, a most unholy man, well-versed in the dark arts. For many years, he lived among our scholars and holy men in the Caliphate. This is how he discovered the Marid's existence, secretly gleaning that we had locked it away to… to keep the world safe. So he made his plans, and when he deemed the time right, he stole the demon, carrying it away within his own corrupt body."

"Yet he died," said Asgrim.

Abid nodded sagely. "Yet still he died, for no mortal man can long carry such an evil within. Perhaps he didn't realize this. Perhaps the Marid lied to him. I do not know. But we have been trying to recapture the demon for many, many years now, to take it back to the Caliphate, where it can be safely held for all time."

"This is why you've raided this island before, isn't it?" Asgrim asked.

"This is true, Captain. Twice now, we've tried to take the demon back. But each time, I am ashamed to admit, we failed. After our last attempt, the Franks sent soldiers to move the monastery. We would have sent an army, but it would have meant war with the Frankish King Charlemagne, a war we did not wish to fight."

Asgrim snorted. "Not yet, you mean."

"Islam is peace, Captain. The Caliph wishes the demon returned to its prison, but does not desire another war. So—"

"So you tricked me into raiding the island for you, hoping I'd defeat the garrison."

Abid opened his hands to Asgrim and nodded. "We knew you were bold where we were not, that you could accomplish what we did not have the strength to do."

Asgrim sighed and leaned forward, jabbing his empty beer mug at the man. "Saracen, don't blow air up my ass."

Abid's face went grey, then he smiled again, bobbing his head quickly. "You are, of course, correct and astute, Captain. I flatter you needlessly. But the silver is real, and we are prepared to pay you handsomely for your services."

"What do you want?" said Asgrim. "Speak plainly for once in your miserable lying life."

The two men locked eyes, and Asgrim was certain there was anger hidden behind Abid's. A long, uncomfortable silence passed before Abid inclined his head and spoke again. "We seek to recapture the Marid, to take it away from this land and return it to the Caliphate, where it can no longer pose a threat to the world. If you help us in this task, we shall give you all of our silver, a thousand coins, enough to become the wealthiest of all sword-Danes."

Asgrim leaned back and considered the Saracen. Harald leaned in and whispered into his ear. "I don't trust him. Make him show us the—"

Asgrim lifted a hand to silence Harald. "How, Abid? How will you capture this Marid? It's already killed scores of men." He turned and jabbed a finger at Sea Eel, still beached on the sand. "It is stronger than you can possibly imagine, immensely powerful—far more powerful than any single man, than dozens of men combined. No man can hope to stand against it."

"We have our ways, Captain, powerful ways. My colleague Yusuf is far more than just a servant. He is a potent mystic, famous among our people. I have brought him all this way for just this reason." Abid paused, his fingers brushing something on his chest beneath his robes. He leaned forward and lowered his voice, but spoke with conviction. "We can capture this spirit and take it from here, saving all of the people who live on this island. And believe me, if left alone, it will kill them all. It will kill you and your men, as well. And once there are no more souls to consume, it will move on to the mainland and continue its evil. Only we have the means to defeat it."

Once again, Asgrim remembered Freya's warning: If it reaches the mainland…

He stared out at the dark forest, knowing the spirit, this… *Marid*, was still out there, mocking him.

So many dead: the priests, the Frankish soldiers, those poor village girls, his own brother… even Alda, who had saved his life, who had touched him without flinching. What kind of a man was he?

"All right, Saracen. We'll help you. And in return, you will give me half the silver now."

Abid's face paled. "But, Captain—"

"Half the silver *now*, or our business is done." Asgrim put on his most threatening smile. "Well… *almost* done. There's still the matter of your treachery."

Abid suddenly sat erect, clearly understanding Asgrim's threat. He dipped his head and raised his hands, palms toward Asgrim. "We have a deal, Captain. As God is our witness, we have a deal. You shall have half the silver now, the rest when the *Marid* is captured."

When Asgrim stood up abruptly and reached across the fire, Abid's guards leapt to their feet, their hands reaching for their swords, but Asgrim merely gripped the other man's forearm and squeezed it.

"We have a deal," Asgrim repeated. Then he leaned in closer and put his mouth near the Saracen's ear. "But if you betray me, I promise I will cut you open and pull your intestines from your fat belly. You will be a long time dying." Asgrim stepped back and opened his arms wide. With a huge smile on his scarred face, he said, "Well, now. I guess we're all friends again."

SEVENTEEN

The shoreline,
August 14, 799,
Dawn

Early the next morning, they headed inland, hunting the spirit. The night before, Asgrim had asked for volunteers, fearing few, if any, of the men would willingly go with him. When the men, including Harald, confronted him en masse, each one demanding to go, Asgrim had stood speechless. He chose ten of the most experienced men and put Harald in charge of the others, ordering him to make sure *Sea Eel* was ready to sail on his return.

Often, the web the spinners weave is a twisted one. Only days before, Harald had tried to kill him; days later, Asgrim trusted him with his ship.

Steiner Ghost-Foot was one of the men Asgrim had chosen to accompany him, and the man silently led the party into the island's interior. Asgrim followed closely behind with his other nine men, as well as the Saracens: Abid, the mystic Yusuf, and the four foreign warriors.

A cool breeze blew in from the sea, carrying with it the smell of the open water, and Asgrim longed to be done with this island and to sail away with the wind in his face once more.

Each of his men wore their captured Frankish armor and carried shields, swords, and fighting axes. Four of his men also carried longbows with arrows nocked and ready for release. They had brought supplies for two days, which was more than long enough to search the tiny island. Besides, Asgrim doubted the spirit would hide from them; it didn't seem to fear men. Now, however, they traveled with a Saracen sorcerer, a man that could, supposedly, capture the spirit. But if the sorcerer was that powerful, why did Asgrim's guts feel rock hard? Why did he sweat so early in the day when it was still cool?

Achmed, the Saracen warrior who led the others, carried a round shield on his back that was completely covered by a black cloth tied in place by cords. The man took great care with it, and Asgrim could tell without seeing it that it was heavier than other shields. Heavy shields were a disadvantage in a shield wall, where the fighting might last an hour or more. Asgrim would have considered the man foolish for carrying such a heavy piece of armor, but his instincts told him the Saracen warrior was anything but foolish. Tall and heavily built, with a warrior's wide shoulders, Achmed's dark-brown eyes seemed to watch everything, like a bird of prey. Several times, Asgrim had caught the man sizing him up. No. He was no fool. This man would be a hard opponent. In fact, the other three warriors also carried themselves with the same confidence that only comes from experience and skill. The four of them drifted through the woods, moving almost as silently as Steiner, despite wearing glittering scale mail and pieces of plate armor.

Asgrim dropped back to walk beside Abid. "Your men seem competent… for easterners."

If the Saracen picked up on the insult, his face didn't show it. Instead, his eyes lit up with pride. "They are the Talons of the Falcon, holy warriors trained from infancy to be the perfect warriors. The sword of the Caliph himself, his own personal bodyguards."

"Yet now they guard you, a merchant?"

"No, Captain. I am merely God's humble servant, one that speaks your western tongues and has moved among your kind long enough to learn your infidel ways. These men are here to protect Yusuf." Abid glanced toward the skeletal Saracen mystic walking behind them. Yusuf stared at the ground as he walked, seemingly oblivious to his surroundings. "These men make sure *he* accomplishes his task. Without his knowledge and skills, we would all be damned to a horrific death."

"And Yusuf is here to capture this… *Marid*?"

"Indeed, Captain. And we must do all we can to ensure his safety—even if it means our lives."

"Can we not simply destroy it? Slay the Frankish knight that carries it?"

Abid shook his head. "It would simply pass to another vessel, Captain. It is too powerful for any of us except Yusuf. But even he—with his occult training and protections—must proceed with great caution. This particular *djinn* is pure evil, a demon of unimaginable force."

As Abid spoke, Asgrim noted that the other man's fingers drifted once again to touch something around his neck and under his robes.

What's he hiding under there?

"And what is your plan, then? How will you capture the spirit?"

"We shall find it, or it shall find us," said Abid. "We are servants of God, and our presence will offend the *Marid*. Eventually, it will come against us."

"This is your plan? Walk about this island until it attacks?"

"Yusuf is a *most* holy man, Captain. All his life has been spent in the service to God, delving into his mysteries. He has garnered great power, divine knowledge."

"From what I understand, so did this Saint Philibert," Asgrim said. "And look what his supreme knowledge brought him."

A trace of anger flashed in Abid's eyes, and this time, his voice carried a hint of the heat he was trying to hide. "Philibert was *not* a holy man. He was a pretender, a seeker of dark power. But he was not without his tricks. My own father sat at the Caliph's court as a trusted advisor when Philibert the Black first came among us, pretending to offer secret knowledge. And he impressed all with his false magic, claiming God as its source. But he lied. He lied about everything. He even pretended to know the secrets of immortality. The old Caliph himself believed his deceit." Abid snorted. "We should have cut Philibert's black head from his shoulders. Instead, he was given great privileges."

"And this is how he found the spirit?"

"It is so, Captain. Ages ago, our most holy men trapped the *Marid* within a special vessel, a silver vase capped by a blessed ruby that was once worn on the finger of a very holy man. Through murder and deceit, Philibert removed the ruby, letting the *Marid* possess him. Philibert then fled from the *Caliphate* in a ship he had waiting for him. Long had he prepared his treachery. By the time my people realized what had happened, the traitor was days gone. It took us years to find this island and even more years trying to recapture the *Marid* ourselves. As my honored father lay dying, I promised him I would return the *Marid*—even if it meant my own death."

"It might," said Asgrim. "I don't think you understand how dangerous it is."

Abid's eyes shone with the light of his fervor. "Oh, we understand how powerful it is, Captain. Never doubt this. Before my people trapped it, the *Marid* laid waste to scores of towns and villages, slaughtering all."

And how was it set loose upon the world in the first place? Asgrim wondered, but didn't ask, suspecting there would be no true answer forthcoming.

"It skinned a number of the monks—and my men," Asgrim said.

"It wears men." Abid nodded sagely. "Either their living flesh or their dead skins. Sometimes, it simply skins them and then discards their remains. My father spoke of entire towns where every single inhabitant—man, woman, and child… even the animals—were skinned. I do not know why. Perhaps it simply *wishes* to do so. Perhaps such things amuse it. The ways of demons are hidden."

They had traveled deep into the woods. Ahead, Steiner paused in mid-step, his hand raised in caution.

They waited in place, silent and unmoving. No birds chirped in the trees; no animals rustled in the foliage. All other living creatures seemed to have simply vanished. Once again, Asgrim felt the air grow cold and moist. Although they were inland, he smelled the sea. He was certain that if he closed his eyes, he would hear the waves, as he did when holding a horn to his ear. A tremor ran through his muscles, and his hand shook as he reached for *Heart-Ripper* and drew the weapon.

His eyes drifted to Abid's, and he saw the fear in the other man's face. The *Marid* was here, hidden among the trees, watching them.

It wanted them to know it was there, Asgrim realized. It could disguise its presence when it wished to do so, as it had on the beach when it spoke to Asgrim.

Asgrim snapped his fingers and hissed at the men to get their attention. Their eyes wide with fear, they looked his way, and Asgrim motioned to them to form a circle and face outward. The Saracen warrior Achmed instantly nodded his understanding and grabbed men by the shoulder, forcing them into position. Abid and Yusuf darted into the center. Yusuf removed a pouch he had been carrying and hurriedly rummaged through it. All of the men readied their weapons, all except Achmed, who did not even draw his large curved sword. Instead, the Saracen warrior simply removed the large shield from his back and stood with it at the ready, his hand on the black cloth that covered it.

The unnatural silence stretched on, and Asgrim fidgeted in place, squeezing the handle of his sword and staring into the trees around them. And then, as if it had simply materialized from nothing, he saw the *Marid.* It still wore the body of the Frankish knight Cuthbert and stood just next to a large twisted tree not twenty paces away. Pink leaves drifted through the air beside it, falling from the branches overhead.

Asgrim's heart hammered beneath his chain mail so hard his chest hurt. Realizing he had been holding his breath, he exhaled forcibly and shook his shoulders, his vision locked on the spirit.

The knight looked worse than ever, more like a moving corpse than a living man. The pale skin stretched so tightly over its skull that it looked ready to pull loose. Even from where he stood, Asgrim smelled rotting flesh.

The *Marid* stepped closer and bowed deeply. "*Greetings, wolves of the northern seas, and you, as well, monkeys of the Caliphate.*" His voice throbbed with power, like a force that pushed at them.

Yusuf spoke for the first time, but Asgrim didn't understand his eastern words. The tone, however, was clear, commanding—even if it did waver slightly.

The *Marid* smiled, exposing his white teeth, looking like a hungry predator. *"How rude, charlatan of the Caliphate. Your new northern friends don't speak your foul tongue."*

Yusuf responded again, with more emphasis this time. The *Marid* laughed and shook his head. Achmed's grip tightened on the cloth covering his shield.

What has he hidden beneath that?

The *Marid's* eyes darted toward Achmed, and he scowled. "*Those tricks will not work. I will never serve your pathetic little kingdom again.*"

"Co—com… come forward, demon," stuttered Abid. "We have God's protection. We do not fear you."

"*Yes you* do, *fool. And you are wise to do so. Your God isn't here. But I have no time for fools like you. I am here for the northman, the wolf of the sea.*"

The *Marid's* gaze turned to Asgrim, who stepped back, weak in his knees.

Be a man, damn you!

He forced himself forward again and slammed *Heart-Ripper* against the metal boss of his shield. The resounding clang rang out throughout the trees. "Gods damn you to hell, *draugr!* Let us do battle, then."

The *Marid* smiled. *"Come and find me, wolf of the sea. You know where I'll be."*

With that, the *Marid*, the spirit that wore men, turned and disappeared into the forest.

EIGHTEEN

The woods,
August 14, 799,
Midday

The *Marid* made no effort to hide its tracks. They led directly to the burned shell of the monastery. But then, somehow, Asgrim had always known they would. It seemed fitting that this ended where it had begun.

A cold sweat blanketed his skin, and his mind wrestled with his fears. Despite the presence of the Saracens and their mystic, the *Marid* had no fear of them; that was plain. Why not? If they had captured it once already long ago, shouldn't the spirit fear them? Why would it taunt them and then lead them straight to its haunt?

This felt like a trap. But he wanted—*needed*—the rest of that silver.

Or did he? He already had five hundred pieces of it, each one stamped with the markings of the Saracen kingdom. That was already more coin than he had ever taken before, far more than he needed to pay his wergild and go home. He could just kill the Saracens and keep what they had paid him.

No. He wasn't going to break his word. Besides, he needed vengeance. That damned spirit had forced him to kill his own brother, and then it had killed Alda, who, unlike Asgrim, had been a good person. There had to be a reckoning for that.

So be it.

Perhaps it was simply his fate to come back to the monastery.

Fate. Asgrim snorted, not caring when the others glanced his way. So far, the three old crones had led him on a merry chase, all in the name of this nebulous fate.

Plow fate!

He considered the Saracens. If the *Marid* was leading them to a trap, the mystic Yusuf did not seem overly concerned. Perhaps he was just too stupid to be frightened. Asgrim was damned sure he saw fear in Abid's face, and he *knew* that one was crafty enough to recognize the danger. The four Saracen warriors, the Talons of the Falcon, he couldn't get a feel for. They were still a puzzle. They moved through the forest like hunters closing in on a wounded animal, wary yet certain they would soon have it cornered.

The sun was high overhead when they came out of the woods and onto the edge of the square salt fields that surrounded the black monastery of *Noirmoutier*. The air still carried the stench of the burned wooden buildings, but the stone walls of the monastery remained, scorched in places, but undamaged, still strong and menacing. Not long ago, he had looked upon this monastery as a prize to be plundered, but it had been a trap.

The walls should be torn down, Asgrim thought. Nothing good would ever come from the haunted place.

He tied his helmet tightly beneath his chin, ensuring he could see through its eye-guards. The Saracen warriors prepared themselves by kneeling and praying, their heads bobbing. The sorcerer Yusuf sat by himself a short distance away and began to chant softly, his eyes closed, his lips moving quickly. Asgrim's men stood and stared at the Saracens, then followed Asgrim's example and began to ready their arms and armor for battle. But they moved slowly and awkwardly, as if they were half-asleep. Then they stood in a small knot, drawn together by mutual fear, gazing at the burned walls of the monastery and whispering among themselves.

Asgrim joined them, and they parted for him, making space at their center. In their grey faces, he recognized their mounting terror. These were brave men who had fought in the front rank of many shield walls, yet each one looked ready to soil himself. Asgrim understood that perfectly. A man could fight any other man and at least have a chance at defeating him. But what man could do battle with the otherworld? What man could fight a *draugr*, an undead spirit that could rip the mast off a ship and then ram it through the hull?

Sigmund Sigmundson lifted his chin and tried to smile, but failed utterly. "Wha—what orders, Captain?"

Their courage hung by the barest shred, ready to pull apart.

Asgrim reached out and wrapped an arm around Sigmund's neck. He pulled the other man's head in until their helmets touched. "You are a good man, Sigmund Sigmundson, a better man by far than most others. Never forget that."

Sigmund nodded and this time, managed a feeble smile.

Asgrim let go of the other man, pulling back to speak to the others. "That damned spirit waits for us in that fucking monastery. Each of you knows this to be true."

He paused, letting his eyes meet each of theirs. "I won't lie to you. That thing terrifies me, and I'd like nothing more than to return to *Sea Eel* and sail away from this gods-cursed island. But I won't. I can't. And it isn't the silver."

Asgrim smiled. "Well, not *just* the silver."

Some of the men actually smiled this time, even Steiner Ghost-Foot, who always looked as if he was sucking lemons.

Asgrim let the smile vanish from his face as he turned and pointed to the black walls of the monastery. "But I'll have retribution. No one—not even a *draugr*—gets away with slaughtering my men, my own brother, and skinning innocent women. We're going to teach this eastern spirit that there's a price to be paid for fucking with sword-Danes."

The men nodded. The terror was still in their faces, but it had been joined by resolve. Not much, perhaps, but he saw more than there had been a minute before.

"These Saracens seem to feel confident in themselves," said Steiner, glancing toward the kneeling warriors. "Perhaps their magic *is* strong enough to stand against this spirit."

"If it isn't," said Sigmund, "we're not going to—"

"If it isn't," said Asgrim, "we won't see nightfall. But all men die. Not one of us will live forever in this world anyhow. Fine! We fight, perhaps we die, but we face our fate like men, like Danes."

The men pulled in closer to Asgrim, drawing strength from him. They nodded, meeting each other's eyes.

"Perhaps I'll see you in Valhalla this night," Asgrim said.

"Aye, Captain," they muttered, turning to one another and wishing him well, slapping each other on the back, promising to drink a beer together in the hall of heroes this night should they fall.

Asgrim swelled with pride. The gods only knew men like this deserved their place among the other heroes in Odin's mead hall. He pulled away from his men as Abid approached.

"The *Marid* will be waiting for us within those walls," Abid said, his voice trembling. "Soon, God willing, we shall have it again, and then we can leave these lands."

"And give me the rest of my silver," Asgrim said.

"Indeed, Captain."

"It's leading us here. You do know that, right?"

Abid's eyes darted to the walls of the dark monastery, and his fingers once again brushed something beneath his robes. "Who can say what such a creature thinks, Captain? Most likely, it tries to frighten us away, but God watches over us, and he shall see us victorious. Mark my words, before the sun sets again, we shall have recaptured the *Marid*. God keep us safe."

"I hope you're right, Saracen. I hope your one god does indeed watch over you, because I don't think my gods are here. I think I've sailed too far south."

"There is only one God, and Mohammad is his prophet," said Abid.

Asgrim snorted, rolling his eyes. "Let's go get this damned spirit and get away from this cursed island—before the Franks come back with more soldiers."

When all the men were ready, and Yusuf had completed his mystic preparations, they stepped off, Asgrim leading toward the black monastery. Steiner Ghost-Foot walking beside him, to his left, carrying a bow and nocked arrow. Asgrim was not surprised. Steiner was a brave man, but Asgrim *was* surprised to see the Saracen guard commander Achmed just to his right. Just for a moment, their eyes locked, and Asgrim recognized a kindred soul, another battle captain. Abid and Yusuf followed closely behind, surrounded by the other warriors.

One of the Saracen warriors said something, and Achmed paused, then glanced back at Abid and spoke in a rush, concern clear in his tone.

Asgrim scowled at Abid. "What is it?"

"There are tracks on the ground, many warriors," said Abid.

"Aye," said Asgrim, "Ours. We were here a week ago."

"No, Captain," said Abid. "He says the tracks are recent."

Asgrim glanced at Steiner, who was now down on one knee, examining the soil. The scout looked up at Asgrim and nodded, his face betraying his embarrassment. "He's right, Captain."

Asgrim felt the hair on the back of his neck rise. "How many, and how long ago?"

Steiner examined the ground for several more moments, then moved to a different location about ten feet away and did the same again. Finally, he looked up. "A dozen men, maybe more. Probably two to three days ago."

"What men?" Asgrim asked.

"Steel-shod boots."

The Franks. They had been here. But before or after Asgrim had routed them? Or could these be new Franks, more reinforcements from the mainland?

Asgrim's gaze searched the walls of the monastery, looking for indications of a trap, signs of men watching them from hiding. He saw nothing; not even a bird flew over the silent black walls.

Finally, Abid spoke: "These Franks. Could they be waiting for us?"

Asgrim chewed his lower lip, then exhaled. "It possessed the monks when they dug up the old bones from the crypt, then the Frankish knight who fought the monks—even my own brother. Could it do the same to others it came across?"

"Most definitely, Captain… unless one possesses protection."

Asgrim scowled. "Protection?"

"We can keep you and your men safe, Captain. We protected you once already when the *Marid* first appeared. We have… secret ways."

"I don't like secrets, Saracen," Asgrim spat, glaring at the merchant.

The warrior Achmed stepped closer.

"My apologies, Captain," said Abid quickly. "I did not think to tell you. My companion, Yusuf, can keep us safe from the *Marid's* evil, but not the others on this island…"

Asgrim nodded and then faced the rest of the men. "Be ready. The Franks may still be here, hiding. Be prepared for anything."

He stared for several long moments at the empty walls of the monastery before nodding to himself. "Let's go, then."

No one challenged them as they approached the blackened walls. Up close, the stench of burned wood was overpowering. Asgrim's skin crawled, and he expected men to burst out from hiding and attack, but none did. He was the first man through the monastery entrance, walking into the courtyard where they had originally found the bodies. Only scorched earth and soot-stained walls remained. But the air became cooler and damp with the promise of the sea—a sure sign the *Marid* was nearby. His sense of unease grew. The rest of the men followed closely, trying to watch all the doors and windows of the inner courtyard at once.

"It's here, isn't it?" asked Steiner.

"Yes," said Asgrim.

"The *Marid* is powerful and arrogant," said Abid, "but it has underestimated the power of God before. It does so again, you shall see."

Asgrim felt a dull weight within his gut, as if he had swallowed a large stone. "I hope you're right."

From behind them, the sorcerer Yusuf began chanting in his foreign tongue. The words made Asgrim feel uneasy, although he had no idea what the man was saying. Yusuf continued for some time, and Asgrim and the others waited, watching, tensed for battle. Finally, Yusuf spoke. Abid listened and then translated for Asgrim.

"The *Marid* is indeed present, Captain. Yusuf believes it is inside, through that doorway, below us somewhere." Abid pointed to the main entrance.

“The monks’ crypt is down there,” said Asgrim.

Abid nodded.

“You better be right about your magic, Saracen.” Asgrim turned and glared at the sorcerer. “We’ve come this far. Let’s finish this.”

With that, he stepped inside the black monastery. After only a moment’s hesitation, the other men, led by Steiner and Achmed, followed him.

Within the cursed walls of the monastery, the air was even colder, and Asgrim could actually see his breath in front of his face. Everything that could burn had been consumed by the fire his men had set, leaving only the blackened walls intact. The level above them was exposed. The wooden floor had been consumed by the flames, falling in and creating piles of blackened rubble that the men were forced to step carefully around.

The stairway leading down to the crypt, though, was clear. Asgrim snorted. If that didn’t scream trap, then nothing did. He stood at the top of the stairs, glaring down into the darkness below. The air thrummed with menace and the cold promise of death. He gripped *Heart-Ripper’s* handle harder, squeezing it until pain spiked through his hand and forearm. Trap or not, he wasn’t leaving this cursed place until he had his revenge for Bjorn… and for Alda.

His men shuffled nervously behind him. They had to move now, before their courage frayed too thin. Men could only stand so much.

“It waits,” said Abid, from just behind Asgrim’s shoulder.

“I know,” answered Asgrim, feeling a rush of chill air circle about his legs. “Someone light a torch.”

One of his men handed a flaming brand to Asgrim. He slung his shield over his back by its straps and then took the torch. Asgrim stood in place, blinking rapidly, staring at the darkness. The spirit was right below, expecting them. It doesn’t fear men. Why should it?

If they went down there, they would all die. There was no question of this.

Fate. Fate was inexorable.

As he took the first step, the slap of his hard leather sole echoed down into the well of the stair. A damp wind wound about his legs. Steeling his resolve, he took another step, then another. Slowly, he descended. The torch guttered. Achmed and Steiner followed so closely behind that he felt their hot breaths upon his neck. Behind them, his men were quiet, save for their footfalls on stone and ragged breathing. At the bottom of the stairs, Asgrim stepped into the large crypt. The air was so cold that he shivered; ice covering the stone walls of the crypt glittered in the torchlight.

The *Marid* stood waiting for them, in the exact spot where the statue of Philibert had been. The spirit even imitated the statue's exact pose, his arms crossed, his head raised to the ceiling above, but with an evil smirk on its cadaverous face, it watched the men approach. The statue itself lay shattered on the floor. Asgrim stopped about five paces from the *Marid.* The men followed, packing the chamber behind him. Yusuf began chanting again, and Asgrim felt an army of insects crawling across his skin.

"*Greetings, warriors,*" said the *Marid,* lowering its gaze to them, but still smiling cruelly. "*I had feared you were no longer coming, that I would have to go and root you out from whatever hole you were hiding in.*"

"We… we do not fear you, *draugr,*" said Asgrim, hearing the lie in his voice.

The spirit didn't answer, but merely shook its head. Yusuf chanted louder. The air throbbed with power and menace.

"*I find the presence of these eastern fools distasteful,*" said the *Marid.* "*But just the same, I am glad that you brought them with you, Asgrim Wood-Nose.*"

Heart-Ripper wavered in Asgrim's hand, and for a moment, he felt the desire to lower it and welcome this creature. Then Yusuf's voice rose in intensity, and the feeling passed.

The *Marid* frowned. "*You think these fools with their charlatan tricks can protect you? Why? And what is it, exactly, that you think you need to be protected from?"*

"You're evil," answered Asgrim. "And you killed my brother."

"No, northern wolf, I did not kill your brother. You did."

"But… but it was your—"

"Oh, don't be so tedious, northman. I gave your brother the gift of serving me. You took his life."

Abid spoke in his foreign tongue, softly, in almost a whisper. Asgrim heard it only because the man stood just behind him with Yusuf. It must have been a command to Achmed, because the other man edged closer to the *Marid*, stepping just past Asgrim with his hand on the cover of his shield.

The *Marid's* eyes flicked to watch Achmed, and it grimaced. *"Whatever deal they made with you, you should know that they will break it. They have no intention of letting you or your men live."*

"Tricks, *draugr*. Tricks and lies," Asgrim spat.

"No, northman. But you suspect as much already, don't you? They seek to force me to serve them again. And if they succeed, their first command will be to slay you and all your men."

"Lies, Captain," hissed Abid. "It is a deceiver. It is frightened now because God's power will soon protect the world from its evil."

The *Marid* laughed, and it was an unpleasant sound. It shook its head and glared at the Saracen before returning its attention to Asgrim. *"You are no fool, northman. You understand this man lies. They will not protect anyone, merely use me for their own gain. Their Caliphate's power will grow over the entire world. But I will not be used, not again."*

"You *will* serve God, demon!" shrieked Abid. "You will submit."

"*Never,*" said the *Marid. "Instead, I shall take you and your ship, northman. I will use your body to replace this vessel of flesh, which even now is failing and rotting. You and your northern wolves will serve me. And why not? You and I are more like brothers than you and your real brother ever were. We serve the same purpose, red death, carnage, chaos, and destruction. Oh, yes, we shall burn the world and destroy every village, town, and city along the coast. And our strength will grow. More ships, more men, and more death. And you, Asgrim Wood-Nose, will become famous. Your name will live forever.*"

"I… I don't," Asgrim's glance went from the *Marid* to Abid.

"*You are one of mine,*" said the Marid, "*You are death from the sea, just as I am. You know this to be true.*"

"I'm not… I…"

Was he like this thing?

"I could have taken you and all your men that night in the fort. But I waited because I knew I'd have to deal with these Eastern fools sooner or later. And now you've brought them to me. And their magic shall not work a second time."

"Don't listen to its lies," said Abid.

The *Marid's* eyes narrowed as it turned to Abid. "*Tell me, Eastern man, did you bring my old prison with you?*"

"Enough, demon," said Abid.

Abid yelled something in his Saracen tongue, and the crypt erupted in confusion. Achmed stepped in front of Asgrim, blocking his view as he yanked the cloth cover from his shield. Asgrim saw a flash of silvery metal. The *Marid's* face went pale and then flushed with rage. Yusuf also stepped forward, chanting furiously, almost shouting, and held a small silver jar over his head with both hands. The *Marid* drew back, its eyes widening.

But then someone screamed in pain from the rear of the chamber, and Asgrim saw forms battling near the foot of the stairs.

"Behind us!" Asgrim yelled. "We're under attack."

Frankish soldiers poured down the stairs, attacking those closest to the crypt's entrance. The Franks were unarmed, attacking the Danes and Saracens with their bare hands, biting and clawing at them as if they were animals. Asgrim saw one of his men go down under the weight of three Franks who had swarmed over him.

They hadn't been in the ruins of the monastery, but Asgrim had no doubt that these where the same Franks whose tracks they had found earlier—the survivors of the battle at the village, now possessed by the spirit. They must have been hiding in the woods nearby, awaiting some occult message to attack once the Danes and Saracens had entered the crypt.

He had been a fool to come straight down here first.

A wild-eyed Frank charged Asgrim, reaching for him with claw-like hands. Asgrim rammed his burning torch in the man's face, letting it fall to the floor as he stepped to the side and brought *Heart-Ripper* down on the back of the man's neck and yanked the blade back, nearly severing his head. Everywhere, men fought against the crazed Franks, with more still swarming down the stairs. There was barely room to move in the crowded crypt, and Asgrim almost tripped over a body lying on the floor. Achmed maneuvered to stay in front of the *Marid*, still holding the spirit at bay with whatever magic his silver shield possessed. Yusuf struggled to maintain the jar over his head amid the men fighting around him and jostling him. Abid stood just behind Yusuf. Terror filled his wide eyes. Then a half-naked Frankish soldier grabbed Abid and pulled him down, biting at his throat. Abid screamed, and the Saracen's feet pounded the ground. Asgrim moved to help, but someone suddenly grasped at the shield on his back, pulling him off balance. He slipped his arms free of the shield's straps and spun in place, lashing out with his sword and cutting a Frankish arm off at the elbow. But then at least three more Franks rushed forward, colliding with him, and he went down under their combined weight. Panic gripped him as their fingers jabbed at him like knives, trying to get through his chain mail coat and tear into his flesh. He kicked and thrashed, cutting at them with *Heart-Ripper* and pounding at them with its hilt. He needed room to get up, to keep fighting, but he couldn't get it. Only his armor saved him from their attack, but that couldn't last. One of them bit at his thigh, and stabbing pain ran up his leg.

Then, miraculously, one of the Franks he fought collapsed against him, unmoving, and another was suddenly wrenched free. Asgrim managed to shove *Heart-Ripper* against the throat of the last Frank and wrenched his blade back, sawing the Frank's throat to the bone. Hot blood sprayed his face, but he was suddenly free of his attackers. He staggered to his feet just as Steiner killed the Frank he had pulled from Asgrim, cutting the man open from chest to navel and spilling his guts onto the stone floor.

Panting, Asgrim nodded his thanks, but then three more Franks threw themselves on Steiner from behind, dragging him to the ground. Asgrim tried to help, but even more Franks appeared, cutting him off, trying to drag him down, as well.

Gods damn it! How many of them are there? His men! His men were being slaughtered.

Asgrim kicked one of the Franks between the legs. Even possessed, the man dropped. Another rushed him, but Asgrim brought *Heart-Ripper* down on the side of the man's neck, hacking through bone and muscle. He tried once more to reach Steiner, but the wild mass of fighting men had pushed them farther apart, and he couldn't find him in the cramped confines.

He needed to do something, to take charge, but chaos ruled. Sigmund sat atop the chest of one of the Franks, repeatedly pounding the man's already-crushed skull against the stone floor, seemingly oblivious to the fact the Frank was already dead. A moment later, another Frank fell upon Sigmund's back, and Asgrim was pushed away from him by the press of the fighting.

One of the Saracen warriors, Asgrim couldn't tell which one, swept by him, his large sword whistling through the air as he sent Franks reeling from its deadly path. Incredibly, as the man fought, a Frank clung to his neck, trying to pull him down. Another had wrapped his arms around the man's leg, and still, the Saracen fought on.

This is impossible. They had to get out of the crypt. They had already lost this fight, didn't the Saracens see that? If they stayed, they died.

Only dim light remained in the crypt from the torch lying on the stone floor, which had been sent skidding against one of the walls. Asgrim's breath rasped in his throat, and he glanced about wildly. He backed away from the fighting, looking for a way out of the horror. He knew he was panicking, and he knew he was letting his men down, but he couldn't help it. He *had* to get out of there. His legs struck something, and he fell backward onto the ground, dropping *Heart-Ripper*.

In the near darkness, he just made out the face of Abid lying beside him. At first, he thought the merchant dead, as his throat had been bitten open and blood drenched the front of his fancy robes, but then the man reached out with a trembling hand and grasped at Asgrim's leg. He had seen enough death to know that Abid was on his way to whatever Saracen afterlife awaited him. But the dying merchant's eyes shone with purpose and intensity, and his lips quivered as he tried to talk, to tell Asgrim something, but in the midst of the confined battle, Asgrim could make out none of his whispered words. Whatever Abid had to say, he was going to take his message to the grave with him. In his other hand, though, the Saracen merchant gripped a large round silver medallion that he weakly thrust at Asgrim. That must have been what he had worn beneath his cloak. Whatever magic the talisman possessed hadn't saved him, but Asgrim took it from him anyhow. Abid smiled, closed his eyes, and collapsed dead. Asgrim quickly draped the medallion's chain over his own neck and forgot about it as he looked about the chamber, trying to figure out what to do next.

Nearby, Yusuf continued his frantic chanting. Achmed still held the *Marid* at bay. But at that moment, a Frank threw himself from behind onto the Saracen warrior's back and pulled him down. Achmed's shield flashed silver as the man went down. It skidded across the stone floor, clattering to a stop against Asgrim's leg. The *Marid* launched itself at Yusuf with an unearthly howl and ripped the man open from throat to groin with one sweep of its hand. Yusuf dropped the silver jar. It clanged against the stone ground as Yusuf fell to his knees, his entrails dangling, his face twitching with disbelief.

The *Marid's* laughter rang out within the near-dark crypt as it stepped forward and crushed the silver jar with its boot.

Achmed rose, throwing the Frank away from him. Two more launched themselves at him, and Achmed kicked the first one square in the chest, sending the Frank flying back. At the same time, the Saracen captain reached above his head and drew his long curved sword—just in time to strike out at the second Frank and send the man reeling back, his chest cut open.

Gods, the man had been fast! Faster than Asgrim could have moved.

Just for a moment, Asgrim and Achmed's eyes locked, and Asgrim felt courage and hope flow back into him. But then the *Marid* stalked forward and gripped the back of Achmed's head, lifting him from the ground by his conical steel helmet. Achmed's feet kicked wildly as the spirit lifted him higher. And Asgrim's newfound hope vanished when the spirit crushed Achmed's helmet and skull in its grip.

His eyes darting about, Asgrim saw that the battle was over. His men were all dead, and the Franks began to converge upon him from every direction.

He had failed, and there was only death in this crypt. Only death.

As the press of possessed men advanced, blood dripping from their chins and fingers, his courage and his hope slipped away completely. There was nothing left but to die—and he had no weapon. Frantic, Asgrim's hands patted the ground, seeking *Heart-Ripper*. He couldn't find his sword but, in desperation, grabbed the silver shield Achmed had dropped. He held it in front of him, certain he would be dead in moments, his throat ripped out by the possessed Franks.

But instead of attacking him, they stopped, staring at him stupidly, as if they were so drunk they couldn't move.

Asgrim bolted, the shield held in front of him. He ran right past the closest of the Franks who still stood frozen. Other Franks reached for him as he stumbled through them, bloody fingers grasping. But as soon as their wild black eyes saw the shield, they paused. In moments, Asgrim was past them and running up the crypt stairs and then outside, into the dizzying bright sunlight.

Only a coward fled from battle, and he was most certainly running away.

He kept running, unable to stop, sprinting past the monastery entrance and into the fields. Behind him, he heard pounding footsteps. Glancing over his shoulder, he saw two Franks chasing him.

His heart hammered wildly as his terror drove him on, across the salt fields and into the woods, with the Franks close behind and getting closer. What a sad, pathetic end to the famous Asgrim Wood-Nose: to die empty-handed and fleeing in terror from an enemy. He prayed his father and brother couldn't see him now. Or his mother.

Especially his mother.

He knew he was pathetic, but he couldn't help himself, He couldn't stop. And they would get him. This was clear. He was too exhausted from running in armor while carrying the heavy silver shield. He could tell they were almost on top of him. In moments, he would feel their fingers on his back, pulling him down, ripping into him, as they had done to all the others.

It wasn't bravery that made him stop and face them, but merely desperation. He spun, trying to set the shield in front of him, but they were too close, and they collided with him, knocking him onto his back. Despite his efforts, he dropped the shield. Then they were on him, snarling like wild animals, trying to get at his throat with their teeth. He had no strength left. It was all he could do to hold them back, but he couldn't do so for long. One of them pounded at his head, shrieking like an animal, and Asgrim's helmet came loose. He tried to twist in place, but the Frank managed to strike him in the temple with his fists, once, twice, three times. His vision began to grow dim.

And then he heard a woman scream in rage. Something smashed against one of the Franks, and the man collapsed against him. Someone moved nearby, but the other Frank was still clawing at his throat. Asgrim's fingers brushed against his helmet lying beside him, and somehow, he wrapped his fingers around its rim. He smashed the helmet repeatedly against the side of the Frank's head, gaining more and more traction with each blow. Suddenly, he was free of the Frank's weight. His rescuer had dragged the wild man from him by the ankles. Seeing bright spots in his vision, Asgrim crawled to the Frank, raised his iron helmet above his head in both hands, and brought it down on the man's head, shattering his skull.

He rolled over onto his back, breathing huge gasps of air. The woman leaned over him.

It was Alda; she was alive! How was that possible?

A moment later, she was cradling his head against her chest, tears running down her plain but beautiful face; her long red hair was loose.

"Right… all right… saved me," he whispered through his pain.

And then he passed out.

NINETEEN

The beach,
August 14, 799,
Sunset

All day long, Harald Skull-Splitter's doubts nagged at him. When the sun began to set, he was certain something had gone horribly wrong. He paced and worried, occasionally stopping to stare out to sea. As night came on, he could now only just make out the shape of the Saracen ship anchored off shore. He shook his head again and cursed.

The men watched him from the camp. No doubt they had the same concerns he did. They wanted to leave, but they were worried for the captain. The hull was repaired—at least well enough to sail. Dragging the longship back into the water would take only an hour at most, but they would need two more to load provisions onboard. Soon, they could be far from the cursed island, out on the waves.

He sighed and ran his palms through his hair.

There was no way he was going to break his oath and betray the captain again, never again.

Harald was no war band leader; he understood this now. Asgrim Wood-Nose was a real leader. Harald knew no other man alive who would have saved the men after they had mutinied and tried to kill him. And instead of killing Harald for his betrayal, he had elevated him among the others, which was an honor he knew he didn't deserve.

No. He wasn't going anywhere, and neither was *Sea Eel*. If the captain wasn't back by morning, though, Harald would take the rest of the men and go find him. If the gods want them all to die on this fucking island, so be it.

Feeling a sudden chill in the air, he rubbed his forearms. Then he saw his breath in front of his face and realized his doom had come. Forcing down the panic that set his heart hammering, he turned and faced the trees behind him. A man stood watching him, not more than ten paces away, wreathed in shadow. With fingers going numb from fear, Harald drew his new Frankish sword. He opened his mouth to yell out a warning to the others, but he suddenly couldn't speak. His sword fell to the sand, forgotten. Then Harald dropped to his knees beside it and stared stupidly at the man, not understanding what was happening. The man approached Harald, and as he did, Harald saw he was more corpse than man. His muscles trembled, jerking as spasms ran through his body, and he began to gasp for air.

The man stopped in front of Harald, watching him with black eyes.

Draugr, thought Harald.

Behind the corpse-man, stepping out of the trees, a score of others appeared: Frankish soldiers with glazed eyes. Harald knew his shipmates must have seen them, but no one called out in challenge. No one came to help him.

Doomed, they were all doomed.

"*You shall be the first of my northern wolves*," said the *draugr*. "*Together, we shall haunt the waves, raiding and killing all along the coast*." The *draugr* paused, looking past Harald at the Saracen ship. "*But first, we need to kill some men.*"

But Harald Skull-Splitter was no longer there. The mindless drone, the *ghul* that now inhabited his body climbed to its feet. The only emotion in its head was the need to serve its master, to rend, kill, and cover itself in blood.

And somewhere, Harald Skull-Splitter's soul screamed.

* * *

Asgrim found himself deep in a forest, one he knew well, despite the darkness of the night that surrounded him. He had grown up in this forest; he could never forget it. He was home, in Hedeby, near his father's farm… no, *his* farm. His father was long dead. Soon, he would lead the expedition to Ireland, claiming more honor than his father had ever known. But at that moment, Asgrim didn't care. He stalked through the woods, naked steel in hand, his anger rising. Fury and rage drove him on, propelling his footsteps; and far too much alcohol drowned his restraint.

Freya, damn you, damn you.

She had betrayed him, seeking comfort in the arms of another who was her true lover.

Frodi should have been more of a man. Had Frodi truly loved Freya, he could have challenged Asgrim. Then they could have laid a cloak out on the ground and danced the swords together, as Asgrim had done so many years before with Hrolf the Elder.

And Frodi would have died, as sure as the sun would rise and fall.

If Asgrim knew this, Frodi must have, as well. So instead, he took Asgrim's wife as a secret lover, meeting deep within the woods, where they thought no one knew. Asgrim now slipped through those same woods, *Heart-Ripper* in hand.

Fools! How did they think this would end?

And to add to the indignity, Asgrim had found out about them that night, the very moment of his greatest glory. The beer and wine had flowed like water at the celebration in his mead hall. Fawning over him, everyone had congratulated him on being selected as leader of the expedition. He was the luckiest of men, blessed by the gods with a magnificent destiny of conquest and glory.

And a faithless whore of a wife.

Earlier, when he had stepped away from the celebration, stumbling outside for some fresh air and a piss, his head had been spinning. Never had he been so drunk. Someone had brought some Rakish ale, and Asgrim had drunk more than his share. He found himself swaying. How much had he had? As he was relieving his bladder, he fell forward against the wooden wall of his barn, and urine ran down his hose, soaking his skin. He hadn't even been aware that Olaf was standing next to him until the other man started talking. Asgrim turned and stared at him stupidly, trying to understand what he was saying. He had never liked Olaf, who was lazy and too smart for his own good. In battle, Olaf always managed to be somewhere other than where the fighting was fiercest. He had signed on with Asgrim to sail to Ireland, but Asgrim didn't like him or trust him. Still, he had his own ship.

Olaf smiled, and Asgrim concentrated on his lips, trying to make sense of what the other man was saying. As the words slowly sifted through Asgrim's brain, a cold fear settled through the haze of alcohol and was replaced almost immediately by a growing rage. Olaf turned and pointed into the woods, telling Asgrim that no man would ever challenge his right to vengeance. Olaf didn't dare say it, but the insinuation was there: how could Asgrim ever lead an army if he couldn't control his own woman?

Asgrim drew *Heart-Ripper* and stumbled into the woods.

Whore. Slut. Betrayer.

He would show her. No woman, no man, no one betrayed Asgrim and made a fool of him. He reeled drunkenly, almost collapsing before catching himself against a tree trunk.

Bitch.

Child. Innocent. Lover.

Closing his eyes and moaning in torment, he shook his head from side to side. Then he ripped open his shirt and beat *Heart-Ripper's* pommel against his chest once, twice, three times, drawing blood and causing himself to stagger from the pain. But the throbbing cut through the torment in his soul and gave him clarity.

Then he heard a woman cry out in passion. They were just ahead, through the trees. Olaf had told the truth.

Panting, Asgrim let his fingers trail through the blood on his chest, leaving tracks. Was he surprised? Had he always known, or at least suspected? Perhaps. Maybe he just hadn't wanted to see it or to acknowledge it and thereby make it real, something that would need to be dealt with.

His rage throbbed and flared. Asgrim Wood-Nose, the ugly freak no woman could ever love—he wasn't lucky. He was cursed. He pushed through the bushes, coming up on them from behind. They lay on a blanket, naked, with their backs to him. Sweaty and red, Freya sat atop Frodi, riding him. Frodi's eyes were closed and his face was rapturous.

He had always liked the young man. More than just handsome, he was also polite and earnest. Why? Why was he doing this to Asgrim? Why were the two of them doing this to him? The world seemed to spin about him. Why had all women treated him like a monster?

And he knew the answer: because he *was* a monster.

At that moment, Freya, who had never made any noise other than a whimper when she had lain with Asgrim, cried out once again in ecstasy. Asgrim didn't even remember making the decision to move; it just happened, as if he were standing separate from his own body and watching someone else—a stranger—step forward, pulling *Heart-Ripper* back.

With an agonized scream, Asgrim thrust the crucible steel forward through Freya's naked spine, going all the way through her body and into the young man's. They screamed in agony and thrashed about, but Asgrim leaned into the blade as he yanked it up to tear a gaping wound in their bodies. He pushed so hard that the blade went all the way through them and into the blanket and then the dirt beneath it, pinning them together. Asgrim released them and staggered back, crying out in rage and horror as he yanked *Heart-Ripper* from them. Panting, he stared stupidly at them. Had he really just done this thing, this monstrous thing? It seemed impossible.

The young lovers lay together, Freya still atop Frodi with her face in his neck; Frodi stared stupidly at Asgrim. Still somehow alive, his lips quivered, opened slightly, and then closed again. Then his eyes rolled up, exposing just the whites, and his death rattle slipped from his throat. Blood gushed from their bodies, soaking the blanket and mingling together in a rapidly spreading pool. So much blood had come all at once, so fast. Asgrim had killed them both almost instantly.

But then again, he was so very good at killing people.

He dropped to his knees at their feet, into the spreading pool of blood that soaked through his hose. *Heart-Ripper* dropped from his nerveless fingers.

"Damn you, damn you, damn you," he cried out in a hoarse whisper as tears ran down his cheeks.

He closed his eyes, and the world spun about him. A vast, growling wind gripped him, lifted him into the air, and spun him about like a top.

And then he found himself somewhere else, sometime else, back on the same unnatural shoreline on which he had found himself before when the spirit of Frodi had spoken to him the first time, to tell him Freya awaited him. Once again, he was surrounded by fog and an uncanny silence.

The afterlife. The spirit world.

"Brother," a familiar voice called out.

Bjorn stood in the water, his skin grey and his eyes pits of darkness. His brother was dead, a shadow of the man he had been.

"Bjorn," whispered Asgrim. "Why are you here?"

"I cannot go on," said Bjorn. "There is no Valhalla for me."

"But you died in battle. How… how is that—"

"The *Marid's* taint passes through worlds and into the lands of the dead," Freya's voice announced from behind him.

Spinning in place, Asgrim saw her standing near the edge of the water, her hands clasped in front of her. A spreading stain of blood soaked through the front of her gown. He closed his eyes, feeling the crushing weight of his crimes.

"Freya," he mumbled, "I'm sorry for what I did. I'm so sorry."

She cocked her head to the side, watching him with a puzzled gaze. "Perhaps," she whispered. "But your sorrow changes nothing now."

And she was right. He moaned and nodded, knowing some crimes could never be forgiven. He motioned toward Bjorn with his head. "What madness is this, then? Why isn't my brother in Valhalla? How can an eastern spirit interfere with a warrior's journey to Valhalla? The Valkyries—"

"Did not come for me, brother. I died when the *Marid* took my body, not when you cut it open. There is no Valhalla for me," said Bjorn.

"No," whispered Asgrim.

A surge of emotions rushed through him, making the world seem to spin and wobble, as his mind grappled with this information. He hadn't killed his brother, then; he wasn't a kinslayer. But his relief was almost immediately overwhelmed by the realization that his brother would never see the afterlife he deserved.

This couldn't be.

"We are all lost now, Captain," said Harald Skull-Splitter, stepping out of the fog, moving to stand beside Bjorn.

"Harald…" said Asgrim. "But…"

More figures stepped out of the fog. The remainder of his crew joined Bjorn and Harald. All were dead. They stood in a semicircle facing him, silently watching him through dead eyes.

"No," whispered Asgrim. The weight of responsibility crushed down on him. "*All* of you?"

Freya sighed, her expression so sad. "The *Marid* knew it had to deal with the Saracens that would be coming for it. It knew that if it didn't, they might recapture it someday, force it to serve them again. Now, that fear is gone, so it can concentrate on what it always wanted, *you and your ship*, to use the shells of your men. It is a demon of the sea and needed a way to raid along the coast. I told you it had to be stopped. Now, it will use your ship, killing everywhere it goes. And the spirits of those that it kills will never rest."

"We shall never rest," said Bjorn.

"Never," said Harald.

"Never," echoed the voices of his crew.

"No," whispered Asgrim. "I've led you all to this horror?"

Dizziness overcame him, and the world seemed to spin about him. "What… what do I do?"

Freya stepped closer. "You must not let it leave. Only *you* remain to stop it now. Only you."

"*How*? How does one man fight such a thing? It beat us all—even the Saracens. And they used magic," said Asgrim.

"The Saracens sought to capture it, to use its power," said Freya. "But the *Marid* cannot be held by men, not forever. It must be banished, sent back to its own realm."

"But how?" asked Asgrim.

"I wish I could fight with you again, brother," said Bjorn, stepping closer now, reaching out with his large arms and placing them on Asgrim's shoulders, "just one last time. But I'm dead. *You* must find a way. It's only you now."

Asgrim shuddered at his cold touch.

"Only you," said Bjorn. He turned away and walked into the ocean, disappearing into the fog.

"Only you, Captain," said Harald Skull-Splitter as he, too, turned and vanished.

"Only you," said his dead crew, disappearing.

"I can't fight such a thing," said Asgrim. "It's not possible."

Freya watched him. She wore no expression on her face. "You've led such a wicked life, Asgrim Wood-Nose, hurt so many. Yet you're not truly evil, are you? Merely weak, so very weak."

"I'm sorry," said Asgrim. "I'm so sorry for what I did to you. If I could take it back…"

Freya considered him for a long moment, and then she shook her head, turned, and walked away into the mist, leaving him alone.

"I don't know what to do," Asgrim said. He dropped to his knees in the water. "I don't know what to do."

Then, as if from far away, he heard Freya's voice one last time, almost a whisper. "It is a sea demon. It gains its strength from the ocean."

As his world turned dark, he heard a woman call his name.

* * *

Alda cradled Asgrim's head in her lap and begged him to stay alive and to stay with her. She knew she was acting overly emotional. He wasn't wounded, merely exhausted, but she couldn't help how she felt. She had been hiding alone in the woods for more than a week, terrified that the devil that had possessed the knight would find her and skin her, as it had the poor village woman who had come seeking her healing skills and had been caught in her place. Always sensitive to the otherworld, Alda had felt something evil coming for her that day. Horrified, she had fled into the woods, desperate to get away and to save herself. Much later, when her panic subsided, she crept back to her home and found the butchered remains of the woman hanging from a tree. Horror, grief, and shame overcame her, and she fled again, nearly mindless, into the woods.

Many days later, she saw the northmen again, moving toward the cursed monastery—and Asgrim was leading them. He was back with his own kind. To her surprise, feelings of intense happiness flooded through her when she saw him, tall and proud, as he led his men; and for the first time in days, she smiled. After they passed, she followed them, needing to be near him—even if he didn't want her. She couldn't help it.

When he had reappeared from the ruins of the monastery, pursued by those black-eyed soldiers, she had not hesitated to come to his aid.

Asgrim mumbled and stirred in his sleep. Alda smiled down upon him and smoothed his hair away from his forehead. Leaning over, she kissed him once upon the lips and softly whispered his name.

The world was indeed wondrous and strange when a Frankish woman fell in love with a Viking warrior.

* * *

Asgrim awakened to Alda's touch, hearing her repeat his name. Bolting upright, he pulled her to him in a tight embrace, crushing her against his chest. "I'm sorry," he said. "I shouldn't have left you. I thought you dead."

She said something, pleading with him in rushed words. He didn't understand, but he knew what she was asking just the same. She wanted to leave this place, to flee with him. He wanted that, as well. Together, they could find one of the stray Frank horses, wait for low tide, and then ride away from this island of horrors across the spit of land that reached to the mainland.

Who could blame him? No man could fight the dead.

He would have the love and companionship he'd always wanted, perhaps even a child, perhaps more than one. It was his chance finally, his time. What could stop him?

Fate.

Even now, the three spinners held their scissors over the thread that was his life, mocking him, offering him what he most desired, and then denying it to him.

No. Not fate, but duty and responsibility. Damn the crones.

He held her at arm's length, staring into her eyes. "I'm sorry," he told her. "I want that, I want a life with you, but it's not for me. I don't deserve it. I owe the dead."

Tears ran down her cheeks, and she buried her face in his neck, sobbing into his beard, somehow understanding what he was going to do.

What he had to do.

TWENTY

The Black Monastery,
August 14, 799,
Evening

With Alda accompanying him, Asgrim returned to the black monastery one last time. This time, though, the *Marid* was no longer present; it had used the monastery to ambush the Danes and Saracens, then moved on—no doubt to Asgrim's ship. The air within the monastery was still tainted with its evil; perhaps it always would be. In the crypt, he retrieved *Heart-Ripper* from among the dead, quickly grabbing it and turning away, stepping around the corpses.

The Saracens' magic had not protected them, but Asgrim still wore the eastern talisman he had taken from Abid, thinking it couldn't hurt. It was a simple enough piece of jewelry: a palm-sized, round piece of silver covered with Saracen markings and what appeared to be stars. Perhaps it wasn't magic at all, but simply a family heirloom or a keepsake of Abid's. He let it hang beside his Thor's hammer.

On his way out, he paused at the bottom of the stairs and let his gaze rest on the bodies of his men, lying among the Saracens and Franks they had slain. Those had been good, brave men, and they deserved more than to be left here to rot in this evil place. But he could do nothing for them, and at least they had died fighting. He hadn't seen Steiner's spirit in his dream, or any of these men. Perhaps that meant they had been spared the horror the others had not and were already in Valhalla. He just didn't know. Besides, he would probably join them soon enough. He climbed the stairs.

Once out of the crypt, he searched what was left of the monastery's worksheds. The main complex was now only rubble and stone; however, some of the buildings that had stood separate from the monastery—the kitchen, smithy, stables, and workshops—still remained intact. In a storage shed, he found what he was looking for, a bundle of reed torches and a single clay jar half-filled with oil for the monks' lanterns.

He would burn *Sea Eel* before allowing the *Marid* to take it.

Asgrim tried to send Alda away from him, but failed utterly. She refused to leave his side. He became angry, raising his voice and pointing toward the Frankish village, but she shook her head and took the jar of oil and bundle of torches from his hands. Then she waited for him, staring at him in challenge. He watched her stubborn face for long moments and then nodded.

She had her own fate, too. Who was he to refuse her?

In darkness, they set out for *Sea Eel.* How had it come to this? How could he be the last Dane? Once, men had believed him lucky. No more.

They covered the distance quickly, moving through the forest toward the beach. Soon, he heard the crashing of the waves. Just before coming out onto the shoreline, he stopped among the trees and dropped to one knee. He poured a splash of the oil over one of the torches, let it soak for a moment, and then used his tinder and flint to set it afire. It caught quickly, burning black smoke. He handed it back to Alda, along with the jar, and then removed the silver shield from his back, adjusted it onto his arm, and drew *Heart-Ripper*. The Saracen's talisman hung from his neck on top of his chain mail coat, his hammer of Thor beneath it.

"Are you ready, Alda?" he asked, meeting her eye.

His intent was clear and, her lip quivering slightly, she nodded.

This one is a queen among other women, Asgrim thought. She deserved better than to die with him.

But no man can change his fate.

He set off toward the beach. Alda followed so closely behind him that she was almost rubbing up against his back. Asgrim stepped onto the pebbled shoreline and faced his destiny.

Sea Eel had been re-launched and sat with her prow pulled up onto the shoreline, ready to sail away. The Saracen's dhow was gone. Had the remaining Saracens escaped? He hoped so. Somebody should escape.

Frankish soldiers and Danish raiders moved about the shore near the longship, preparing her. Even from where he stood, Asgrim could tell that something was wrong with the men. They moved woodenly. They were *draugr* now, taken by the *Marid*. He saw no sign of the spirit as he began to walk toward his ship.

When they were about twenty paces away, the first of the possessed men, a Frank, turned and pointed at them. Then the others, both Frank and Dane, ceased their labors and stared at them, as if uncertain what to do. The smoke from the burning torch Alda carried wafted past him. As if possessed of a single mind, the men stumbled toward them with hatred and murder in their dead eyes.

Doubt rushed over Asgrim, and his breath caught in his throat. The shield would work, or they were dead.

The air felt thick around him, and then the shield began to vibrate, pulsing with energy. As the first of the *draugr* reached him, the walking dead man staggered to a stop, lowered his arms, and stared stiffly at the silver shield. Then another, one of his former crew, froze in place just behind the first. Every single man who approached Asgrim halted, each one staring stupidly at the shield. The eastern magic *was* working. Asgrim stepped past the first man, turning to keep the shield facing him as he went. Alda turned with him, her chest against his back, her breath hot on his neck.

When the shield was facing away from them, the *draugr* began to move again, to approach him, only to stop once more when Asgrim turned the shield back toward them. Spit dribbled down their chins, and they stared at him with dead, all-black eyes. He edged past the living corpse of Harald Skull-Splitter, hating himself.

Had any captain ever failed his men as profoundly as he had?

They reached the prow of *Sea Eel* and turned to keep the shield toward the crowd of *draugr* gathered in a half-circle in front of him.

Where was the damned *Marid*?

He shoved the point of *Heart-Ripper* into the sand so the blade stood upright, within easy reach. Then he reached behind himself, still keeping his gaze on the dead.

"The oil, woman. Give me the oil."

She took several seconds to comprehend what he was asking for, but then she fumbled the jar into his hand. He took it and poured it against the wooden strakes of his longship. The stench of the oil washed over him.

Years ago, the act of building this ship had brought him back from the dead and connected him with his father.

He sighed and held out his hand for the burning torch.

"It's only a ship," he said, not believing it for a moment.

And then his eyes rested on the false keel, on his and his brother's still-legible initials that they had carved into the wood so many years earlier, and he hesitated, dropping his hand and staring.

* * *

The *Marid* stepped from the sunken shell of the Saracen's *dhow* that sat on the silt-covered floor of the ocean. Schools of fish swam past, averting their course well away from the *djinn*. After slowly slaughtering and skinning the crew of the *dhow*, it had no reason to sink their ship, as well, but it had done so anyway, perhaps out of spite.

And it had much to be spiteful for. Long had it been forced to serve their *Caliphate*. But with that day's events, those humiliating days were truly over. Never again would it serve man. It was truly free. The easterner's precious silver jar that had served so long as its prison was destroyed and could never hold it again, and their finest mystic was dead. Now, with the northerners' ship and the husks of their bodies to act as crew, it could savage the coast, kill, and burn, and—

Something was wrong.

It had filled the corpses of the Danes and Franks with minor *ghuls* from its own dimension, near-mindless thralls who were consumed only by the need to kill and obey. But now it sensed their confusion and uncertainty.

The northman was back. Asgrim Wood-Nose was still alive.

Impressive.

The *Marid* examined its rotting hands. The corpse of Cuthbert was falling apart, as they all did in time. It masked its aura and walked along the ocean's floor toward the shoreline.

Time for a new body.

* * *

Asgrim held the burning torch in front of him with one hand, watching the *draugrs* step away from his ship. The Saracen's silver shield had held them at bay, but suddenly they all simply stepped back, in one large group, away from him and Alda.

He stepped away from *Sea Eel's* oil-soaked hull, still keeping his shield directed at the dead men.

"Why are they moving away?" he asked.

Alda squeezed his waist and said something in Frankish, probably admonishing him to finish the job and set fire to his ship. And he knew he should, but…

"It's my last connection with him," he said. "All I have left."

She pleaded with him again, grabbing his arm holding the torch and trying to drag it toward the ship.

He couldn't. He just couldn't. He turned to face her, to try to explain.

And as he did, he saw the *Marid* walk out of the surf behind him, not ten paces away, opposite the group of *draugrs*.

He hadn't felt its presence; only chance had caused him turn at that moment. The *dhow* hadn't sailed away. The *Marid* had sunk it.

The spirit glared at Asgrim with its all-black eyes. Its gaze went from Asgrim to the burning torch in his hand.

Asgrim locked eyes with the *Marid*. "No one sails my ship but me," he said as he rammed the burning torch against the oil-soaked hull of *Sea Eel*.

The ship's hull ignited in a flash, forcing them away from it. The *Marid* screamed in anger and rushed forward. Asgrim dropped the burning torch in the sand and grabbed *Heart-Ripper*. Holding the silver shield in front of him, he turned to face the *Marid*.

The *Marid* staggered to a stop, covering its eyes with its forearm as it turned away. Behind Asgrim, the flames crawled up the side of *Sea Eel*, quickly spreading across the longship.

"*Fool!*" shrieked the *Marid*. "*What have you done to my ship?*"

"No," snarled Asgrim. "*My* ship."

Bizarrely, Asgrim was calm as he stepped forward, swinging *Heart-Ripper*. The *Marid*, still facing away from the shield, blocked the sword strike with an upraised arm. Impossibly, the blade did not cut through the spirit's arm, but rebounded off the bone. The jarring impact almost made Asgrim drop his weapon. It was like chopping at a tree trunk.

Impossible!

The *Marid* shrugged off the wound, lashing out at Asgrim and solidly connecting with his shield. Asgrim flew back through the air, his vision suddenly blurry. When it cleared, he saw the silver shield had been ripped from his arm. Its straps were broken and the metal had bent in half. The *Marid* stalked forward, and Asgrim knew he couldn't get up in time. But at that moment, a burning torch flew through the air, striking the *Marid* in the face, sending sparks flying. The *Marid* slapped at its burning head, glared at Alda, and then drew its sword. Asgrim climbed back to his feet, *Heart-Ripper* in his grip, and moved to place himself in front of her.

The spirit glared at him. "*Northman, that Saracen talisman you wear only stops me from taking your body. It won't prevent me from killing you. And you will die slowly, as will your woman. I shall wear her skin as a nightshirt.*"

Asgrim spat at the sand near the *Marid's* feet. "Gods curse you. Come on, then!"

Enraged, the spirit advanced, but then it halted. A confused expression spread across its face as it looked past him. Asgrim glanced behind himself, and his mouth dropped open in disbelief. *Sea Eel* blazed and crackled as the flames consumed her. But walking from the burning longship, literally stepping into thin air, was his brother Bjorn, followed by his dead crew. The spirits—and spirits they had to be—shone like flames, but they were translucent, little more than smoke. And behind them, standing on the burning deck of his ship were Freya and Frodi, watching the dead advance toward Asgrim and the *Marid*.

Bjorn grinned. "*We fight together again one last time, older brother. One more chance for the Valkyries to take notice of our courage.*"

And then Bjorn stepped right into him, somehow passing through him and becoming a part of him. Strength and power flowed through Asgrim. Then Gorm Louse-Beard stepped into Asgrim, who again staggered under the sudden rush of strength that flowed through his muscles. A heartbeat later, Harald Skull-Splitter, his spirit face beaming with anticipation, also joined with him. In moments, every single crewman whose body had been possessed by the *Marid* joined with Asgrim, filling him and giving him unimaginable strength.

Asgrim turned and faced the *Marid*, knowing he did so as an equal. The spirit glared at him. Its eyes betrayed its doubt. "Fool. Your northern magic will fail you, just as the easterners' failed them."

"We shall see, *draugr*," said Asgrim.

They came together, swords flashing, hitting so hard that sparks flew through the air. They struck at one another with such force that the bones of lesser men would have shattered under the impact. Again and again, they fought in a cycle: attack, parry, counter-attack, withdraw. And then the cycle would begin again. Move, shift, strike, block, strike, and strike again. Asgrim's world became very simple and very focused: kill, kill, kill.

The *Marid* was skilled with a blade and was unbelievably good, but Asgrim fought with the borrowed strength of his men and the need to defeat this thing. Despite Asgrim's borrowed strength, the *Marid* was still more powerful, and slowly, the spirit began to force Asgrim back. It took the offensive and kept it, striking again and again, and Asgrim could do nothing more than ward off its blows. Asgrim knew he would make a mistake before long, and the spirit would strike him down. He was becoming tired, and the *Marid* had to realize that. And then Asgrim remembered another duel many years before, against a man that he had thought too old and too tired to stand against him, and he grasped at the only chance he had. Asgrim lashed out at the *Marid's* front leg, purposely overextending himself. As he expected, the spirit stepped back, parried his blow, and then struck back at Asgrim's exposed leg. Pain shot through Asgrim as the *Marid's* longsword scraped along his thigh, and the spirit grinned with triumph. But the *Marid* had not expected the hook punch Asgrim had already launched with his empty hand. His blow caught the *Marid* solidly in the jaw, and despite the agony in his leg, Asgrim pushed with his thighs, drawing power from them. Asgrim heard a loud crack as the *Marid* staggered back, its jaw broken. Asgrim lashed out again, this time with *Heart-Ripper,* and cut the *Marid's* sword hand off at the wrist, sending both sword and fist flying to the sand. The *Marid* stared at the stump of its severed sword arm, and then howled in anguish and rage, rushing Asgrim. But instead of meeting the attack, Asgrim dropped to one knee and then rose up, catching the *Marid* over his shoulder and sending it flying through the air behind him.

The *Marid* slammed against the side of the blazing longship. In a blur, Alda rushed past Asgrim, hurling the mostly empty jar of oil at the spirit. The jar smashed into the spirit's forehead, shattering and sending the remnants of the oil over its head. Flames caught in its hair and then spread over its body. It jumped to its feet, spun in place, and then staggered toward the ocean.

"*Asgrim,*" Freya's spirit called out from the burning deck of the longship. "*It is a creature of the sea. It draws its power from the ocean.*"

Asgrim leaped onto the back of the burning *Marid*, ignoring the pain from the flames. He spun the spirit about and shoved it back, back, back—until its body slammed into the burning hull of *Sea Eel.*

The *Marid's* black eyes stared at Asgrim through the flames that devoured its dead flesh. Its open mouth was a black hole, where teeth cracked from the heat.

"You want my ship, *draugr*?" snarled Asgrim. "Take it, then!"

Asgrim slammed *Heart-Ripper* through the *Marid's* sternum, pinning it to the hull of the burning ship.

He staggered back, falling onto the sand. And all at once, his borrowed strength drained from him. The *Marid* screamed and thrashed, but could not pry itself free. Bright green flames sprouted from its body, covering it in an intense heat. Just before Asgrim had to cover his face and look away, he saw a flash of the spirit's true form, its pebbled green skin covering a torso that looked more like an eel than a man. The monster's head was overlarge and hairless, and its all-black eyes were the size of a man's palm.

Hands grabbed him and pulled at him. Utterly spent, he was only vaguely aware that Alda was dragging him from the inferno that had been his ship. Around him, the dead Franks and Danes dropped to the sand, unmoving.

The green flames blazed out and were replaced by orange and red tongues of fire. The *Marid* was now an unmoving black cinder.

He heard Freya's voice, so faint that it seemed to drift in the air. *"Asgrim Wood-Nose, she is proud of you."*

Sea Eel burned to the water line.

The Marid was destroyed, banished.

* * *

Alda took him back to her hut to treat his injuries. There, in her small hut, she wrapped his burned hands in cloth and covered them in an ointment that relieved the worst of the pain. Then she stitched the long gash in his leg. He would recover, but he would probably walk with a limp for the rest of his life—a small enough price to pay for defeating a spirit as powerful as the Marid. With the help of his dead men and the guidance of Freya, they had survived. He was grateful, and, in truth, he had much to be grateful for. Alda had found a half-burned box in the charred remains of Sea Eel. Inside was a leather sack holding the five hundred silver pieces Abid had paid him, which was more than enough to pay his wergild and start a new life with Alda, a life free of violence and raiding.

He was done with his past. It was time to start over, to make a family, and to bring life into the world rather than take it. He prayed his brother and the others who had come back from the dead to help him had, this time, been taken by the Valkyries to Valhalla.

Later, when the tide was low, they rode a captured Frankish horse across the sandbar and toward the mainland.

"We'll go somewhere else," he said. "A new chance for both of us."

She didn't say anything, but he felt that she understood him. She leaned her cheek against his back, squeezed him tightly around the waist, and sighed. He felt her breath on his neck.

Despite his pain, he smiled and kicked the horse into a trot. Alda yelped and clung tighter to him.

What man could change his fate?

He could.

ACKNOWLEDGEMENTS

To Jennifer Carson, the best beta reader anyone could ever want. Thank you so very much.

ABOUT THE AUTHOR

A former soldier, William Stacey served his country for more than thirty years, including multiple combat tours in Bosnia and Afghanistan. William loves exercise and all things martial and is a black belt in karate. Black Monastery is his debut novel.

If you've enjoyed this novel and would like to be notified of new books of adventure and horror, please visit my website at www.williamstacey.ca and sign up for my newsletter.

Made in the USA
Middletown, DE
12 July 2017